USA TODAY BESTSELLING AUTHOR
DALE MAYER

Lifeless in the Lilies

Lovely Lethal Gardens 12

LIFELESS IN THE LILIES: LOVELY LETHAL GARDENS, BOOK 12
Beverly Dale Mayer
Valley Publishing Ltd.

ISBN-13: 978-1-773363-62-2
Print Edition

Books in This Series

About This Book

A new cozy mystery series from *USA Today* best-selling author Dale Mayer. Follow gardener and amateur sleuth Doreen Montgomery—and her amusing and mostly lovable cat, dog, and parrot—as they catch murderers and solve crimes in lovely Kelowna, British Columbia.

Riches to rags. … Chaos calms. … Suddenly it's quiet. … Too quiet if Doreen's involved!

What was supposed to be a leisurely stroll through a peaceful cemetery after a recent funeral turns into the start of a new case. Someone clobbers Doreen over the head and leaves her facedown among the funeral flowers.

Is it random violence? Revenge? A warning of worse to come?

No one knows, not even Doreen, but one thing is certain: the attack enabled the disappearance—perhaps the abduction?—of Doreen's beloved African gray parrot, Thaddeus. Frantic, Doreen foregoes a trip to the emergency room in favor of heading straight home, where she hopes Thaddeus will return sooner rather than later.

When he does show up, riding a branch down the river, coming right home, he's different, and all he can talk about is Big Guy. He's also sporting an SOS message fastened around his ankle… Doreen sets out to retrace Thaddeus's path, while Mack hunts down her attacker.

Between birds and boys and Corporal Mack Moreau's brother, the lawyer looking into her divorce situation,

Doreen has her hands full. And that's before her former lawyer shows up unexpectedly at her home! Off-balance by all these events, Doreen opens her door to someone with a serious grudge to take her down …

Sign up to be notified of all Dale's releases here!

https://geni.us/DaleNews

Prologue

Saturday Late Morning …

THE FUNERAL FOR Rosie happened Saturday morning, two days after the last debacle. Doreen walked away from the graveside. Rosie's ashes had been laid to rest, and the crowd had dispersed. Her autopsy stated her death a suicide, having ingested the remainder of her husband's old heart medicine and a cocktail of other drugs she'd hoarded.

That wasn't why she would be remembered though. No, Rosie had been accused of killing the three little old ladies—the kiwi clique—and her husband, David, which had the entire community up in arms, not to mention the added news of Marsha going to jail for murdering her husband too.

Doreen had quietly stepped out of the hype reverberating around town. She watched as Nan walked away ahead of her. Her grandmother would go to a celebration-of-life ceremony, which Doreen had also backed away from, hoping to go home and to just relax.

The last few days had been more media sensation than anything. The police were still piecing together the bits and pieces from Rosie's life, but it was a pretty simple case, where the same drugs had been used in all three of the women's deaths, the first one being an accident, and Rosie using that as an opportunity to point fingers at Marsha and to take out the other women Rosie considered her enemies.

The return of Rosie's cancer had apparently given her the freedom to make a few changes in her life—such as getting rid of the kiwi clique that had been a pain in her butt. And gave her a supposedly God-given opportunity to point the finger at the one other woman who could ruin her life by telling everyone what their husbands had done. Rosie had never wanted her grandson to know and had lived in fear of what he'd do if he found out. And the police had found the same drug had been given to her husband, who she'd killed years ago. It looked like it was a pretty simple open-and-shut case, but the end result had left the community in shock.

And, of course, the local fair would never be the same again.

As Doreen walked by the multiple fresh graves, she stopped to look at various stones and monuments, seeing patches of lilies at various places.

Finally she ended up in a complete circle, as she stood over Rosie's grave. "I hope you're at peace now," she said sadly. "It's not the end I would have wanted for you."

She reached out and picked up a lily and sniffed it, wondering why lilies always represented death. As far as she was concerned, flowers should be for life and rebirth. But so often they were used for funerals. She placed it back into the vase and straightened them out.

She didn't have her animals with her, out of respect for the others attending the ceremonies dotting the cemetery. It's a good thing she'd left them at home, as No Pets Allowed signs were everywhere. But being without them? ... Well, she felt a little lost herself.

Not to mention how worried she was about the upcoming meeting with Mack's brother, the lawyer. But she'd dragged out as much time as she could here. She needed to go home and to eat before the two men arrived, and she had to face the unpleasantness of her now-defunct marriage.

She stared at the lilies for one last long moment, sighed, and turned to step away. As she did, a shadow fell over her side, and she felt somebody reaching out for her. She turned with a smile, only to cry out at the blow that came out of nowhere and struck her on the back of her head. She didn't hear anything but the sounds of footsteps thundering away, as she crashed into the pile of lilies at the graveside.

The pain was crushing.

Poor Mack. He would be the one to find her.

Lilies. How appropriate.

Her last thought before the blackness took her over? She had already come up with a name for the investigation into her own death.

Lifeless in the Lilies.

Chapter 1

Saturday Noon …

DOREEN WOKE TO sunlight and blue sky, which was immediately overlaid by chaos and a confusion of barks, snaps, yells, and growls. She groaned and rolled, shoving blades of grass into her face. A heavy hand landed on her shoulder. "Stay where you are. You've been hit."

Her eyelids fluttered open to see Mack crouching beside her. She frowned at him. He immediately frowned back. She closed her eyes and whispered, "What happened?"

"That's what I would ask you," he said, his tone grim.

Her eyelids shifted open again, but it was a struggle to keep them that way. "I don't know," she cried out, only to shudder, as her voice added to the din. "It's so noisy. What's with the noise?" She moaned as the cacophony around her increased.

He leaned over and whispered, "If you've got the energy, you'll want to call off Mugs."

Immediately her eyelids snapped open, and she struggled to sit up. But, as she did, Mack struggled to hold her down. "Stay still," he ordered.

She growled at him. "Let me go."

Hearing another bark beside her, she twisted her head to see Mugs, snapping at a crowd of people and keeping them all back. She whistled only once, yet Mugs caught the sound in his floppy ears and raced toward her. She collapsed back in the grass and stretched out a hand, placing it on his head. But that wasn't enough. Mugs buried his face and his snout against her neck and in her hair, snuffling all up and down her side.

She chuckled. "I'm okay, buddy. I'm okay."

A collective sigh of relief came from the crowd around her. Something else warm and fuzzy was up against her other arm. When she shifted to look, she saw Goliath curled at her side. She looked up at Mack. "Well, at least they're here, looking after me."

He nodded, but his tone was grim, as he said in a quiet tone, "I haven't seen Thaddeus. He's gone missing."

Her eyes popped open. "What do you mean?"

He shook his head. "Either he's gone walking or somebody has taken him."

She stared up at him, her heart already filled with joy at having Mugs and Goliath here, then shifting to panic-stricken mode after realizing that Thaddeus may not be. "That's not good," she whispered. Yet something else shifted in her brain. "I didn't have them with me." She shrugged and said, "Or maybe I did. I have no idea."

"Let's leave that for the moment. Tell me. What are you doing here?" he asked.

She focused on him, but her mind went blank. "What am I doing *where?*" she asked cautiously.

His eyebrows shot up. "You're at the cemetery."

She frowned, as she thought about it. "Oh." Her gaze caught sight of the crushed lilies beside her. "*Oh,*" she said.

She reached up a hand to her sore head, then realized what happened. "Someone hit me," she snapped, glaring up at him. "Did you find him?"

He raised his palms. "Of course I didn't find him," he said. "We barely found you."

She stared at the ground, her head twisting to look at the crowd gathered around. "Who found me then?"

He pointed off to the side, where a little boy stood close to his mom. "Well, Mugs technically, but also that little boy did."

"Wow. How long ago?" she asked, struggling to sit up again. This time Mack helped her, slipping an arm underneath her back and helping her into a sitting position. She shuddered as the pain ricocheted down her back. "Did he see what happened?"

"He said he came here because of Mugs."

She looked over to see Mugs, snuffling the little boy's hand, and the boy's expression of absolute rapture on his face as he petted him. "Mugs does have that effect on some people."

"Only some," Mack said gently. "A lot of people have learned to run."

"He doesn't attack everybody," she said indignantly, not liking the way Mack was thinking.

"No, maybe not," he said, "but he's certainly attacked enough."

"Well, you could say the same for Goliath for that matter."

"Absolutely I would," he said, with a humorous tone.

Ambulance sirens screamed in the distance.

"Wow, somebody else got hurt too?"

"Nope," he said, "that ambulance is for you."

"I'm fine," she said, with a dismissive wave of her hand.

"No, I don't think so," he said gently. "We'll get you looked over."

She leaned up against his knee, tilting her head to look up at him. "I'm really okay, you know?"

"Really? The blood dripping down the side of your head disagrees."

She winced. "Will they cut my hair again?"

"That's hardly the issue," he said.

She twisted and then gasped at the pain. "But it's not far off," she muttered.

Just then the ambulance arrived. Two men hopped out and raced toward Mack.

"You know what? I only get that kind of attention because you're here."

He sighed. "I am the one who called them."

"You're overreacting again," she grumbled.

"Again?" he said in an ominous voice.

She grinned. "Well, maybe. But you guys should be out looking for Thaddeus."

"Don't you worry about Thaddeus. We'll find him," Mack murmured. "I want you to go to the hospital and to get checked over."

"But we don't always get what we want," she announced, as she struggled to stand. Just the thought of going to the hospital made her ill.

"Oh no, you don't," he said, keeping her seated on the ground. "You're not getting out of it this time."

She tried to ignore him, but, with the paramedics hurrying toward her, she knew that she couldn't avoid it. Mugs immediately stood and barked at the two paramedics. She called him over, and he came back to her, wagging his tail happily. She gave him a cuddle.

"It's okay, buddy. They're here to help me." He woofed several times and shoved his face up against her. She hugged him close, and a paramedic crouched in front of her.

"Let's take a look at the injury."

She studied his face. "I think I recognize you."

"You should," he said. "I been out to look at injuries you've received several times now."

She winced. "It's not good when the paramedics get to know me by name," she announced.

"It's not good when the cops get to know you by sight either," Mack muttered, as he pointed off to the side, where several policemen were, including Chester and Arnold, holding back the crowd.

"Oh dear," she said. "Will I owe them more beer and pizza now?"

Chester, who must have been close enough to hear, turned and grinned, giving her a thumbs-up.

Mack burst out laughing.

She sighed. "I am a little tired," she admitted.

"Well, as long as I know you didn't do this on purpose."

She rounded on Mack, then cried out in pain at the sharp movement. "Why did you do that?"

"Why did I do what?"

"Make me turn like that," she said.

"I didn't make you turn," he said, sighing. He moved off to the side, so the paramedic could get a better look at her head. "Besides, why were you outraged at my comment?"

"Do you really think I did this to myself?" she asked in an ominous tone, glaring at him.

"Of course not," he said, "but you did agree to meet with my brother this weekend."

"Well, I can't do it now," she said, reaching a hand to her head. "I'm hurt."

He snorted at that. "A minute ago, you were just fine."

"A minute ago, I forgot about your brother," she snapped back. At that, one of the paramedics tugged on her, and she cried out in pain.

"I'm so sorry," he said, "but we'll need to take you in. Do you want to walk to the ambulance, or shall we bring over a gurney?"

"Oh my," she said. "I don't even want to go in the ambulance."

"Too bad," Mack announced, as he stood and gently lifted her to her feet. "Now, can you walk on your own, or shall we put you on a gurney and wheel you through the crowd?"

"Now you're just being mean," she announced.

"Of course I am," he said. "I live to bug you and to be mean, apparently."

She turned to look at him and said, "That's a failing. You should fix it." The paramedic looked at her, bemused. She glared at him. "It's really not nice to knock people when they're down now, is it?" He immediately nodded, and her eyebrows shot up. "It is?" He shook his head. "Are you confused?" she asked.

"Oh, yeah," Mack said. "We all are. And I'm taking the decision away from you." In one smooth movement, he bent and swooped her up into his arms and strode toward the ambulance.

She immediately clutched his shoulders. "You could have at least warned me," she cried out.

"Why would I bother?" he snapped back. "You just would have argued. And you're not getting out of meeting my brother this weekend either."

She poked his chest. "Bully."

He just shook his head at that. The crowd parted as voices called out.

"Will she be okay?"

"Is she all right?"

"I hope she's okay."

"Do we know what happened?"

"Did she get hurt?"

"Did someone hit her?"

But Mack gave no answers. And she didn't have any to give. She waved to the crowd and was emotionally taken aback when she saw so many people waving their hands, with bright smiles on their faces. "Wow," she said. "Are they happy that I'm hurt?"

"Of course not, silly," he said, with an exasperated sigh. "They're happy that you'll be okay."

She leaned back slightly, so she could look up into his face. "But how do they know that?"

The paramedics just looked at each other, then at Mack. He shrugged and said, "Don't even bother. She's just being difficult."

She sniffed. "Can Goliath and Mugs come with me at least?"

"No animals in the ambulance," the two paramedics said immediately.

She stared at them. "Then rest assured, I'm not going either."

"Too late for that," Mack said, as he stepped into the ambulance, still carrying her.

She glared at him. "Who made you the boss?"

"A lot of people," he said in that ominous voice of his.

He sat her on the gurney and stretched her out, so she was lying flat. Immediately he was replaced by the paramedics, who quickly buckled her in.

"Mack?" she said desperately, hating that note of worry in her voice.

He stopped, then looked at her and smiled. "I'll take care of the animals."

"But Thaddeus," she said. "Where is Thaddeus?"

He shrugged. "He wouldn't have gone far. He was here earlier."

"But you don't know," she said. "You just don't know."

"I promise we'll find him."

And, with that, she had to be satisfied. As she laid back down, she felt the pain racking through her system. "Why do I always have to get hurt?" she muttered.

"I'm pretty sure Mack would say it's because you always put your nose into things you shouldn't," the second paramedic said.

She stared at him in surprise. "But I wasn't even doing anything. I was just at a funeral."

"Maybe so, but you've been stirring up all kinds of chaos."

"I haven't been stirring anything up," she said tiredly, as she collapsed against the weird crackling of the plasticky pillow under her head. "All I'm doing is shining light on some cases."

"And that's what I mean about stirring things up," he said cheerfully. "Not everybody likes to have you bringing light to dark shadows."

"Well then, they shouldn't have done something wrong in the first place," she announced. Just then the ambulance started up, leaving her with the one paramedic. She sighed.

"It always hurts worse when I go to the hospital."

"Well, it shouldn't," he said. "The people there can help you."

"Well, it does hurt. Everybody pinches and prods and pokes with their needles," she said. "It just hurts."

"Well, tell them not to hurt you," he said.

"Like that'll help." The jostling ride was blessedly short, and, before she realized it, she was shifted onto a bed in the emergency room. She laid back down, now with an equally stiff, equally uncomfortable sheet over her, and felt the shakes setting in. By the time a nurse came to check her blood pressure, pulse, and temperature, she gave an exclamation and turned and disappeared. Doreen wasn't sure what was wrong, but, when the efficient woman returned with a heated blanket a few minutes later, Doreen cuddled under it and moaned with relief.

"It's the shock," the nurse said sympathetically. "You should warm up soon."

"Is it just shock?" she asked, her teeth chattering. "I guess I was lying there on the ground for a little bit too."

"Do you know how long that was?" the doctor asked, as he walked past the curtain.

"No, you'll have to ask Mack."

"I can do that," he said. "But you were unconscious?"

"According to them, I was, yes," she said. "I just don't know how long."

"Good enough," he said. "Let's take a look." His *taking a look* was just like she had expected. By the time he was done, she felt the tears in the corner of her eyes, and she struggled to not let them pour out.

"We'll get you fixed up," he said. "You'll need a couple stitches, and we'll get you a shot for the pain."

She wanted to nod but didn't dare move because, ever since he had examined her head, the pain was so much worse. She didn't quite understand how that worked, but it always seemed to be that way. And it wasn't fair. She felt the tears of self-pity on her cheeks and knew that wasn't normal for her either.

By the time the doctor returned, he and the nurse wielded needles and other tools from a tray the nurse had brought in. Doreen looked at the tray, him, and bit her lip.

He just waved a hand. "Don't you worry about this," he said. "It'll all be fine."

"Are you sure?" she asked. "That looks painful."

"You've already been hurt," he said with a smile. "We're just fixing it up."

She knew that in theory but wasn't so sure how that would work in practice. When the curtain was pulled back again, and Mack stepped in, she glared at him. "You don't belong here," she announced.

He glared at her. "Yes, I do."

The doctor turned to him, smiled. "Hey, Mack."

"Hey, Doc. How's she doing?"

"Still as charming as ever."

"Absolutely she is," Mack said, grinning. "It would go a bit easier if she wouldn't be."

"Too bad," she announced from the bed. "Remember what I said."

"Oh, I remember," he said. "You'll be you, no matter what."

"And you wouldn't like it any other way," she said, giving him a big fat grin.

Mack chuckled at that. "That's okay," he said, "because I know the doc here will put some stitches in that head of yours and fix you up."

She glared at the doctor.

"Yep," he said in response. "Stitches. Probably about ten."

Her smile fell away. "No! That'll hurt," she cried out.

"It might," he said, "but we'll numb it, so it won't hurt as much."

She groaned and laid back down. "I don't have a choice in the matter?"

"Nope, and it's the best thing for you," he said. "This will heal much faster."

"How much hair will you cut away?"

He chuckled. "No matter how minor the hair removal, the women are always concerned about their hair," he said, with a smile.

She shrugged. "I don't really want to walk around with a bald spot on my head."

"I don't think that's the most important issue right now," Mack said in a repressive tone.

She glared at him. "Nobody asked you."

"Nope," he said, "nobody did. But, if you don't want me calling Nan and telling her about this, then you'll behave yourself, starting now."

"That's just blackmail. That's what it is."

"Maybe, but, as long as it works, I don't really care."

And again she glared at him, but it was futile. Because he really would call Nan. "You'll just make her worry needlessly," she muttered. "Besides," she said, as an afterthought, "she probably already knows."

Chapter 2

Saturday Early Afternoon …

O F COURSE DOREEN was right. Nan did already know, and she was in a fine mess by the time Mack finally drove Doreen home. As she slowly made her way out of the truck, refusing to wait for him to come around and help her, the front door of the house burst open, and chaos ensued, as the animals flew out toward her. Nan stood on the front step, shaking her head. She looked at Doreen's face and cried out, "Oh my. Oh, dear. Oh, my dear."

Mack walked around the truck, wrapped an arm around her shoulders, and helped her up the steps. In the meantime, Mugs barked and jumped all around both of them.

"It's okay, Mugs," Doreen murmured, feeling a whole lot woozier than she had expected. Once inside, she collapsed on the first pot chair and reflected on the fact that she'd gotten rid of all the other furniture. "It'd be nice if I had something comfy to sit on," she muttered.

Mack snorted at that. "If you hadn't sold everything, you might have."

"Well, I don't know if it's sold or not," she said. "I haven't heard from Scott in weeks."

"Oh, dear, I hope it's okay," Nan said.

"I would hope so," Doreen muttered. The moment she sat down, Goliath jumped into her lap. Tears collected in the corner of her eyes, as she hugged the great big behemoth. She looked over at Mack. "Thaddeus?"

He shook his head slowly. She buried her face against Goliath, her shoulders trembling. Nan clucked at her side, gently patting her shoulder. "We'll find him. I know we will."

Doreen nodded. "I know. I know," she said, "but ..." And she let her voice trail off. It must be the painkillers making her mumble like an idiot. She wasn't normally like this.

Nan stepped back and said, "I'll put on the teakettle." She turned and raced into the kitchen.

"How do you find a bird?" she asked Mack.

"Well, everybody knows about him, and everybody knows what he looks like," he added. "And, yes, we've put out an alert, asking everybody to keep an eye out for him."

A few minutes later, as she sat here, cuddling Goliath, Nan returned with a tray. Doreen looked at the tray and asked, "Where did you find that?"

Nan seemed momentarily confused. "I don't know," she said with a shrug. "I just reached into the cupboard, where I always kept it, and there it was."

Doreen frowned and studied the tray, but she didn't know if it was something that maybe Mack had kept and decided that they needed when they were sorting stuff or if they had missed something else in the kitchen. Nan looked around for a place to put the tray, and Mack hopped up, grabbed a chair from the kitchen table and brought it over and put it there for her.

"You know what?" he said. "You might feel better if we sat outside."

"We might," Doreen said, with a yawn. "But I don't have anything to sit on out there either."

"There is that," Nan said. "When you get the money for the antiques, you'll have to buy yourself some outdoor furniture."

"I need to buy some indoor furniture first," she said, with a note of humor. "A couple chairs in this living room really don't do the job."

"Not if you'll be a socialite," Nan said, with alacrity.

Doreen gave a tiny shake of her head. "I'll admit that I've had more people through this place than I thought possible over these last few weeks," she said, "but that won't continue."

"No, maybe not," Nan said, "but you'd be surprised. People will start to gather around you now."

"Why would they do that?" Doreen asked, looking at her grandmother in surprise.

"Because you're becoming somebody," Nan said, with that wise look in her eye. "Everybody wants to be around somebody."

"I'm a nobody," she said, with a yawn. "And apparently those painkillers are really having an effect on me." She reached up and rubbed her face gently.

"Maybe you should go lie down," Mack said.

She shrugged, then shook her head, wincing. "It's pretty early though."

"Still, a nap won't hurt," he said.

"Maybe not, but it feels like I already had one out in the grass."

"That one was unintended," Nan said. "By the way, I

would make you something to eat, but there's not much food in the house."

At that, Doreen grimaced. "I haven't done any grocery shopping."

Nan stood here, her hands on her hips, her fingers moving up and down, almost like a piano rhythm. "Are you eating?"

"Of course I am," she protested. Nan looked over at Mack, then peered down at Doreen. "But are you eating enough?"

"Well, I stopped losing weight," she said, "so I would presume so."

But Nan didn't appear to be satisfied with that either. "Do I need to go grocery shop for you?"

"Not at all," she said forcibly. "I'm fine."

Nan sniffed. "I don't want you so worried about money that you're afraid to spend it."

"Now that's a lesson she needs to learn," Mack said. "She is definitely afraid to spend it."

"Well, it's just that I don't really know where the next dollar is coming from," Doreen protested. "So it's a little hard to go out and just spend money, if I don't know that I'm getting more."

"I was hoping you'd be getting on okay by now," Nan stated, her worry evident in her tone.

"Well, if I get the antiques sold, I will be," she said. "And I'm not doing badly, but I don't really have much in the way of prospects for getting a decent job. People look at me differently now."

"Of course they do," Nan said. "Like I said, you're somebody."

"I'm somebody without a job," she said in exasperation.

"Where have you tried?" Nan asked.

"I haven't really," Doreen said glumly. "I started on my résumé and then didn't know what to say because there's really nothing to put down. How do you list *socialite* as an occupation?" Both Mack and Nan stopped, then looked at each other and over at her. She shrugged. "So you can see the problem, right?"

"But some places don't need any experience, my dear," Nan said. "You could probably get a job at the grocery store."

"I probably could," she said, yawning. "And I promise I'll look at it, when I am feeling better. I need just a few days to get over this."

"No, you need more than a few days," Nan said. "You've been going nonstop for a long time."

"Maybe," she said. "And now I have another problem to deal with."

"What's that?" Nan asked, perking up. "Anything I can help with?"

Doreen thought about it for a moment, then realized that wasn't fair. "No," she said, "Mack won't let you."

At that, Mack turned and looked at her. "What are you talking about?"

She glared at him. "I'm talking about your brother."

He gave her a hard look. "No, you're right. Nan can't help with that."

"Oh my," Nan said, looking at Mack. "Can you help her?"

"That depends on what my brother has to say," he said.

Nan looked positively thrilled.

Doreen just looked at her grandmother sourly. "You know how hard this will be, don't you, Nan?"

"Absolutely it will be hard," she said immediately, with a nod of her head and a commiserating look in her eye. "But it's necessary."

"Why is it necessary? I could just walk away from the whole thing."

"And let him get away with it?"

"At least then I wouldn't have to deal with it or him," Doreen said, sagging into the seat and closing her eyes.

"You can't hide forever."

"I'm not hiding," she said, eyes closed. "Being determined to not get involved is a whole different thing."

"No, it's not," Mack said. "It's hiding."

She glared at him. "You don't know what it was like."

"No, I don't," he said. "And you're right. It's not for me to judge. I can understand you not wanting to get involved, but you're the one who can't put food on your own table, while he's living high on the hog in his massive mansion. He's got all kinds of money that he's not sharing, and you have an equal right to it."

She groaned. "There'll be a payback for arguing. You know that, right?"

"What kind of a payback?"

"He always gets back at people," she said tiredly. "It's not like I'll be happy with any money if I have to look over my shoulder, always thinking he'll find ways to get to me."

There was silence in the room. Nan looked at her. "I don't think you ever told me how bad it was, dear."

"Of course not," she said, with a gentle smile. "I didn't want to worry you."

Nan then just clucked and clucked several times. "Oh, dear," she said. "You know that's not the answer I wanted to hear."

"Maybe not," she said. "But no point in lying at this stage. I was very ashamed of what was going on, and I wasn't sure how to handle my life as it was. I didn't want to get you in trouble, and I didn't want to bother you," she murmured. "You've always been there for me, and I didn't want you to see how badly I was faring in life."

"So you seized the chance, and you walked away from him," she said. "Don't ever feel like you're a failure because of that."

"Maybe, but I haven't done very well since."

"Well, we'll get to the bottom of it now," Mack interrupted. "First, I want you to have a rest and to relax a little bit, before my brother gets here."

She stared at him, her eyes going wide. "When is he coming?" she asked in an ominous tone. "Surely you pushed it off until next week."

He glared at her. "No, I didn't. He's coming this weekend. I just have to confirm with him when."

"Oh, Lord," she said, sagging back again. "And here I was hoping that this might push it off."

"Getting yourself injured by some unknown assailant won't stop me from trying to get you back on your feet financially," he said in a severe tone.

"And you should be grateful for his help," Nan chimed in.

Doreen opened her eyes to see Nan looking at her with worry. Doreen reached out her hand, and her grandmother immediately snatched it up with both of hers. "I'm sorry, Nan. You're right. I just don't want to go through the whole headache of reliving the details."

"But getting to the other side will be so much better," Nan said, patting her hand. "And, if Mack is willing to help you, let him help."

She smiled. "Do I have any choice?"

"No," Mack said in a determined voice. "You don't."

After a brief pause, he added, "Let's get you upstairs to bed."

Chapter 3

Saturday, Midafternoon …

DOREEN WOKE UP from her unexpected nap with a crick in her neck from lying the wrong way while wrapped around Goliath. The house was silent. Nan and Mack were probably gone. Immediately her eyes lit on the empty rod where Thaddeus usually slept, and she snatched up her phone and texted Mack. **Any news on Thaddeus?**

His response came back with a no. She sighed, looked down at Goliath, scratched his tummy, and asked, "Could you find him?"

Goliath twitched his tail, but, other than that, there was no sign that he had even heard her request. But then why would the cat worry? Half the time the two were at odds anyway. But Doreen wanted to believe that they were a bonded family and that Goliath would miss his friend. At least she could hope so. Mugs was stretched out on his back, with four feet to the wind, looking like he didn't have a care in the world.

She frowned at that. "How come you guys aren't worried?" she asked, but neither animal answered. Did they know something she didn't? She wondered because it seemed like they were oddly content. She hopped to her feet and then froze, as the room swayed around her.

"Wow," she mumbled to herself. "That was a little too fast."

Moving slowly, she made her way to the bathroom and used the facilities, then stood in front of the mirror, gasping at the image reflected back at her. "You look like a witch." Her hair stuck out in all directions, and the stitches in her head poked out like black sticks in the air, looking painful.

She wondered about a shower and then figured that there was probably no point right now. Nobody would give her the go-ahead, and she vaguely remembered the doctor saying to give it a couple days. She managed to scrub down her face and neck with a washcloth, getting off some of the worst dirt, mud, and blood, feeling marginally better.

With that, she slowly made her way back to her bedroom, then realized her clothes were bloody and dirty as well, and managed to get changed in an attempt to at least feel fresher. With that much done, she headed downstairs to her trusty coffeepot.

As soon as she had a pot dripping, she opened the back door and let Mugs and Goliath, who had come downstairs with her, outside to do their own business. She walked out to her deck and felt the same pleasure she had felt every other time. She was just so thrilled to have it.

The old rickety table and two chairs were serviceable but just barely. It was in her plans to update them, when she had money, whenever that was. Pulling one chair back, she went to sit on it, when the leg buckled. She cried out and just managed to stop herself from falling.

A closer inspection showed the other chair was in a similar state. The table didn't look much better. Stacking the three pieces against the side of the house, so she didn't forget and try to sit again, she slowly walked the edge of the deck, her hands instinctively going to the railing to give her some support, as she looked out at the beautiful stamped concrete path and edging. Although the edging itself was a little bit on the blurry side along the grass, she was so delighted to have it.

She moved cautiously onto the cobblestones and headed toward the river. Ignoring the bench, she managed to slowly lower herself to the grass and looked at the water. It was still amazingly high and flowed with a ferocity that surprised her. The odd branch went by; a lone duck swam past, and she wondered what the devil he was doing out there in the strong current. There must have been a heck of a storm up on the mountain to have this much water down here.

Doreen hadn't seen much in the way of wildfowl, like the ducks, since the river had risen. Which made sense to her, as fighting the current had to be exhausting. But then, maybe like her, that solo duck was trying to buck the system.

She smiled at that, thinking she could certainly relate. She knew that Mack wouldn't give up on her seeing his brother. And she had no business giving up on Mack either, as he'd been there for her every step of the way, even if she hadn't been terribly welcoming. Mugs walked over and nudged her gently. She scratched his long silky ears. "Hey, buddy," she said. "Any idea where Thaddeus is?"

They sat in a morose silence, as she waited, enjoying the peace and quiet, though her heart was heavy as she thought about her missing pet. Who would have thought Thaddeus would be the one to go missing? But then, talking parrots were something else to begin with and probably not all that common. Just as she sat here, considering that she should make her way back up to the house because the coffee would be ready, she heard a shout upriver.

She saw two teens chasing something in the river or across the pathway. She leaned forward, trying to see what they were up to. As they got a little bit closer on the far side, they pointed at her. She looked at them and called out, "Hello?"

They shouted at her across the river, but she couldn't hear for the roar of the water. She slowly stood, as they pointed frantically at something coming toward her. She looked up, and there was Thaddeus, riding on the back of a branch down the river.

Just like a homing pigeon, Thaddeus was on his way right to her. Or, as she judged the speed of the water, right past her. She instinctively stepped out into the water to catch his branch as he raced past. She caught it but fell into the tumbling icy water herself.

Gasping and crying out, she fought the current and only managed to get herself pulled several houses downriver, where the waterway took a slight bend in the angle it flowed. Gasping in the cold water, she stood. Shakily, she struggled onto the riverbank, hung on to the side of the fence, realizing she was almost to the corner where they headed down to Nan's. Thaddeus and Goliath raced toward her, and Mugs led the charge. They all barked, meowed, and cawed terribly at her. She stood here for a long moment, feeling icy cold, but then her gaze landed on Thaddeus, and her face lit up.

"Thaddeus," she cried out and held out her arm. Perfectly dry, Thaddeus hopped off the back of Mugs, where he'd been perched, and landed on her arm. Quickly he raced up her arm to her shoulder and gently stroked her cheek.

"Thaddeus, oh, Thaddeus, you're here." Laughing and

crying, she stroked his head and his body. "Oh, sweetie, what happened to you?"

Somebody else called out, "What happened to you?"

And, sure enough, there was Mack, glaring at her.

She stared at him in surprise. "Look!" she cried out. "Look who's here!"

He looked at Thaddeus, at her, and shook his head. "Where did he come from?"

She gave him a lopsided grin. "You won't believe me."

He gave a long-suffering sigh that she had come to recognize. "Nope, I probably won't, but try me anyway."

She glared at him. "You could at least keep an open mind."

"Ahem," he said, with a quick nod at Thaddeus. "Do you want to get to the point?"

She explained about the boys drawing her attention, the branch coming downriver with Thaddeus, and how she ended up in the cold water. He stared at her, looked at Thaddeus, then at the various debris flowing by, and said, "You realize he could have flown off the branch at any time, right?"

She considered Thaddeus for a moment, then turned toward Mack. "Oh." But then she added, "He doesn't fly well, and there's no telling what he has been through."

"Maybe not," he said, "but, if he got onto a branch, I'm sure he could have gotten off."

"He was scared," she said defensively.

"So you jumped into a raging river at high water levels to save the bird?"

"Yes!" she said determinedly. "And I would do it again too."

He groaned. "Well, at least you're safe, although that

head wasn't supposed to get wet for a couple days, was it?"

She shrugged, then grinned. "If you don't tell the doc, I won't tell him either."

Rolling his eyes, Mack reached out a hand and said, "Come on. Let's get you back home again."

"It's only around the corner," she said, as she walked with him, but her clothes were soaking wet, and she felt the chill, even though it was a hot summerlike day.

"As soon as we get home," he said, "you need to get into dry clothes."

"I will," she muttered. But she was overjoyed at having Thaddeus back. "What do you think happened to him?" Then she noticed something around his ankle. "Mack, look," she said. "Something's on his ankle." She reached up to check his leg, but Thaddeus flapped his wings at her.

"Thaddeus is here. Thaddeus is here," he cawed out.

"I know, Thaddeus," she said. "Let me see what's on your ankle."

But he shook his head and afterward shook his leg, as if something were irritating him. Which something was of course—that band on his leg. She looked at Mack. "Do you think you can get it off?"

He reached up with one hand and gently stroked Thaddeus, then said, "Let me check your leg, big guy."

"Big guy," Thaddeus crowed, and then he stood tall, flapped his wings. "Big guy, big guy, big guy."

She laughed. "Oh, I'm so happy to have him back again," she said to Mack, who quickly unclipped what was on his tiny leg.

"I am too," he said. "He's quite the character, and I'm glad somebody didn't try to keep him."

She looked at Mack, fear in her eyes. "Do you think

Thaddeus was kidnapped? *Bird-napped?*"

Mack stopped, looked at the band in his fingers and the folded piece of paper, and said, "I don't know about bird napping to keep him, but it's obvious that somebody had him. Otherwise how did he get this?"

She gave her head a shake. "I must be more tired than I thought because that didn't even make sense until you said it."

He hooked an arm around her shoulders and said, "Come on. Let's get you back up to the house."

Soaking wet, with every step, she left a puddle. The shivers occurred long before they hit her property.

He looked at her in concern. "I'm just glad you made it out of that river," he said. "It's flowing really high. Even now," he said, looking at the pathway that was just underwater.

"I know," she admitted, struggling to stay upright. But having Mack beside and slightly behind her was like having a huge timber of support. They finally made it back to Nan's house, and he helped her up the little grassy bank, so she was standing at the top. He bent down and picked up Mugs and Goliath, then put them back on the grassy edge too because they were scrambling around, so excited to see her safely home again. Quickly they all trooped to the house.

Noticing she was still shivering, Mack nudged her to the back door. "Go on, get up to the bedroom and get changed."

"Only as long as you don't open that note right away," she said, pinning him with a gimlet eye.

He rolled his eyes. And then he sniffed the air. "You have coffee on," he said in delight.

She glared at him. "I know, and I didn't even take a cup down to the river with me."

He chuckled. "All the more incentive to get up and get changed," he said. "I'll pour two cups."

With that, she made her way to the stairs, leaving a wet trail behind her. Up in her bedroom, she struggled out of the wet clothing and into dry clothes, thinking she would have to do laundry at this rate. She gently patted her wet hair with a soft towel, careful of her stitches, before she made her way back down. "How is it I can be so cold on such a beautiful warm day?"

"Well, not everybody is taking swims in icy water."

"I didn't think it could be anywhere near that cold," she muttered. She accepted the cup of coffee he handed her gratefully and sat down at the kitchen table and hugged it close.

"Glacier fed, remember? And those ugly storms in the mountains explain the flash flood down here," he said, as he sat down beside her. His gaze was concerned, as he looked her over.

She gave him a wan smile. "I'm much better now," she said firmly. "Especially now that I have Thaddeus with me."

Thaddeus immediately hopped up on the table and walked toward her. "Big guy, big guy," he cried, earning a chuckle from both of them.

"You are my big guy," she said, reaching over to gently stroke his chest. He hopped up on her shoulder and crooned against her cheek. She closed her eyes and leaned into him. "I missed you, big guy."

"Thaddeus missed Doreen."

Her eyelids flew open, and she stared at Mack. "Did he just say that?"

Mack looked confused. He looked at Thaddeus and back to her. "What did you say, Thaddeus?"

But Thaddeus just looked at him and said, "Big guy, big guy."

"Doreen loves Thaddeus," she said and then repeated it over and over, but he looked at her like she was a lunatic. She sighed. "I'm sure he said, Thaddeus missed Doreen."

"Well, I'm not sure," Mack said. "It sounded something like that, but I'm not positive that's what it was."

In her heart of hearts, she knew that's exactly what it was, but if Mack hadn't heard it himself, he wouldn't believe her. Still, it didn't really matter. She knew. As she sat here, she looked at the band Mack now held and asked, "What is it?"

"What it is," he said, "is a piece of paper held on by this little clip." He held it out.

Like a paperclip. "Wow, it's amazing that he didn't lose it."

Mack nodded. "It is meant for something small, like this note."

"Maybe," she said, "but his leg is very small too." Leaning forward, she watched as Mack carefully opened up the tiny piece of paper, only about three inches by one inch when totally unfolded. As she stared at the message written there, she gasped. "Oh, my gosh," she cried out. "Surely that can't be what I think I'm seeing."

"I'm afraid so," he said, his voice grim.

She snatched the piece of paper from his hand and stared at the message.

Help. I'm being held captive.

Chapter 4

"SOMEBODY IS BEING held captive. Thaddeus found them, and now they're asking for help." Doreen stared at Mack in shock. "There's no way to know where Thaddeus was."

"No," Mack said, "that's a problem."

She looked at the piece of paper, then turned it upside down and flipped it over. "What are we supposed to do with this?" she asked. Then she remembered the boys who had been chasing Thaddeus—or at least following him downriver. "There were two boys," she said thoughtfully.

Mack immediately leaned forward. "What two boys?" She told him what she'd seen, and he asked, "Would you recognize them?"

She stared at him and shrugged. "I'm not exactly myself right now," she said apologetically. "And they were quite a ways away." She paused. "And once I caught sight of Thaddeus riding that branch," she said, "I didn't even think about the boys."

"Of course not," he said. "Do you remember how far up the river they were?"

She nodded. "At least a little way up the river," she said,

"not far. Maybe thirty or forty feet, but they were on the other side."

He thrummed his fingers on the table, before jumping up and saying, "I'll go take a look."

She hopped up too. "I'm coming with you." He spun and glared. She took a step forward and glared right back at him, shoving her chin up pugnaciously. "And I'll bring Thaddeus."

His eyebrows shot up, as he contemplated Thaddeus and then her. "Fine," he said, "but we'll just see where the boys might have gone."

"Fine," she muttered. She quickly swallowed half the cup of coffee in her hand and said, "What a waste of coffee."

"Put it in a travel mug," he suggested.

She looked at him, smiled, and said, "See? I'm really not myself right now."

He just rolled his eyes and waited long enough for her to pour the coffee into a travel mug, then topped it up from the pot. And then the three of them trooped down to the creek again. Only the rest of her clan wasn't having anything to do with that. As soon as they hit the river, Mugs barked, and Mack realized that the whole group had come along.

He pointed at the river, turned, looked at her, and said, "That's another reason why you need to stay here."

"Not happening," she said.

"And what will you do to get them across the river?" he asked.

She smiled, immediately scooped up Goliath, and shoved him into Mack's arms. "That's what I'll do," she said. She then snatched Mugs, who was much heavier, and picked him up herself. "I should have given you Mugs though," she muttered, earning a snort from him.

"Serves you right for trying to get into trouble all the time."

"I'm not trying to get into trouble."

"That's the problem," he cried out, as he walked across the small bridge, which even now had water splashing over the top of it. "You get into trouble without having to try."

"That's just mean," she said. "I didn't get into trouble. Trouble found me."

He sighed. "But it always finds you," he muttered. "How is that possible?"

"I don't know," she admitted. "I mean, I was just trying to say goodbye to a friend at the funeral," she said. "Who could have seen me there?"

"Anybody who was at the funeral," he said.

She nodded, considering that. "Did you ask if anybody saw what happened?"

"We've got officers right now out checking cameras, looking and questioning anybody who was there earlier today," he said, "and, so far, nobody saw anything."

She shook her head. "How is it always that way?" she muttered. "It's almost like criminals know exactly when nobody is watching."

"Well, of course," he said, "it's not like they'll do anything wrong while people are watching."

"Yeah, but they can't be in the shadows all the time," she said. "Besides, isn't it true that a lot of crimes happen in broad daylight, and people just don't recognize what they're seeing?"

"Well, it's possible," he said, "but an awful lot happens when nobody is looking too. It appears to be innocuous because they are very good at what they do."

"Well, I just got hit," she said. "They didn't kill me, and

they didn't try to move me, so I'm not sure what the whole purpose was."

"I'm not sure either," he said, "but not to worry. We'll get to the bottom of it."

And she knew he would. If there was one certain thing about Mack, he was nothing if not tenacious. And, if he said he'd do something, he would do it.

At the other side of the little bridge they turned right and headed upriver. Even there it was soggy and wet, and she knew she would have to change out of her pants again when she got home because the cuffs were already wet. Then she noted that Mack had soaked his shoes and socks too.

"You'll ruin your shoes," she announced.

"They're already ruined," he snapped. "That's hardly an issue right now."

"Are you sure though?" she asked worriedly. "Those are expensive shoes."

He stopped and looked at her, then smiled and said, "Yes, but that's also an occupational hazard," he said. "You have to work a budget into your life for clothing and necessities."

She shrugged. "You can only work a budget if you have an income."

He pondered that for a moment, as they walked forward, and he nodded. Up ahead, the pathway raised ever-so-slightly, and it was dry all the way. He immediately put Goliath down, and Mugs followed very quickly. When Doreen straightened up again, she looked at Mugs and said, "You're going on a diet."

"He's getting fat," Mack noted.

Mugs started barking and tore out after Goliath. Thaddeus, who was on her shoulder, readjusting his position after she stood up, said, "Mugs is fat. Mugs is fat."

She looked at him in shock. "You did not just say that," she cried out. "That's so mean."

"*He-he-he.*"

She shook her head. "You can't call Mugs fat," she told Thaddeus. "That is unkind, and it'll hurt his feelings."

At that, Mack turned and looked at her and said, "Did you just say that to a bird?"

She glared up at him. "Mugs has feelings too. You can't just call him fat."

Mack didn't say a word but pivoted and strode forward.

She guessed that meant that he didn't really believe her. She raced to catch up with him, grabbing his elbow. "Mugs has feelings too. We can't disregard that."

"Mugs will be just fine. Keep feeding him, and he'll be happy."

"Well, of course," she said, "but I can't have him getting fat." She quickly added, "He isn't now either."

"Of course not," he said.

"Well, he isn't," she said. "And I can't have you saying that he is."

He just groaned. "This is another stupid conversation."

"Well, I didn't start it," she said.

"Well, if you didn't, who did?"

She looked at him, thought about it, and said, "Thaddeus did."

"Oh, for crying out loud," Mack said, and he strode away even faster.

Chapter 5

Saturday Late Afternoon …

DOREEN KEPT STOMPING behind Mack, as they made their way to the first cross street. "I don't remember it taking this long," she said, as he turned to look at her.

"It's not that long. We had to go past the block because it's partially flooded."

She nodded. "You'd think, after all this time, they would have put better drainage in here."

"Mother Nature always wins out when it comes to flooding," he said. "It's not bad right now, but, every once in a while, we do get a year where it can be really ugly."

"I don't want to see it like that," she muttered.

"Have you checked your sump pumps lately?"

She stared at him in shock, then shook her head. "I have not."

"We'll do it when we get back. That's why you have them though, for unexpected water surges like this," he said, as he looked around the area. "I would have thought that this would have calmed down by now."

"I would have too," she said.

"But we've had an awful lot of rain," he said, shrugging.

"These floods come out of nowhere but go down almost as fast."

She nodded. "It seems like it's been a season of everything."

"You've had quite the time since you got here, haven't you?" he asked, tossing a grin her way.

"Well, it has been that," she said. "I'm not exactly sure what kind of a season at this rate, but it's certainly been different."

"It's better than what it would have been if you'd stayed with your husband," he said.

"Well, that goes without saying," she said, blowing a fluff of hair off her forehead. As they walked forward, she said, "I think the kids were up around here."

"This far?" he asked. Stopping to look back at her place, it was just barely visible through the trees.

She nodded. "That's why I didn't get too good of a look at them."

He nodded and stopped to survey the area. "Maybe we'll just walk up a little bit and see what we can find."

She kept pace with him now, not carrying Mugs any longer, although her wet jeans were getting more uncomfortable to walk in. They passed the Environmental, or ECO center, as the locals called it, and moved toward a residential area. When they reached the corner, she looked at it and noted, "A bunch of houses are in here. Those kids could be from some of these."

"Well, they could be," he said. "We'll take a look." As they moved up and around the area, they saw some kids playing. "Recognize anyone?"

She shook her head slowly. "Honestly it just happened so fast."

"Of course," he said. He walked up, waved at a couple kids. One waved back, but another just stared at him. The others kept playing, ignoring the adults.

"I guess your reception isn't always positive, is it?" she asked Mack.

"It's not negative either," he said. "It depends on how the kids have been raised. As to whether they're afraid of the police or not."

"I can't imagine raising children to be afraid of the cops," she said, with a shake of her head. "Besides, you don't look like a cop, but you do look like authority."

"Maybe not, but it happens."

"I guess I just think it's wrong."

He smiled. Then a child who had been sitting nearby got up and tore off in the opposite direction.

"Well, that's not a good response," she muttered.

Mack stopped and studied the kid, as he disappeared around the corner.

"Do you know him?" Doreen asked Mack.

He shook his head. "No, I don't think so, yet something is a little familiar about him."

"Well, I imagine, after a number of years, you get to know everybody here."

"Unfortunately that's not the case," he admitted. "I'd like to say it is, but certainly a lot of people live here that I've never come across."

"Well, that's a good thing then because that means they haven't been involved with the police."

"Well, that's the theory anyway."

Something in his tone of voice made her stop and glance at him. She looked around at the other kids, who were smiling, but they were looking at Thaddeus. "This is

Thaddeus," she said. "He's my parrot. Do you have any idea which two kids saw him on the river earlier?" They just stared at her with odd looks on their faces, mostly blank. "I don't think we're terribly welcome here," she said quietly to Mack.

"I think you're right," he said, his hands across his chest, as he surveyed everybody in front of them. "The question to that then is, why not?"

She shrugged. "Maybe it's more of a poor area or maybe it's just a smaller area, where they're warier of strangers."

"I wouldn't have said so," he said, "but sure. Up ahead we do have a lot of apartment buildings."

"That doesn't mean that it's a low-income area though. And I'm sure not one to be talking," she said, "because I've probably got less money than any of them." He chuckled again. She smiled. "I'm glad I can make you laugh at least."

"You always make me laugh," he said, looping an arm around hers.

She smiled, and they walked up a little closer to the kids. "Do you think they'll talk to us?" she asked.

"I doubt it," he said.

Just then a door banged on a house nearby, and a big burly man—wearing jeans, suspenders, and a dirty T-shirt—stepped out, glaring at them.

Mack smiled. "Hey. Nice day, isn't it?" he said.

"Well, it was until the pigs showed up."

She stiffened and gasped. "Did you just call me a pig?"

He glared at her. "Who are you, toots?"

At that, her jaw dropped. "My name is Doreen," she said, inclining her head regally, completely at a loss as to how to deal with him.

"That's nice," he said, shaking his head at both of them.

"You're not wanted here, so get lost." And, with that, he stepped back inside and let the door slam again.

"I don't think I've ever met anybody quite so rude," she mused, staring at the door.

"Get used to it," he said, "particularly if you think you'll align yourself with the cops. An awful lot of people out here don't like us."

"But you're very nice," she said in astonishment.

He laughed. "Doesn't matter if I'm nice or not. I'm a cop, and, if they're trying to avoid the law, they don't like cops. Likely they've had a bad experience."

"Exactly, but that's still no reason to treat you like that," she said in outrage, and it was getting harder and harder to keep her temper contained.

"Whoa," he said, looking at her sideways. "Don't you go getting all riled up now."

"Why not?" she said. "That was really unfair of him."

He snorted. "That's hardly an insult in today's world."

"That doesn't make it right."

"Maybe not, but it doesn't make it terribly wrong, and we won't cause an issue over all this." She crossed her arms over her chest and glared at him. He just rolled his eyes. "Come on. Let's head home."

"No, somebody here put out a cry for help," she said. "Remember? That's why we're here."

"We don't know that it's from here at all," he said, with quiet emphasis. "Remember that. We don't have any reason to be bothering these people."

She raised her hands in frustration and turned, as if to leave, then stopped when she spied the same little boy. "Don't look now," she said, "but that little guy who took off is watching us from around the corner."

"Of the same house?" he said, slowly turning.

"No, the neighbor's," she said.

"Good," he said, "maybe I should go take a look."

"Maybe I should," she said. "He might do better with a woman than you."

"Maybe not," he said.

"Well, I can tell you that he'll do better with Thaddeus than both of us," she muttered.

That stopped him in his tracks. "You've got a point there," he said, with a nod. "Go ahead and see what you can do."

Chapter 6

DOREEN, AFTER CHECKING to ensure Thaddeus was securely on her shoulder, called Mugs and Goliath to her side and walked slowly toward the little boy, who stared at her from around the corner. Once he realized she was approaching him, he backed away.

She immediately held out a hand. "It's okay. We won't hurt you," she said in a gentle voice. "Do you want to come meet my animals?" The little boy's eyes grew round, but he nodded. She smiled and crouched down just a few feet away from him. She didn't dare check to see what Mack was doing, but hopefully he had sense enough to stay back a little bit.

Thaddeus leaned forward. "Big guy, big guy!"

The little boy looked at him in surprise and then quickly gazed at her and back to Thaddeus.

"Yes, he talks," she said, with a beaming smile. "At least sometimes he talks. Just when you want him to talk, he doesn't though." The little boy giggled. She smiled. "Do you want to say hello to him?"

The little boy crept out a step and then another. He extended his hand, and Thaddeus reached forward—but with his beak—so the little boy got scared and pulled back.

She immediately reached out a hand. "Hey, it's okay. Thaddeus won't hurt you."

The little boy looked at her uncertainly, but then Mugs walked over and leaned up against him, almost knocking the little boy over. He chortled with laughter and bent down to pet Mugs.

"His name is Mugs."

"Mugs," he repeated, patting the dog awkwardly.

"That's right, and the cat is Goliath. Because he's so big." He looked at her in surprise and saw Goliath sitting between the two of them. She said, "You can pet him too, if you want."

He looked surprised, then gazed down at the cat, and back at Mugs, who he was still awkwardly trying to pet. She spoke to Goliath. "Well, the least you could do, Goliath, is walk a little closer for some attention."

The big cat shot her a baleful look, his attention on the house and something moving in the window. Again she didn't dare focus on that and kept her gaze on the little boy, staying crouched in front of him. When he reached out a hand toward Thaddeus, she took several small steps closer, so that Thaddeus was closer too. "Just reach out your hand flat," she said, holding hers out to show him. "Hold it out so he can check to see what's on it." When he did, she crept a little bit closer and said, "Thaddeus, say hi."

Thaddeus cocked his head, looked at the little boy, and said, "Hi. Hi. Hi." The little boy laughed and laughed.

"Isn't he fun?" she said, with a smile. At that point Goliath, who hadn't bothered to move, was now right at her feet. "If you want to come forward and say hi to the kitty, you can."

He looked at the kitty and then at Mugs, who was still at his feet.

"Or you could say hi to Mugs or Thaddeus again," she said, with open hands. "They're all quite friendly."

He giggled, but his hand stayed on Mugs, who didn't appear to mind the attention at all. As a matter of fact, he looked close to knocking the little boy over and just lying on top of him. She frowned at Mugs and said, "You be nice, Mugs."

Immediately the little boy stopped petting the dog. She faced him, smiled, and said, "No, I don't mean that he'll hurt you, but he especially likes little boys. He might want you to lie down on the grass, so he can lie on top of you."

At that, the little boy burst out laughing, as if he couldn't imagine such a thing. But she'd seen Mugs do some pretty wonderful and weird things over time.

She smiled at the little boy and said, "My name is Doreen. What's yours?"

He giggled. "Isaac."

"Well, Isaac, it's very nice to meet you. Is this your house?" She pointed to the closest one.

He shook his head, but he didn't say anything more. He kept patting Mugs. Just then came a shout from inside one of the houses. Isaac looked at a window, startled, then looked at her and bolted backward. Mugs immediately tried to run after him, but she called him back.

"Mugs, you come here." He stopped, looked at her balefully, and she shook her head. "We can't go back there. It's not our place."

The little boy disappeared down a pathway. She slowly got up, gathered Mugs and Goliath, and withdrew, so that everybody would know that she was leaving. Casually she turned, making sure the animals followed her, as she retreated to where Mack stood beside a driveway, his hands on his hips.

"That didn't appear to do much," he muttered.

"Well, we know his name is Isaac," she said, quietly motioning toward the street, so they could walk back home. "Also we don't know who's in his house, but the noise that came from inside scared him, and he took off like crazy."

Mack nodded. "I've never seen him before."

"Is Isaac an unusual-enough name that you could check birth registrations to see who he might belong to?"

He looked at her in surprise. She shrugged. "No," he said. "It would help to have more than just a first name."

She winced. "Of course it would. I wasn't thinking. I guess there are probably hundreds and hundreds of Isaacs."

"Tens of thousands across the country," he said. "It'll be pretty hard to find the one who might be here."

"Well, only like one hundred thousand or so people live here, so what will that be? Like maybe fifteen Isaacs?"

"Probably at least fifty," he said, with a chuckle. He waved toward the river. "Shall we?"

She nodded. "Or we could walk all the way around," she muttered. "I would like to know what's on the other side of that pathway."

"And we can do that too," he said, "but I'm a little worried about you and your energy level."

She frowned as she thought about it. "I'm not doing too bad right now," she said cautiously. "I just wouldn't want to go too far."

"We shouldn't have come out at all right now. It's too soon after you got hit," he said, as he looped his arm through hers. "We should be getting you back home again."

She shrugged, really worried now. She hated to admit it, but she felt a little bit shaky on the inside. But, of course, Mack had already noticed. Almost instantly his gaze zeroed in on her face. "Damn, I knew we shouldn't have come."

"When we get an anonymous message asking for help," she said, "it's not like we'll sit at home and do nothing."

"Well, I agree with that. But you're not the one who should be out here."

"It'll have to be me," she muttered. "I don't even want to contemplate who may have had Thaddeus while he wasn't with us."

"And the trouble is trying to backtrack his whereabouts earlier today," he murmured. "Because, if that crazy bird can fly just a little bit, he can also get into a lot of trouble a long way away."

"Isn't that the truth? He can get in trouble in my own backyard," she said, snickering. "I love him dearly, but we don't always know where his mind is at."

"That's true." Mack sent a quick text and slowly led her toward the street. "Another road is over here," he said. "We'll go up this way and come around."

She nodded as they headed to where the river had another bridge, and, by the time they crossed it, she started to shake. He led her to a nearby bench and had her sit down. She looked at him and said, "I can keep going, you know?"

"You can," he said, "but you don't have to."

"Of course I do," she said. As she looked down the road, her shoulders slumped. "I just wish it wasn't quite so far." At that moment, a vehicle approached and stopped in front of them. She looked at the cruiser in surprise. "Did you call them, or are they here because we look suspicious?"

He laughed. "I asked them to give us a ride."

"Are you tired?" she asked excitedly. He looked at her, his head tilted, and she sighed. "Of course you aren't," she muttered. "You called them for me because I am running out of steam."

"I called it for you," he said, "because you were recently attacked and shouldn't be out here at all."

As she looked up, she saw Arnold, working his way around the front of the car, hitching his belt up under his belly. "Arnold, you'll need bigger shirts." She motioned at the way the buttons were straining.

"Nope," he said, with a big grin. "I'm changing my laundry detergent because my shirts shrank in the wash."

She opened her mouth to say something, but Mack gently nudged her hip with his hand. She shot him a look, and he gave her a veiled glance in return. She nodded at Arnold and smiled. "That sounds like a good idea." She pointed at the cruiser. "Are you here to pick us up?"

"Yep," he said, patting his belly. "Come on in, and let me get you home."

She and her animals hopped into the back seat, giving Mack the front passenger seat.

"Off we go," Arnold said, pulling away from the curb.

Doreen heard the two men discussing the message Mack had found on Thaddeus. She leaned forward. "We also have to consider that it might have just been a prank."

"Agreed," Arnold said. "But why?"

"The printing was very precise," Mack said. "It was hardly shaky or rudimentary."

"So somebody with good handwriting then. That's great," she muttered, as she sagged against the back seat, Mugs and Goliath beside her, with Thaddeus firmly gripping her shoulder, as if he wouldn't ever get off. He kept adjusting and squawking as they drove around.

"You know what? Thaddeus seems to be quite upset," she said, studying the bird on her shoulder.

At that, Mack twisted in his seat and turned to look at him. "Hey, Arnold, let's turn around and go back."

Arnold pulled off to the side and asked, "Go back where?"

"To the area where we saw the little boy, to see if Thaddeus reacts at all."

Arnold shrugged. "Hey, I'm off in an hour. As long as you take up my time for the next hour, I'm good," he muttered. "Last thing I want to do is go back to the office."

Mack sighed. "The trouble is, we still have tons of work at the office too."

"Ha, there is," he said, "but, as long as I'm driving you guys around, I don't have to do it." With that, he pulled a U-turn in the middle of the street and headed back to the bridge. He pulled out into the main traffic and, following Mack's instructions, headed into the area they had just come from.

"What is this area called?" she asked.

"Not sure it has much of a name," Arnold said. "High Road is off to the left. You've got one of the cross-through roads up here, and we're close to Apple Park, which is the big park for the games," he said. "The big ECO center is behind us, or, at least, it is now," he said, as they drove past.

She nodded. "Okay, so where are we heading?"

"This is down in the High Road area," Mack said, as Arnold took a few more turns.

"Huh. Would Thaddeus really have been this far away?"

"You've got to understand that the cemetery you were at is just over this hill here," he said. "It's not very far at all."

"Oh," she said, falling quiet. "That's Spall Road, right?"

"Yes," he said, "and High Road is just down here a bit farther."

She sagged back. "I don't know this area at all," she announced.

"Which is why we're here, taking a look now." And slowly, with Mack watching Thaddeus for a reaction, he had Arnold move up and down several other blocks. But now Thaddeus had settled on her shoulder and remained quiet.

She looked at Mack and said, "You know how contrary he is."

"I know," Mack said. "I was just hoping that maybe, for once, he would cooperate."

Arnold snorted. "I don't think so," he said. "Every time I try to get that bird to cooperate, he gets even more difficult."

Doreen felt like she had to defend Thaddeus against these two guys and their accusations. "I don't think he's trying to be difficult," she said, "but more like he thinks you guys have got this now, so he can sit back and not do anything." At that, Arnold looked at her in the rearview mirror, his eyebrows shooting straight up. She sagged. "Yeah, I know. I hear you. That sounds ridiculous, even to me."

"I don't know about that," Mack said. "We're only just learning what this trio of yours can do. And, so far, they've been one surprise after another. Look at how I got them from home to help me find you. Mugs found you right away."

She stopped and stared at him. "Oh, my gosh," she said, sitting straight up. "I forgot."

He stared at her. "Forgot what?"

"I forgot that I wasn't even at home. That I'd left the animals behind," she said. "I was at the cemetery without them, wasn't I?"

Mack nodded. "Nan called me to say she was worried about you. That she'd tried to call you several times, and there was no answer. So she'd walked up to your place and couldn't find you. And your car was gone, which I've had returned by the way," he said. "So I grabbed the animals, hoping they could help show me where you were, and they did. Knowing you planned to attend the funeral, I started there."

"Well, how did you get Mugs to know?" Arnold asked Mack.

"Of course he knew, by his sense of smell," she said, scratching Mugs's head. "Thanks, buddy." He woofed and stretched out his front paws, the big thick heavy pads landing on top of her thigh. She gently stroked his long silky ears, smiling down at his huge chocolate-colored eyes. "You are one heck of a good sniffer dog."

"Well, you can't forget Goliath either," Mack said, "because he stayed right with Mugs. They brought us to the corner of the cemetery, where you were."

"You're pretty special too, Goliath," she said. At that, Thaddeus leaned down and crooned against her ear. "Thaddeus loves Doreen. Thaddeus loves Doreen."

Feeling her heart wrench and knowing how close she'd come to losing him, she reached up, kissed him gently, and stroked his head. Before she realized it, they were pulling up in front of her house. Mack got out, opened the back door to let out Mugs and Goliath, and then slowly helped her up and out. He thanked Arnold, and, after speaking with him through the front passenger window of the car, he straightened and nudged her toward the door.

"I'm fine," she said. "You go off and do your thing."

"There isn't anything to go off and do," he said, staying beside her. "I'm off work now myself."

"Oh, good," she said, and then she looked at Arnold. "Does he have to return to the office?"

"Sure, but his day is almost done anyway."

"So, does crime stop when you guys are done?"

"As you well know," he said, "it does not."

"I'm surprised you guys get time off."

He snorted at that. "Really?" he said. "We need time off. Particularly since you came into town."

"I didn't mean you personally. I just didn't realize that there was less of a police force in the evening, when that's when the crime goes on."

"Well, it might surprise you to know that not everybody is a criminal, and during the day we have a lot more to do than just chase those criminals," he said, his tone humorous.

She shook her head. "I'm not making a whole lot of sense tonight. I'm sorry."

"Nope," Mack said, "and it just adds to my worry that you need to get inside and to get some rest."

"I'm going to," she said, but even the front steps looked to be too much for her. Slowly she made her way up, though she knew he was waiting and watching … and worrying. "I'm getting there. I'm getting there."

"You are, but you're also showing me how much you need to be off your feet for the next few days."

She shrugged. "I can't even think about anything else but that note," she said.

"I'm on it," he said.

She shot him a look. "Again, you can't do a whole lot without Thaddeus."

"I can," he said. "I'll take a look at that area from where Thaddeus disappeared, which is at the cemetery," he said.

"And he wasn't gone all that long, yet somehow made his way back home, which is the surprise."

She frowned at that. "It's not that big of a surprise. He's got great instincts." She tried not to make her tone accusing, but it was hard when Thaddeus had disappeared earlier today.

"Hey, you don't need to say anything," he said, obviously picking up on her tone. "Believe me. I'm fully aware that I lost him at the cemetery."

Immediately she felt bad. "No," she said, "he has a mind of his own. And, when he gets on the scent of something, he's gone, whether you like it or not. It wasn't your fault."

"That's generous of you. I'm just glad we got him back," he said.

She nodded, then walked into the living room and sank down on the pot chair.

"You shouldn't stop here," he said. "Go on up to bed."

She looked up at the stairs and said, "I can't. Too many steps."

He looked at her in surprise. "Are you feeling that bad?"

She frowned. She didn't want the sympathy or for him to worry too much, so she struggled from her chair and said, "No, I'm not that bad. I'm just tired. Once I have a rest, I'll be fine." Grateful he didn't follow her up the stairs, at the top of them, she leaned over and said, "See? I'm fine."

And, with that, he nodded. "I'll check up on you later."

"Fine," she said. "Don't wake me up though."

"I won't," he said. Then he quickly turned and walked out the front door.

She used up the very last of her strength making it into her bedroom, where she sagged down onto her bed and pulled a blanket over her. She smiled to herself, as she felt all the warm bodies curling up around her, and she crashed.

Chapter 7

Sunday, Early Morning…

WHEN DOREEN WOKE up, she was surprised to hear birds singing and to see an odd half-light to the sky outside her bedroom window. She rolled over, stretched, and moaned happily. She felt pretty decent. She heard a snuffling sound at her side and looked to see Mugs rolling over onto his back, his feet skyward. She extended her hand and just barely reached one silky ear.

"Well, I feel better, so we must have had a good nap, and obviously it's got to be past dinnertime." Her stomach growled in agreement. "But do I have any food though? That's the next question. Nan didn't think so."

She slowly sat up, moving gently because Goliath was curled up against her, and she didn't want to disturb him. She reached for her phone and stared at it in shock, then turned it off and back on again.

"The dreaded thing must have frozen," she muttered. But, no, when it came back up again, it still said 5:20 a.m. She shook her head. "Wow, did I really sleep from late afternoon yesterday clear through the night?" She slowly made her way out of the bed and headed to the bathroom.

When she was done, she walked out and stood at the window. Sure enough, she could just barely see the rays of a rising sun in the distance.

She turned and looked at the rest of the animals; they were still in the bed, as if not at all willing to get up quite so early. She looked down and was still dressed in the clothes she had gone to bed in. With that realization, she slowly stripped, her pant legs still damp. She hadn't even shucked them off.

Muttering to herself, she curled back up in the bed and laid here, comfy and cozy, cuddling the animals for a while. She drifted in and out of sleep, not really tired, not really awake, barely snoozing, letting the events of the previous day pass her by. How smart of Mack to come to the house to pick up the animals to help find her. It had worked, and then, while at the cemetery, somehow Thaddeus had either been taken, moved off, got lost, or something.

But no doubt a message was tied around his ankle when she found him, and, with that line of thought, she mentally dived into endless pathways, finding no answers, as she tried to figure out why somebody would have done that. If they could write that much, couldn't they have written more, to at least give them some idea of where they were? But they hadn't, and it was just somebody's cry for help, sending Doreen nowhere. No directions had been given. No address. No landmarks. So it wouldn't be an easy trick to find who had written the note, much less where to find him.

As she lay here, her mind immediately went to the little boy who had been scared of Mack yet interested in her animals. He hadn't been well dressed and was so scrawny, like a couple steps up from starvation, but then little boys could be chubby or they could be thin. And, in this case, he looked like he was suffering. That made her sad too.

She hoped he wasn't in any danger. Maybe he wasn't going through a bad patch with the family, though her instincts told her otherwise. And the fact that Isaac had given her his first name but not a last name didn't help. There had to be something she could do for him; she just didn't know what. She also didn't know that he needed anything, since it was just a single snapshot in his lifetime. Maybe he'd had a bad night or had just lost someone close. No way for her to know.

She stretched several times, then sat up and did a couple yoga poses, proud of herself for actually remembering them. Feeling better, she got up and stepped into the shower. By the time she came out, all dried off and dressed, it was quarter to seven.

"That's a much more civilized time to be up and about," she said to Mugs. But he didn't respond, not so much as a tail wag. She reached down and scratched his available belly, then did the same for Goliath, getting a weird meow from him in surprise.

She laughed and walked over to where Thaddeus sat on his big roost and said, "Coming with me, Thaddeus?" He opened his eyes, blinked several times, then sleepily walked onto her shoulder, where he curled up in the crook of her neck. She headed downstairs to put on coffee, then opened up the back door for the fresh air and sunshine. It would be a very different season when fall hit and then winter settled in. She could really use a few more weeks of the sun.

Per the calendar it was barely summer, but the weather here in Kelowna felt like late summer. When the coffee was done, she propped open the screen door, and, with Thaddeus still the only one around, she picked up her cup and headed out to the river. She felt better but still tired and knew it would be a couple days before she had her full *oomph* back.

At least that's what had happened the last few times she'd been injured. Particularly with head injuries. She hadn't ignored her wound during her shower, but she certainly hadn't given it as much care and attention as she could have. But then again it seemed very much like she'd had so many of these types of injuries that she was almost blasé about them. Except for the pain.

Outside, she sat down on the edge of the riverbank and smiled into the morning sun. The river that had caused her so much cold discomfort yesterday, today it twinkled as it moved through the rocks. The water level had dropped off too. She understood that it depended on the rain and the mountains, and that it could rise and fall on a regular basis in a pattern that the weather forecasters could probably understand, but, for her, it was new and different every day.

It was much less of a force today though. She watched as several ducks swam upriver toward her. She smiled in delight, and, when they got closer, she immediately checked to see where Mugs was. And, sure enough, he was headed down the sidewalk to join her. When she called out to him, he picked up the pace, and, with his ears and jowls flapping in the wind, he raced toward her. Sitting on the sidewalk, cleaning himself, was Goliath. Mugs bounced by Doreen, half knocking her over. She laughed, pulling him into her lap.

"You're a sleepyhead," she muttered, as she scratched him.

He gave a light *woof* and snuggled in closer. She held him close, grateful for how much he had enriched her life.

He'd been her saving grace when she'd been married, but she felt completely differently now because she was a whole different person. Yet Mugs had come from that life to this one right along with her. He was part of her history, but, more than that, he was a big part of her future.

When her phone buzzed beside her, she looked and laughed when she saw it was Mack. She quickly texted him back. **I'm fine.**

Sleep?

Slept well, woke up early. Just now having coffee at the river.

Great.

He didn't say anything else, so she just put her phone beside her, and, with the dog still half on her lap and half on the ground, she just enjoyed being alone for a few minutes. Finally Goliath walked over and rubbed his body all along her side. She chuckled and gave him a good cuddle too. Thaddeus was busy walking back and forth along the edge of the river. She slowly reached for the rest of her coffee, tossed it back, and said, "What's up, Thaddeus?"

Thaddeus spun, as if startled at hearing his name, but he stared at her. "Thaddeus. Thaddeus."

"Yes, you're Thaddeus," she said cautiously, as she looked at him. "What's the matter. Are you upset?" At that, his head bobbed up and down, as if he were answering her. She wasn't sure what was going on. "Thaddeus, are you okay?"

"Thaddeus upset. Thaddeus upset."

She reached out her hand, and he hopped onto the back of it, then walked up her arm.

"Thaddeus not happy."

She wasn't sure if he was using the language the way it

was intended, but he was breaking her heart with his words. "What's the matter?" she whispered, as she gently nuzzled up against his cheek and head.

"Thaddeus upset," he repeated over and over again.

"What would make Thaddeus *not* upset?" she asked, but, of course, he couldn't answer. She groaned. "I don't know what's wrong," she wailed.

He nudged her. "Thaddeus upset."

"I got it," she said, "but I don't know how to fix it." It seemed like that acknowledgment helped though because he settled down on her shoulder again. It wasn't long before her phone rang, and she looked down to see it was Nan. She picked it up. "Hey, Nan. I'm doing fine."

"Are you?" her grandmother asked worriedly. "I really don't like that you keep getting all these head wounds."

"I know," she said gently. "And I'm sorry. I don't even know what happened."

"Well, that's why I'm partially bothered. I mean, you were at a funeral, for heaven's sakes, and I was there too. But you left ahead of me," she said.

"I was just wandering around after Rosie's funeral. It was just, I don't know," she said. "It was such an odd thing to realize all that woman had done."

"I know," Nan said, her voice heavy. "Did you get any sleep last night?"

"After Mack brought me back," she said, "I laid down for a nap and ending up sleeping all night."

At that, Nan stopped and then hesitantly asked, "What do you mean, after Mack brought you back?"

Doreen stopped and realized that Nan didn't know about the last bit of excitement. "Oh my," she said. "I do have something more to tell you." Then she explained about the triumphant return of Thaddeus and also about the discovery of the message on his ankle.

"Oh, my goodness," Nan cried out. "That's such a clever bird."

"He sure is," Doreen said, laughing. "Even now he's sitting on my shoulder, and a few moments ago he kept saying, 'Thaddeus is upset.' But I can't figure out why he was saying that."

"I've never heard him say that phrase before," Nan said. "That's a little scary."

"I know," she said. "It's definitely distressing, and I don't want him to be upset, but I don't know how to make him feel better either."

"I wonder how he could possibly tell us about that message on his ankle."

"I don't know," she muttered. "Mack will look into it, as well as more about the little boy." At that, she stopped and asked, "Do you know anybody with a little boy named Isaac?"

"No, I don't," she said, "not a one, and I do know lots of little boys."

"Well, you know lots of little boys who have probably grown up to have little boys of their own," she reminded Nan. "You've been here many a year."

"Yes, indeed," she muttered, but her voice was distant, as if she were thinking. "But I don't think I've ever met an Isaac."

"Well, this little guy was maybe five," she said. "He looked so skinny. His clothes were dirty, but it looked like recent activity, as if he'd just spilled his breakfast or something."

"Well, five-year-olds do that on a regular basis," Nan

said, "so that's perfectly normal."

"The other kids didn't seem to be bothered by his presence there."

"But that's kids too," Nan said.

Doreen thought about it and realized her grandmother was correct. "And none of them may have had anything to do with Thaddeus disappearing and then showing up with the note."

"And, if they had seen him on the river, or even flying in the neighborhood, he would have caused quite a commotion," Nan reminded her. "He's not exactly your normal-looking local sparrow."

Doreen burst out laughing. "Oh, that's so true," she said. "He's anything but ordinary. So it'll be that much more of a challenge to figure out who sent that message."

"And while that's part of the mystery right now," Nan said, "let's not forget that somebody attacked you. That's the real mystery we have to solve here. We can't have somebody going around town attacking you whenever they get mad or upset, or they just happen to see you," she said. "That's not okay."

Not used to hearing that kind of talk from her grandmother, Doreen frowned and said, "Nan, I'm fine."

"You're fine this time," she said in a testy voice. "That doesn't mean you'll be fine next time." And, with that, her grandmother hung up.

Surprised at Nan's reaction, Doreen put down her phone, only to hear a shout behind her, followed immediately by Mugs woofing excitedly, as he got to his feet and bounced in place, barking at the house. And she knew. She slowly twisted to see Mack coming out of the house with a big mug of coffee.

"Make sure you're bringing a second cup for me," she called out. He stopped in place and frowned at her, and she gave him a frown right back. "My cup is empty," she said, "and I need another."

He disappeared inside, without arguing, and she realized that was one of the benefits of having been injured. He was taking it easy on her. She smiled at that because Mack had been a huge blessing, whether she was hurt or not. She didn't want to carry that thought too much further, but, when he reappeared with two cups of coffee, she felt the warmth in her heart and realized what a great friend he had become.

By the time he reached her and sat down, Mugs had bounced all the way toward Mack, back to her, and then to Mack again. Goliath, in complete contrast, lay where he had been originally and just waited for Mack to arrive. Thaddeus, on the other hand, was curled up on her neck and didn't even greet Mack.

Mack looked at Thaddeus and asked, "Is he okay?"

"I'm not sure," she said. "He's been saying, 'Thaddeus is upset' all morning." Mack stared at her in surprise. She just shrugged. "He's learning so much, but I never quite know how much weight we should give to his words versus how much he actually understands what he's saying."

"It's kind of scary if he can actually talk like that about his feelings."

"I know," she muttered. With her finger, she gently stroked Thaddeus. "It's okay, Thaddeus."

He snuggled closer and said once again, "Thaddeus upset."

Mack looked at the bird in surprise. "What's the matter, big guy?"

Immediately he stood up tall and opened up his wings,

then flapped them several times and said, "Big guy, big guy."

She chuckled. "Well, he certainly seems to be happy with that."

"Exactly," he said, "and now he doesn't look depressed at all."

"And I never quite know what to think of that," she muttered. "Is he okay, or is he just being silly?"

"Well, I don't think *silly* is even part of it, but it could be that he's just as tired as you are."

"That may be," she muttered. "I did sleep well though. I crashed after you left. I didn't even get changed. I just fell into bed and woke up this morning, still in my wet jeans." As he laughed at her, she wrinkled up her face at him.

"But you've changed now," he said, "so maybe you can stay out of the water today."

"Well, that's the plan," she said. "I don't really like going in when it's cold like that."

"And yet you keep doing it."

"That was not my fault yesterday," she exclaimed.

"Maybe not," he said, "but who still got wet?"

There was really no argument for that; besides, nothing she could say would change his mind anyway. She looked at him. "How about you? Did you get some sleep?"

"I did," he said, "although Thaddeus has been on my mind a lot."

"And that message?"

He nodded. "I talked to the captain when I got back into town, to figure out what our options are."

"Does anybody have any ideas?"

"A whole group of us sat around, discussing it. We don't like the implication that a prisoner is here, who hasn't found a way to tell us anything except through a bird, but then why give such an incomplete message?"

"Time," she said. "I figured that they didn't have much chance to say anything. And there was no room on that tiny slip of paper. But how will we track him?"

"Thaddeus."

"I'm not sure that this is necessarily an adult. It could easily have been a child."

"But it was very precisely printed," he said.

She thought about that and nodded. "That's quite true too." She shrugged. "I don't know then. I just don't know what to say, but it does seem to me that when she wrote that part of the message, either she didn't have time to write more or she didn't know how to get more down."

"Or—" Mack said, interrupting her.

She looked at him in surprise and then it hit her. "Or—"

"She didn't know where she was!" they both cried out together.

He looked at her and then hesitantly said, "Did you notice we both said *she*?"

"I think because, in our world, most times women are the victims," she said quietly.

He nodded thoughtfully. "We do tend to think that way, don't we?"

"So, if somebody is held captive and doesn't know where they are," she said, "what kind of a location could they be in?"

He looked at her in surprise. "What do you mean?"

"Well, presumably they can't see a street sign."

"No guarantee they have any windows at all."

She frowned, thought about it, and said, "Then how did she get a hold of Thaddeus?"

"Good point," he muttered. They sat here, tossing ideas

back and forth, as they sipped their coffee.

"Did you get a chance to look on the map?" she asked.

"Yes, I started with the cemetery, but Thaddeus could have traveled several miles from there. I even called a biologist I know, asking how far Thaddeus could have traveled, since he doesn't fly well, and his feathers aren't fully fledged for whatever reason," he said.

"Thaddeus has a bad wing, so, even with full feathers, he doesn't go that far."

"But he could have gone far enough. The other thing is that he could easily have gotten inside a vehicle with somebody else. Somebody might have picked him up, or he may have gotten in on his own."

She winced at that. "Particularly if the vehicle looked like yours or mine," she said, reaching up a hand to pet the bird. "He's been in both our vehicles enough that it's quite possible."

"I hadn't considered that either," he said. "Maybe he got separated from us at the funeral, then made his way back to the parking lot, and jumped in what he thought was one of our vehicles. It could have been completely by surprise that he ended up wherever this person is a captive."

"And, for all we know, he's the only living thing this woman has seen."

"That's a horrible thought too, isn't it?" He sighed. Picking up his coffee, he took several long sips.

"Did you finish the pot?" she asked.

"Nope, there's another cup for me, when I go back up." She stared at him in surprise. He grinned. "Come on. You're on your second cup, and I've only had one."

There was logic to that, but she wasn't ready to give up on that last cup of coffee in the pot yet. "Sure, but I'm the injured one," she said.

He rolled his eyes at that. "How come you only use that excuse when you want to get something?"

She grinned. "Well, of course," she said. "Besides, I am injured, and I really shouldn't be doing all that much walking." He glared at her. "Well, you know I'm right."

"Right or not," he muttered, "I know that you'll just use that to your advantage."

"Only if there's coffee involved," she said. As she held out her empty cup, she batted her eyes at him.

He rolled his eyes, hopped to his feet, and said, "I should have known better."

"Nope, not at all," she said. "You're just a really good guy."

He snorted at that. "And compliments will not get you that cup of coffee."

"Well, I certainly can't race you back to the house," she admitted. "So it would hardly be sporting for you to steal my cup." She had said it in such a woeful voice that he started to laugh. "I know I couldn't possibly get there before you."

He shook his head and walked back, grumbling. "The things I do for you."

"I know, and I appreciate it very much," she called to his retreating back.

He lifted a hand in acknowledgment but didn't say anything more.

She laughed in delight when he came back out with a cup in each hand, and she realized that he had likely split the cup between them. She could hardly argue with that, as he had gone and delivered it. When he handed it over, she realized that she did have a generous half.

"And, yes, I did take some for myself," he said. "Besides,

the new pot will be ready in a few minutes."

She smiled. "You know what? It feels like a two-pot day to me also."

"Hell, yes," he said. "Some days are just like that."

"Unfortunately it seems like a lot of our days are like that."

"They wouldn't be so bad," he said, "if you would stop getting into so much trouble where you end up hurt."

"I didn't do anything," she muttered. "I went to attend a funeral and stopped to spend a few minutes, contemplating all the cases, the people, and the craziness we've seen already."

"Precisely what I mean," he said.

"Apparently I'm not even allowed to convene with Mother Nature, huh?"

"Without getting into trouble? Apparently not," he muttered.

With the coffee gone, she looked at him and asked, "Did you eat breakfast?"

He shook his head. "Nope, I haven't. I just got up and came over."

"Were you worried about me?" When he nodded, she smiled.

"And Thaddeus," he said immediately.

She reached up a hand to Thaddeus. "Do you hear that, big guy? He was worried about you."

"Thaddeus is upset. Thaddeus is upset."

She hated that he kept repeating that. Of all the phrases he said, that one was enough to make her heart bleed.

Mack studied Thaddeus, frowning.

"See what I mean? It's pretty distressing to keep hearing that too."

He nodded. "It is actually. I'm quite surprised, even though I know, in theory, he can't fully understand everything he's saying."

She rounded on him. "Of course he can."

He just rolled his eyes at her, earning a glare.

"Don't you start making it sound like he's stupid."

"Thaddeus is not stupid," he said emphatically. "He is the smartest bird I've ever met. But he's still just a bird." At that, he glared at her and added, "Don't you start arguing with me about that either."

"Well, of course not," she said, offering a strange look in his direction. "He is definitely a bird."

He groaned. "Some days I know there's just no getting away with anything with you."

"Of course not," she said, shrugging. "And why would you want to?"

"Just trying for some normality, that's all."

"I'm not sure such a thing even exists anymore," she said quietly. He looked over at her in alarm. She shrugged. "It's okay. I'm just a little maudlin today."

"What brought that on?" he asked. "We were just talking, and you looked like you were doing just fine."

"We were," she said, "and it did seem like I was doing fine, but I'm doing less fine as the day wears on. Maybe I just need some food."

"That's a good idea," he said, as he hopped to his feet, Mugs and Goliath immediately joining him. "What do you want to eat?"

She looked at him in surprise. "Are you making something?" she asked, sounding hopeful.

"Maybe it's time for you to make me something," he said.

She wrinkled her nose up at him. "I thought you wanted something edible."

He burst out laughing. "Good point."

Chapter 8

DOREEN LOOKED AROUND the kitchen. "Do you have any idea what we can have?" she asked. "Otherwise I have bread, so we could have toast." He looked at her with a scowl on his face. She shrugged. "Hey, it's what I usually have," she muttered.

"Which isn't nearly enough to keep anybody alive." He looked at her and said, "Did you pick up any other groceries?"

"I picked up a few extras last time," she said cautiously, "but probably not enough to do anything with."

"Show me."

She led the way to the pantry and pointed out her purchases. "A little bit of flour and some sugar."

He looked at her in surprise. "What were you hoping to make?"

"I was thinking of pancakes, waffles, cake, or that sort of thing." Raising her hands at his skeptical expression, she said, "Fine, I don't know. They make it look so easy in the videos, but, for an absolute beginner, it's still complicated."

"It's really not," he said, grabbing the bag of flour and the sugar. "It's really, really simple. But I understand that, for you, it's probably that first step that makes it harder."

She looked on, as he walked over to the counter, brought out a big bowl, and started tossing ingredients in.

"What are you making?" she asked, fascinated as flour hit the bowl, followed by salt and sugar. Then he grabbed a glass measuring cup and dumped in the measured butter and put it in the microwave to melt it just a bit. She watched in fascination as he added the melted butter to all the ingredients in the bowl along with milk and two eggs. It came together into a gloppy mess. Fascinated, she lifted the whisk to see the texture. "What is this?"

"It's pancake batter."

She stared at him in shock.

"Like this, with lumps?" She wanted to whisk it further, but he stayed her hand.

"Leave the lumps in."

"Oh." She dropped the whisk against the bowl and said, "I don't understand how that works. Or why you'd want it to work?"

"If you whisk it too much, it makes thin runny pancakes," he said. "We want our pancakes to rise and to be thick and fluffy." He checked his pan, heating on the stovetop, dumped some butter in, and said, "Do you have anything to go on them?"

She looked at the melting butter and said, "Well, ... butter?"

"Maple syrup, fruit puree, whipping cream, anything like that?"

She shook her head. "No," she said.

"Jam?" he asked hopefully, but she shook her head again.

"No, I finished the jar and haven't got a new one yet."

"Huh." He walked to the fridge, looked inside, and

started to smile.

"Uh oh," she said. "What's that smile for?"

"Are you willing to try something different?"

"Is it edible?"

"Of course it is," he said in outrage. "Everything I make is highly edible."

"If you're making it, I'll eat it." She gave him a fat grin.

"Okay," he said, "but no comments until you taste it."

Worried now, she watched as he pulled out sprouts and eggs. "Okay, now you're worrying me."

Then he brought out the little jar of salsa she'd bought. He held it up and said, "I'm surprised to see you have this."

"I bought it for nachos," she said, smacking her lips. "But, when I brought it home, I didn't know how to make it look like the stuff in the videos."

He cocked his head at her. "What do you mean, the stuff in the videos?"

"Well, it comes out of the oven with melted cheese and all this concoction around it, including bowls of salsa," she said. "But that jar of stuff does not look like what's in the tiny bowls of salsa."

He reached up, covered his eyes for a brief moment, and took a long slow deep breath. "Okay. On the menu this week will be nachos."

"Really?" She stared at him in delight.

He nodded. "That has got to be the simplest meal to create."

"You're only just now telling me that?" she cried out in outrage.

"Well, I'm sorry," he said, glaring at her. "Who knew Miss Hoity-Toity over here with the lobster diet actually likes nachos."

"I've always liked pancakes," she said, "but I was never really allowed to have them."

"That husband again?"

She nodded.

"So, how do you know you like them?"

She stared at him, shrugged. "I don't know. But they look good."

He groaned. "You've never even had them, have you?"

She gave him a sheepish look. "Nope, I guess I haven't. Unless I had them as a kid and have completely forgotten."

"Wow," he said. "Okay, your education is sadly lacking."

"Maybe, but I'm getting there."

He gave her a big grin. "Absolutely," he said. "You are totally getting there." He walked to the stove, and she watched as he dumped ladles full of this lumpy mixture into the hot fry pan.

She raced to the side to watch, as they bubbled and frothed in the pan. "Oh my," she said, "they smell delicious." She watched, fascinated, as he waited a little bit, then tilted the edge of each pancake, as if to look for some magical sign that it was ready to flip, then put it back down again. Her gaze went from the pancake to his face and back again.

"Why are you leaving it? Or rather, why did you lift it?" That started a long explanation on the nuances of pancake cooking. She knew it was far over her head, but, as soon as the bubbles started popping, he got to business.

"That should have been done just a fraction earlier." And he caught the other two just before they popped. She was fascinated to see them immediately poof up into these big lush fluffy pancakes, and she was almost clapping her hands in joy by the time he filled their plates. But there was a spare pancake. She stared at it, then at him and again at the spare pancake.

He said, "I'm bigger than you, so I should get the sixty-forty split."

"But I'm starving," she said, "so I should get the extra one. Plus, I'm injured." He glared at her and then sighed and nodded. Then he handed it to her. She looked at it and said, "Okay, how about we split it?" She used a knife and quickly cut it in half, so that the pancakes were evenly distributed on their plates, and he chuckled.

"I can do without the half."

"I probably can too," she said, "but I don't want to."

He smiled. "There is something special about cooking for somebody who absolutely enjoys food," he said, "so I certainly don't mind."

She watched as he then proceeded to put butter on the pancakes and then covered all of them in salsa. When she saw that her jar of salsa was almost gone, she stared at it sadly. "I had no idea that's all it would do," she whispered.

"You need to buy the big jugs of salsa," he said. "They're much cheaper." She looked at him in surprise. He nodded. "Seriously, if you buy these little jars, you're mostly paying for the little jar," he added. "Otherwise it's much cheaper for the food manufacturers to package big amounts, so it's always cheaper to buy large containers. Everything you bought here would have only cost you a couple bucks more, if you'd chosen the larger sizes."

She stared at a little bag of flour, the even tinier bag of sugar, and the little jar of salsa. "But that's not fair," she said. "I can only afford a little bit."

"And they ding you for it," he said cheerfully. "For the difference in price, you could have gotten a big jug of salsa."

He added the eggs to the skillet.

She sighed. "You know something? I never knew about these tricks to grocery shopping before."

"Absolutely there are tricks to know."

She watched as he took the sprouts from the container and split them into thirds, leaving the last third in the container for her. Then he sprinkled them atop their plates. She stared in fascination as the cooked eggs went on top of that. "I've never seen pancakes with anything green on them. Or eggs."

"Then you've never had my pancakes." He picked up their plates and said, "Grab the cutlery and the coffee, and we'll eat outside."

She said, "Well, I would, but I don't have anything to eat on." With that, he stopped and glared at her, as she shook her head, her palms exposed. "What am I supposed to do? Create a table out of nothing?"

"We'll have to fix that." Then he put the plates on the kitchen table and said, "Come eat." She sat down beside him, slowly watching as he dug in. She tried her first bite and was pleasantly surprised. By the second bite, she was over the oddness of it, and, by the third, she couldn't get enough. She plowed through her meal, until he reached across, grabbed her hand, and said, "Slow down. You'll make yourself sick."

She looked at her plate. Her food was over half gone, and she sighed. "I'm starting to realize how hungry I was."

"You worry me," he said. "There's no need to starve in this town."

"Well, there is if you don't have any money coming in," she muttered.

"Well, if you didn't have pride as such an issue," he said,

"there is a perfectly good food bank."

"See now? I've heard those mentioned and pretended to understand … but," she said curiously, "what exactly is that?"

He looked at her and chuckled. "It's not the kind of bank that you would think," he said. "You don't go make a deposit and a withdrawal."

She stared at him. "So what do you do? And why would we care?"

Still chuckling, he said, "It's a place where people go who can't afford to feed themselves and to get some free groceries."

"Free?" she asked, her eyes opening wide.

"Free," he said, "but you have to stand in line." He wondered if she might hold her nose up at that.

"So it's the inconvenience?"

"I think for a lot of people it's the humiliation."

She stopped and stared, her heart sinking, and then she realized. "Right, because everybody can see that you're standing in line for free food, right?"

He nodded. "Exactly."

"But if I was really hungry—"

"Then you could go get food. I don't know if the food bank here is open every day of the week or if it's only open certain days," he said. "I don't really know how it works because I've never checked it out before."

"And hopefully you never will," she said sadly. "I imagine there are people way worse off than me, so I would feel bad using it."

"And there is that point as well," he said, "but let's not have you starving because you won't go get something that's freely offered."

"Do you know what kind of food it is?"

"Hardly the kind you're used to," he said in a dry tone. "But good wholesome food like eggs, milk, veggies, and rice."

She glared at him. "You don't know what I've become used to," she said. "So far, it's been cereal, toast, and salad, as much as anything."

"Well, and then there is your pasta."

She gave him a fat smile. "There is that. I think I live for that stuff."

"And that would be fine as long as you had other things with it."

"I'm trying," she said, as she finished the last bite of her pancakes and put down her fork. "Man, those were so good."

"Glad you liked them," he said. "It's something I really enjoy, but I don't serve it to others very often."

"I don't even know what others in your world would be," she said. "Who do you cook for?" She had to admit a bit of jealousy churned in her gut as she wondered if he was talking about women. But when did he have time? He spent so much time with her these days that she couldn't imagine that he had room for anybody else.

"Usually my mother," he said, "and, although I don't have a relationship right now," he said, "I have had them in the past."

"Right," she said. "We all have pasts, don't we?" It was hard to hold back the glumness in her tone.

He nudged her arm and said, "I can't finish this last bit. Do you want it?"

She looked at his plate, then looked at him and realized he was just being kind. She immediately sat back and said, "Nope, I'm good, thanks." She patted her full tummy and gave him a big smile. "Honest, I'm full."

"You're lying," he said and immediately took away her empty plate and put his, that still had some food on it, in front of her and said, "Eat." Then he got up and walked over and washed the dishes.

Rather than arguing with him, she quickly finished off his plate, bounced up, and carried the dishes to him. "Thank you."

"You're welcome."

"I'm not actually starving, you know?" He gave her a sideways look. She shrugged. "It's just because of yesterday."

"Uh-huh," he muttered.

She refilled his coffee and said, "There. See? You got one from the new pot."

"And I deserve it too," he said. "Not only did I make you breakfast but I'm also doing the dishes."

She wrinkled her nose at that. "You could leave them, and I'll do them later."

"No, the egg yolk is really hard to clean up when it dries."

"Oh," she muttered, as she watched. "See? There's even a science to this that I don't know."

He stared. "You say the darnedest things."

"Well, I'm not trying to say the darnedest things," she muttered. "But, if you've never done dishes before, how would you know that dried egg is hard to clean up?"

He tilted his head as he thought about it, and said, "You really haven't done anything on your own, have you?"

"Hey, you should have seen the clothes I ruined when I first had to wash them myself."

He stopped and stared. "You've never run a washing machine before?"

"Nope. I didn't even know there was such a thing as a laundromat. Nan walked me through it the first couple times I went because I didn't have one where I was temporarily staying," she said. "That wasn't much fun."

He started to chuckle, his big shoulders shaking.

She glared at him. "Did you know that silk shouldn't go through a washing machine? Particularly not with jeans, and that shoes never go in a washing machine?" She gave him a bright twinkling smile. "Especially high heels? Let's just say, I learned quickly what *not* to do."

By then he was guffawing loudly on the floor.

"Hey, it's not that funny," she said.

"Oh, hell yes, it is," he said, as he stood back up again, wiping the tears from his eyes. He wrapped her up in a big hug and said, "Please don't ever change."

"Change," she said, "is exactly what I'm trying to do."

"Okay. Point to you for that one," he said, still grinning. Just then the doorbell rang.

She looked at the front door and sighed. "I really don't want to see anybody today."

"You have to go see who it is first," he said, and, grabbing a tea towel, he wiped his hands, as he walked to the front door.

"No. If we just ignore it," she said, "they'll go away." He gave her a strange look. She shrugged. "It won't be anything good."

"What makes you say that?" he asked.

"Well, for one, they're strangers. Otherwise they wouldn't have rung the doorbell. Two, it's a Sunday. So they're either selling something or it's somebody I don't want to see."

He fisted his hands on his hips and stared at her. "What

if it's Nan?"

"It wouldn't be Nan. She would have called me first. And she would have come up the river."

"What if it's somebody delivering you something?"

"Well, it won't be something delivered. I didn't order anything because I don't have any money to order anything."

He sighed, opened the front door, then glared at her. "Say hello."

She looked at the stranger in front of her, her mouth automatically doing as he asked. She stopped in shock. "Oh no," she said, shaking her head. "Oh, no."

"Meet Nick," Mack said, "my brother. And you can't avoid it."

"See?" she said. "It's always bad news to open the door on a Sunday." And, with that, she turned and walked back into the kitchen.

Chapter 9

DOREEN COULDN'T STOP glaring at him. Finally Mack sat her down in the living room and told her in a sharp tone, "Be nice."

She upped the wattage of her glare and shoved her chin even higher. He shook his head and shook his finger in her face. She wanted to reach out and snap it off.

"No, I did not set you up," he said. "No, I did not trick you either. And, yes, you need to deal with this."

She gasped. "I was dealing with it."

"Ignoring the whole thing is not dealing with it," he thundered.

That shut her up, but she crossed her arms over her chest and tried to glare harder, but she'd reached her limit. When she heard an odd sound, she shifted her gaze. Looking over, she saw Mack's brother leaning against the front doorjamb. He wore a huge grin on his face, and his shoulders were quaking. She gasped and jumped to her feet. "Are you laughing at me?" she cried out.

He immediately wiped the smile off his face, but he couldn't hold it and started to laugh again. "No. I'm definitely not laughing at you," he choked out, "but I am absolutely loving the interaction between you and Mack."

She frowned. "What has that got to do with anything?"

"Everything," he said, with a gentle smile. He stepped forward into the living room, then stopped, and, in the softest voice she could imagine from a guy his size, he asked, "May I come in?"

She frowned and then nodded grudgingly. "You're already here, so you might as well."

"Oh, gee, how very polite," Mack said. "You might remember that he is my brother and that you do owe him at least some respect."

She crossed her arms over her chest again and said, "Fine, but remember. I'll be true to myself and not to you."

He closed his eyes, pinched the bridge of his nose, and said, "What on earth does that mean?"

"It means that I'm no longer listening to what men like you say."

His eyes snapped open, and he glared at her. In an ominous voice, he said, "Men like me?"

She shoved her hands on her hips and went up on her tiptoes, so she could be a little closer to looking him in the eye. But she had failed miserably and couldn't even reach his chin. "Okay, men like my ex."

"Surely you're not lumping me in with him?"

"Fine." She raised both hands in surrender. "Of course not," she said, "but I spent an entire lifetime of marriage being told what to do and how to act."

"Being polite to somebody who's gone out of their way to help you is just being a decent person," he said, obviously striving to keep his temper under control.

She sighed, her shoulders sagging, as the stuffing went out of her. "Fine," she said. Then she looked at Nick and said, "You've apparently caught me at a bad time. I apologize for being impolite."

At that, Nick burst out laughing. "Nope," he said, "I wouldn't miss this for anything." She narrowed her gaze as he held up a hand. "I'm not Mack, and I'm not your husband. I am simply someone who might be able to help you."

"Lots of people have helped me in the last few weeks," she said, clearly trying to be more gracious. "It would be very nice if you could too."

"I'll take that as an olive branch," Nick said. "Now Mack said you make great coffee." She stared at Nick in shock, then turned to Mack and said, "I make what?"

He sighed. "You do make great coffee now."

She rolled her eyes at him, as she stormed into the kitchen. "Meaning, after you taught me."

"Hey, everybody has to learn from somebody. No reason not to have learned from me."

She groaned, then stepped back into the living room with a glass of water and said, "You can come through to the kitchen."

"Thank you," Nick said in that same gentle voice.

"How come you guys come so big?" she complained.

"We're a matched set," Nick said, "with two years between us."

"Are you older or younger than Mack?" She held up her hand. "No, wait. I already know you're younger."

"Why would you say he's younger?" Mack asked in surprise.

She glared at him. "You are far too dominating to let anybody be older than you." And, on that note, she turned and huffed off into the kitchen. She heard them talking in the background and knew that they were probably laughing at her again. She honestly didn't have a reason for being so upset, except that she had thought that she could get out of this. She knew she was being difficult, but there was just something about seeing Nick all of a sudden like that, without warning …

Joining them, she looked over at Mack and said, "You know we don't have time for this now."

His eyebrows shot up. "We have to make time for this."

She turned to Nick. "We do have a rather important case to be working on."

Nick looked at her in delight. "That's wonderful," he said. "What's it about?"

At that, Mack stepped in. "There is absolutely no end to this discussion," he said, "so we're not even starting down that path."

She glared at him. "It involves me, so that makes it important." Just then, Thaddeus, as if awakened, came from where he'd been sleeping in the kitchen, flying right toward her. When he saw Nick, he stopped, landing on the ground. He looked up at Mack, then at Nick. "Big guy, big guy."

She chuckled, then bent down and scooped him up, putting him on her shoulder. "Thaddeus, this is Nick, Mack's brother."

"Nick," he said. "Nick." And then he reached out a foot, as if to shake his hand.

In absolute delight, Nick gently touched his finger to the bird's foot. "Hi, Thaddeus. Nice to meet you."

Thaddeus immediately bounced his head up and down, up and down, up and down. "Nice to meet you. Nice to meet you. Nice to meet you."

Nick chuckled. "He's quite the character."

"He is, and he disappeared yesterday for a few hours and came back with a message on his ankle, which was a cry for help," she said quietly. "So we're supposed to be"—and she turned to glare at Mack—"looking for this person."

Almost defensively Mack said, "Remember? There's a whole team in my office."

She nodded. "But I bet they haven't done anything about it, have they?"

"I don't know," he said, "but we have to trust them to do their jobs."

"What if the person is dead?"

He thrust his chin toward her. "If they're dead already, we can do nothing to help them, so we've got some time."

She rolled her eyes. "What if they're dying? What if they're gasping for their last breath, just waiting for us to come rescue them?"

"Since we don't know where they are, that'll hardly be helpful," he growled.

She knew she was being ornery again, and it was only the good manners she'd been raised with that slowly pulled some of the stiffness out of her response as she turned to Nick. "Well, we don't need to air our dirty laundry in front of you."

"Hey, the fact that you even have dirty laundry is interesting," he said, waving his hand at her. "Too bad none of this is related to your husband."

"I only wish nothing were related to that man," she said, with an eye roll. "I don't know how much Mack has told you, but he isn't a very nice man."

"I've learned quite a bit about him in the meantime," Nick said. "I have to investigate each person before we can make any decisions on what to do."

"I don't even have any money to pay you, so I have no business talking to you about it in the first place," she said. "Lawyers are expensive, and this conversation has got to be costing somebody hundreds." She stopped, looked at him, and said, "But not me, right?"

At that, he laughed out loud. "No, not you. I'm not charging you for this conversation."

"Oh, good," she said, "because otherwise the door is right there. I've got no money," she said. "And, if your brother doesn't stop drinking all my coffee, I won't be able to have coffee for myself, much less anyone else."

"Oh, for the love of Jesus!"

She turned and glared at Mack, as he raised his hands in frustration.

"Yes, I know Thaddeus is listening."

She nodded. "And you've already taught him enough bad language, thank you." Again Nick burst out laughing. She sniffed, turned, and said, "The coffee is ready."

As the men joined her, she heard Nick saying something about her being delightful, and Mack replying something about Nick having no idea. She was about to take that as an insult, but, when she turned and looked at the glare on his face, she realized it probably wasn't appropriate for her to attack him anymore just now. It was only her insecurities causing her to be so difficult.

"I know that Mack has appealed to your sense of helping out the underdog," she said, "although why you would feel you need to do that, I don't know. But I can tell you that this is a very thankless case."

"Meaning?"

"I don't know how to get you any money for doing the work you're doing," she said. "Honestly, I don't have any."

"Mack was very clear about that," he said, "and we attorneys are not all after money, by the way."

She stared at him for a moment, then handed him a full cup of coffee. "I can offer you a cup of coffee," she said.

"And I'll take it thankfully," he replied. He looked around at her house and said, "You've obviously done much decluttering around here."

"Well, yes, I did. But Mack did the new addition," she said, with half a smile. "He and his buddies did the big deck," she said, then led the way outside. "He's done a ton out here, all last weekend and the weekend before," she said. "It's been amazing."

Nick looked at Mack, who nodded. "A lot of the guys from work came in to help," he said. "The thing is, she has done a lot for the community, and we were happy to have the chance to pay back some of it."

She danced around the deck. "Isn't it beautiful?"

Nick stood at the edge by the kitchen door and said, "It is beautiful. You have a lovely place here."

"I know," she said. "It's my nan's."

"Well, it *was* your nan's," Mack corrected. "It's yours now."

She nodded. "I keep forgetting that," she confessed. "And it's only because Nan is such a beautiful person that I have this home now."

"I'm sure she is delighted to be able to help you," Nick said.

"She is. She has done so much for me. She's always done so much for so many people in many ways," she muttered. Looking down at the poured concrete all the way to the path by the creek, she smiled. "It's really a beautiful place now."

Nick looked around and asked, "Do you have any chairs

to sit in out here?"

She snorted at that. "Not now." She pointed at the set she'd moved off to the side. "The one chair just broke yesterday, almost dumping me on my butt. I need to get a new set, but, when I said I had no money, I meant it. I have no money."

He grinned. "And that's okay. You don't have to do everything all at once."

"Well, that's good," she said. "It's all I can do to figure out how to survive with what I've got right now."

"And it looks like you're doing just fine," Nick said. "Cut yourself some slack."

She smiled up at him. "So you're one of those nice men, aren't you?"

His eyebrows shot up. "Well, I hope so."

She nodded. "As long as you're not like Mack."

Mack straightened from his slouch against the back door and burst in outrage. "What's wrong with me?"

"You won't let me help, lots of times," she said. "You tell me off all the time," she added, then she stopped. "Well, you are helping me learn to cook, and you do help me by paying me to look after your mother's garden." Then she stopped, looked at Nick, and asked, "How come you don't look after your mother's garden?"

He chuckled. "I do look after a lot of things for our mother," he said. "But you're right. Mack is paying you to help with the garden."

"I think he's just doing it to be nice," she said, "at least if I'm being honest. But the thing is, I really do need the money, so I try not to protest too much."

Mack looked over at his brother and said, "I told you that she gets sidetracked easily."

"Oh, and what else did you tell him?" she said in a challenging tone. He just glared at her. "Fine," she muttered, as she sat down on the edge of the steps. "Grab some deck," she said. "That's what I've got to offer."

Both men immediately sat down, one on either side of her.

Chapter 10

DOREEN LOOKED AT Nick. "So did you find out anything useful?"

"I found out all kinds of useful things," he said. "I was trying not to alert him that somebody was looking into his affairs though."

"He is probably already aware," she said. "He does a lot of that stuff himself, so he is always looking to see who's digging around into his life."

"I can see that," he said, "especially if he is involved in anything criminal."

"I don't really know where the law starts and stops with his business," she said. "When you think about it, maybe he's into the not-so-nice business activity, but possibly there is nothing illegal about it."

"Well, I've looked into some of it," Nick said, "but I haven't done a full-blown investigation into any criminal activity he's involved in."

"Can you do that?"

"Well, if I have justification for something like that," he said, "I'd bring in the cops."

"Ah, so you'd bring in Mack then?"

"No, I'd bring in somebody local to your husband's area."

"But then how would you know you weren't working with one of the cops he has in his pocket?"

He looked at her curiously. "Do you really think he does?"

She nodded. "I've seen them."

"Seen who?"

"I've seen the cops at his place."

"But that doesn't mean they were doing anything illegal."

"Well, I think it does," she said. "One time they brought some guy to talk to them, and the guy didn't want to be there. Another time I saw him hand a bundle of cash to one of them. I don't know what it was for, though maybe he was paying a fine or something."

At that, Nick and Mack looked at each other and then at her.

"Fine," she said, willfully ignorant. "That was pretty much my entire life."

"What would your husband have said to you if you'd mentioned it?"

"Well, I did mention it a couple times and got the same type of response. The first time was to mind my own business. The second time was to mind my own business or else. The third time was a smack across my face," she said quietly. At that, both Nick and Mack nodded slowly.

"You never told me about that," Mack said softly.

"I wouldn't be telling you now," she said, growling at him, "if you hadn't brought your brother into this."

"I brought my brother in *to* help you."

"He'll just get hurt," she said. "Did you even think

about that?"

He looked at her and asked, "Do you really think he's in danger?"

She frowned and then shook her head. "I don't know what to think. My ex is not a nice person."

"No, he's not. I did find that out from the various research I got involved in," Nick said. "But I'm also interested in his lawyer."

"Ah, *her*," she said, with a sniff. "She is the one he cheated on me with, and apparently now she's living with him."

"I'm not so sure about that," he said. "A moving truck was seen outside your house."

She looked at him in surprise. "Well, maybe that relationship blew up on them already. I don't know."

"What would cause it to blow up?"

"Disloyalty would be the first thing he'd get rid of her for," she said. "Like, if she slept with somebody else, if she said something she wasn't supposed to. Or even if she just didn't do whatever he wanted her to do."

"Loyalty is everything to him, is it?"

"Absolutely," she said. "I didn't realize just how much I was involved in until after I left, and then I saw it from a little distance." In a sad tone she said, "I was really very naive, and I guess that's one of the reasons why I don't like to talk about it."

"Because you feel guilty?"

"Because I feel stupid," she said in a hard voice. "I've come to realize that, in many ways, I was an abused wife, and I stayed, even though I knew he was involved in something less than stellar. But I don't know if it's criminal. I don't know if he actually broke the law or if he was just one of those snake oil salesmen who skirted the edges of it."

"The second he hit you, he broke the law," Mack said.

"Yeah, but you don't realize that when you're involved in it," she said, "and afterward he would always take me for a holiday or buy something for me, so I wouldn't make a fuss about it."

"Did you ever tell anyone?" Nick asked.

"I did tell a friend at the time once, but she told me to just shut up, to take the gifts, and to try to keep my mouth shut the next time." Both men just stared at her. "It's the way of the world in so many ways," she said. "I just didn't learn very quickly."

"So is that what you did afterward?"

"Most of the time, yes," she said, "but I was still surprised when he asked for a divorce."

"But was it a good surprise or a bad surprise?" Nick asked.

"I was conditioned to think it was a bad surprise," she said. "I didn't realize, at the time, how grateful I would be to be out of there. But, once I managed to get here with Nan, and I saw what my life had become in that gilded cage," she said, "I was quite happy to see my new world. But you don't really find gratitude easily, without something else showing up to point out just how different your life is now."

"But you did though?" Mack asked.

She heard something hesitant in Mack's voice. She turned, looked at him with a smile, and said, "Yes, and I'm fine now. You know that, right?"

He nodded. "You are now."

"That's true, and I guess I wasn't all that fine when I first arrived. I was a bit of a mess, and I know I probably came off to the townsfolk as completely cuckoo," she said, with a headshake. "But you don't really realize just how different your world is. And I wasn't here for at least the first six months of my separation," she said, "so there is that."

"What did you do in the meantime?"

"My husband paid for me to stay in a rental for a short while, but that was expensive and short-lived. So I stayed with a few mutual friends for a bit, but, once they realized our relationship really would end in divorce, and I wouldn't be in the same circles, that support dropped off. I had a carriage house apartment that somebody let me stay in for a time, and another friend let me stay in her summer cabin for a while. After that, I ended up going into less and less pleasant surroundings. Things got ugly as the money he was giving me for living expenses ran out, so did my savings, and the little bit of money I got from selling my few bits and pieces that I managed to take with me," she admitted. "Finally I contacted Nan to see about coming here for a visit," she said, with a happy smile. "Now I have a place that I'm very grateful for, even though some would say it is not even close to the house I used to live in. But I wouldn't trade it for anything."

"At least this one's real," Mack said.

She reached over, squeezed his fingers, and smiled. "It's very real here, as are the people I've found since I've been here. But it'll get ugly and very dirty if we go down this pathway," she said, turning to look at Nick. "That is why I'm so hesitant."

Just then Mack's phone buzzed. He looked at the two of them and said, "Excuse me just a moment, please." Reaching for his phone, he headed down the pathway.

"You seem to be getting along just fine with my brother," Nick said.

"When he's not being difficult," she announced. Nick

burst out laughing. She smiled at him. "You seem like a nice man, Nick. Why would you want to be a lawyer?"

At that, he laughed even harder. "Lawyers can and do offer good and helpful services to their clients."

"Well, my divorce lawyer didn't," she said. "She screwed me over on the paperwork, and then took my husband and moved into my bed," she said, with a shake of her head. "A lot of that I can be grateful for now. But the betrayal—"

"More than the personal betrayal," he said, "was the financial betrayal."

"We have a separation agreement."

"Which is null and void because of her representation in this case."

"Oh, so I don't have a separation agreement?"

"You don't, not a legal standing one."

"So what does that actually mean?"

"It means that you could move back into your old house, if you wanted to."

She stared at him in shock. "That'll get a little too cozy in my bedroom, don't you think?" she muttered.

He burst out laughing again. "Obviously that's not what you want to do, but you have every right to that home, just as he does, because there is no agreement right now."

"What does the other lawyer say? Besides, you say we don't have an agreement, and my ex won't agree."

Nick shook his head. "Doesn't matter. I've submitted several documentation complaints about your divorce lawyer's behavior, and she's coming up for a complaint with the bar herself for another issue. Other than that," he said, "I've started a lawsuit against her on your behalf."

She stared at him in surprise. "But that will get expensive. My ex used to talk about it all the time."

"Talk about what?"

"About suing people and saying he would ruin them."

"Absolutely," he said. "At the same time we have a very strong case against her."

"What is the basis of our case against her?"

"It has to do with her not fulfilling her legal obligations and actually being criminally negligent for filing the paperwork that she chose to file."

"Oh my. So maybe she won't be allowed to live in that fancy house either?"

"I'm going for jail time and to have her stripped of all her legal standing in the community."

"So then she couldn't make a living afterward?"

"Not on the backs of her unsuspecting clients anyway."

"Isn't that a little extreme?"

He shook his head. "No. Fraud is a big deal, and she cheated you out of many hundreds of thousands of dollars, possibly more."

At that figure, her jaw dropped, and her eyes went round. "What?"

He looked at her and said, "You really have no idea how much he's worth, do you?"

She shook her head. "No, I really don't, but it was all in the business."

"That house alone is worth four million."

"Yeah, but he was never going to let me have the house," she said, "not that I want it."

"And that's fine," he said. "He can buy out your share."

She looked at him. "You mean, he would give me money for my share of the house?"

"Yes, which is probably why he went the route he did."

"It's absolutely why he went that route. He often told

me before that I could leave any time I wanted, but I would never get anything from him."

"And he went out of his way to make sure that happened. But they both crossed the line when they cheated you out of everything. If he'd given you a decent or a reasonable settlement, it wouldn't have come to this."

"No, I wouldn't even have considered that this was an issue. What would be a reasonable settlement?" she asked cautiously.

He looked at her with a smile and said, "Several million at least."

She let out her breath in a long slow *whoosh*. "That would be rather unbelievable."

"That's because you don't realize just how much you're entitled to."

"You still have to get it though, and he won't hand it over easily."

"Nope, he probably won't, which is one of the reasons for using your divorce lawyer. To make sure that it was even more complicated."

"And I did sign away my rights."

"But that document isn't legal in standing because she's up for charges on her issues too."

"Interesting," she muttered. "So my divorce attorney actually committed fraud by doing what she did?"

"Absolutely," he said. "She was not representing you. She was throwing you to the wolves."

"Yeah, I felt like it at the time, but, by then, I was only looking for freedom. I wasn't really seeing the wolf pack out there, waiting for me."

"No, and that's why it happened," he said.

"What can we do now?"

"I have a lot of paperwork I need you to sign," he said, and she looked at him carefully.

"But are you any better than she is?"

He stared at her and said, "If only you had asked some of those questions when you worked with her."

Chapter 11

D OREEN WINCED AND nodded. "Right, but I had known her for a long time, and I thought I could trust her. But instead I think she's the one who told him when I was looking at leaving. So he immediately took action. Instead of my jewelry being in the safe, where it was supposed to be, it got moved somewhere else, and the money he had left for my allowance that month disappeared. When I asked him for it, he said I must have spent it. It was a series of little things that all happened within the last few days that I lived with him."

"You're right. I'm sure she was feeding him all kinds of garbage. But the bottom line is that she represented you. You had retained her on your behalf, and instead she used you to get to him."

"Absolutely," she said sadly. "Because people are like that."

"Not all people are like that," he said, gently correcting her.

She smiled. "You're telling me that you're different," she teased.

"I'm very different," he said, "and people like her are the

ones I like to go after."

"Well, that's fine," she said, "as long as they don't know too much about it."

"They're bound to find out when I start filing the paperwork, but that's not your problem."

"Says you. But what if they find me here?"

"Do you not feel safe here? Or do you really feel like he'll come after you?"

"I haven't thought he would be bothered, but he really does care about his money, and he really cares about that house."

"Interesting," he said. "Well, once the paperwork's filed, we can't hide it."

"No, and that'll cause some extra issues for me," she muttered.

"Do you have security here?"

"It's not even that," she said, "because I'm out all over the place. I won't stay behind locked doors. I won't live like that. He used to tell me when I could go out, what I was allowed to do, and when I could do it," she said. "I don't ever want to live like that again."

"And you shouldn't have to," he said. "Never again."

"Says you," she muttered. She looked down at her empty coffee cup and said, "Do you want a second cup of coffee?"

He smiled and said, "I'd love one. And maybe then we can sit down and do some of this paperwork."

Sighing, she snatched their coffee cups and headed for the coffeepot. When she returned, Mack was back, and the two of them were talking.

"You agreed to sign the paperwork?"

"Do you agree that your brother is trustworthy?"

He looked at her, smiled, and said, "Yes, absolutely."

"Fine," she said. She sat down at the kitchen table, and they started through the paperwork, and, by the time they got to the third page, her eyes were glazing over already, and she just signed automatically. When she handed it back to him, she said, "For all I know, I just gave you everything."

"What you did was authorize me to go after her and your husband, at no cost to you."

She looked at him and asked, "So how do you feed your family?"

"I don't have a wife or children, if that's what you are asking," he said, with a smile. "What I will do is make sure that, when it goes to court, and he loses, they cover all the fees."

"Including your fee?" she asked in delight.

He nodded. "That's how it works. They have to pay for the court fees and for my fees as well."

"Good. Then, when he loses, and it comes to that, make sure you charge him lots," she said.

He burst out laughing. Not long after that Nick stood and said, "In spite of a rough start," he said, "I'm really happy to have met you." He reached out a hand, and she shook it in surprise.

"I shouldn't have been so mean," she said, "and you're right. I've been avoiding meeting you." She shot Mack a sideways glance. "Mostly because it's a period of my life I don't like to reflect on."

"That's fine," he said, "but sometimes you can't let people get away with doing all this bad stuff. I've heard from Mack about how good you are at making cold cases not so cold anymore and how people are being brought to justice after a long time. Let's not let this be something that goes on for so long that we can't do anything about it."

She smiled up at him. "Okay. I hear you on that one."

Just then, Thaddeus woke from his nap on her shoulder and looked up. "Big guy, big guy." He looked over at Mack and said, "Big guy, big guy."

Both men laughed. Doreen reached up to stroke his head gently and said, "Now if only you could tell me who put the message on your leg."

"Message? Message? Message?" While he seemed to be confused about the word, he kept shaking the leg that had the message attached to it.

"Thaddeus, do you know who put the message on you?"

Thaddeus rubbed his head against her and said, "Thaddeus loves Doreen."

"And I love you too, yes, but you're darn frustrating. I wish I knew who put that thing on your leg."

"There is that, as one mystery," Mack said, "but there's also the person at large who hit you over the head."

At that, Nick looked at her in concern. "Do you have any idea who that could have been?"

She shrugged. "No, not at all. But, like Mack would probably tell you, I've made some enemies in town."

"But haven't they been locked up?" he asked, looking to Mack.

Mack shrugged. "Sure, but she has also split up some families because of it."

"I guess," Nick said doubtfully. "But that's an awful lot of hate if somebody came after you personally."

"Sometimes people do things just out of emotion," she said. "They see me, and all that anger and pain comes rushing back, and they attack for no other reason than that."

"Maybe," Nick said.

She looked at him. "Does anybody know you're here?"

"My office and a couple other people knew I was coming to visit Mack here."

"I don't think it's got anything to do with my divorce case anyway," she said. "Although you certainly bring in some new suspects."

He looked at her in surprise. "Are you thinking about your ex again?"

"If I wasn't around, what would happen to all that money?"

He stopped, looked at her, and said, "Good point." He turned to Mack. "Are you keeping an extra eye on her?"

"Keeping an extra eye on her is not even close to a solution," he muttered. "She gets into trouble faster than anybody I know."

"That's not fair," she said. "Besides, it's all part of the work we do."

"The work *I* do," Mack said, glaring at her.

She shook her head and sighed loudly. "Fine, so I haven't helped solve any of these past cold cases?"

"This deal with the message Thaddeus brought home isn't necessarily a case at all. For all we know, it's a child's prank. I'm more worried about who attacked you at the cemetery."

She nodded. "But you don't believe that," she said, "and neither do I."

He frowned, dropped his gaze, and said, "But we need a little more than that note in order to backtrack Thaddeus's whereabouts, when we lost him."

"Is there any way to know where he went?" Nick asked.

"No, not really," she muttered. "We went back in that area and found the little boy Isaac," she said, looking again at Mack. "Did you ever find any Isaacs in the area?"

"The guys are working on it." He pulled out his phone and called somebody. "Hey, Chester. Any luck tracking down Isaac?" Mack shook his head and looked over at her. "Chester hasn't had any luck either."

She frowned. "If somebody has a child at home, and they don't fill out the paperwork for that child, then there's no record of his birth, is there?"

He stared at her in surprise and said, "No, not if they were trying to keep the birth secret or just didn't register for some reason."

"Well, what if Isaac isn't registered anywhere?"

"Why would a parent do that?" Mack asked. "We can't just assume that's what happened here."

"No, of course not. But, if we have somebody who's a captive somewhere around here—and you know very well that there are all kinds of nasty scenarios that could make for such a thing—so what if Isaac's birth was just never registered?"

"Then nobody would know," Mack said.

Nick asked, "Any idea how old he is?"

"I'd say four to five," she said. "It's quite possible that he's too young for school. And, if nobody knows about him," she said, looking back at Mack, "they wouldn't be expecting him in school anyway."

"That's quite true," he said thoughtfully.

"We could go back over and make it an official visit," she said. "To at least find out who Isaac's family is."

Mack nodded and said, "Maybe I'll get one of the guys to do that."

"Yep," she said, "you do that." As he walked a little farther away and made the phone call, she chuckled. Looking over at Nick, she said, "He walks away because he thinks he can keep the conversation out of my hearing."

"Does it work?"

"Nope," she said, "because I have a good idea what he's up to."

"But isn't he trying to keep you safe?"

"No, he's trying to keep me out of his business," she said, with a big fat grin. "And that doesn't work."

Chapter 12

MACK RETURNED A few minutes later with a surprised look on his face.

She stared at him, knowing something was up. "What? What is it?"

"The cemetery had some security cameras. The guys have been going through the images," he said, "and a couple faces they don't recognize. Most of the visitors were locals, but a few we can't identify, and they're asking you to take a look."

She looked at him in surprise and then jumped to her feet. "Perfect," she said. "Can we do it now, even though it's Sunday?"

"It's better for us actually, since it's a little calmer."

She smiled and nodded. "Now?"

"Sure," he said, as he looked over at his brother. "Are you coming to dinner tonight at Mom's?"

Nick nodded. "I'll be there," he said, "and, in the meantime, I've got paperwork to deal with." With that, he waved a hand and disappeared out her front door.

She turned, looked at Mack, and said, "In spite of you," she said, "I like him."

Laughing, Mack replied, "Nick is a really good guy."

"I'm just a little leery," she said, although with a relieved smile. "This whole thing is scary honestly. I would just as soon spend the rest of my life never seeing my ex again."

"Nobody said you had to see him," he said in surprise.

"Really?"

He nodded. "Yeah. Ask Nick, but frequently it can all be done without you having to face him."

"Oh, in that case," she said, "I feel much better."

"Good," he said. "Come on. Let's get down to the station."

"Okay," she said. "What about the animals?"

"Let's take them along. I'm still trying to unlock the mystery of how Thaddeus thinks, so we can figure out what's really going on with that."

"Wouldn't that be nice," she muttered. As they headed out to his truck, she snagged her purse.

"Do you need to shop anywhere today?" he asked. "And, by the way, I checked your sump pumps earlier, and both are doing fine."

"Oh, that's a relief." And it was, as she'd completely forgotten about it. "And, as you saw, the fridge is a little bare."

He snorted. "That's more than a little bare," he said, as he opened the passenger door to his truck and lifted Mugs up, so he could sit in the footwell. Goliath jumped up all on his own, and Thaddeus never left her shoulder. With Doreen and all her animals safely ensconced, he closed the door and walked around to the driver's side. As he got in, he said, "How is your head?"

"It's much better today," she said. "Now I can't stop thinking about Thaddeus going off by himself, coming back with a note."

"And how typical of you," he said. "You can't stop thinking about Thaddeus's solo adventure, but getting attacked and hit over the head is a whole different story."

"That's true," she said. "The thought of somebody being held captive just bothers me."

"Are you thinking of your own captivity while married?"

She shrugged. "It's not fair for anybody," she said, "and, if it relates to that little boy, it's even worse."

"But we don't have any way to connect that to him," he said. "Remember my warnings about assumptions."

"I know that," she said patiently. "You're always on me about that, so how could I forget?"

"Of course I am," he said. "And we have to do things legally."

"Right," she said. "It really hampers things, doesn't it?"

He chuckled. "In some ways, yes, it does, but it keeps everybody following the law, so that we don't end up doing renegade stuff, like your ex."

"Good point," she said, with a heavy sigh. "That's exactly what he did. He always wanted to do things his way and never had the patience to follow the law. He often said it was too slow, too fussy, and that he could get things done much faster without it."

"Apparently he did, but there comes a point in the process where you have to pay for that involvement, and the time could be now."

"Maybe so. He is pretty slippery though," she said, "so I highly doubt it."

He smiled and said, "Well, hopefully my brother will give him just enough rope, and maybe, just maybe, he will hang himself." She looked at him in surprise, and he immediately shook his head. "I don't mean that literally," he said. "It's just an expression."

"Where do these expressions come from?" she wondered. "I mean, why would anybody hang themself? It doesn't make sense."

He sighed and said, "Don't worry about it."

With a shrug, she said, "I wasn't going to. I figured you just didn't know where it came from."

He burst out laughing. "Well, actually I do, but I'm not going there," he said. "Besides, we're at the station already."

"That's the thing about a community like this," she said. "Everything is so close by, and everybody is right here."

"Exactly." He hopped out, walked around, and said, "Come on. Let's get the animals. I love the fact that they're welcome in the station. They might as well get their own shields too. They've done so much for the city."

"And it's lovely that you guys believe that," she said. "It certainly makes my life easier."

"True," he said, "but the bottom line is that they've done more good than harm, so we're willing to give them—"

"Enough room to hang themselves?"

Laughing out loud at her quick wit, he then shook his head and said, "No, obviously we don't want them to hang themselves."

"Good," she said, "it's a stupid saying anyway."

He just rolled his eyes, as he pushed open the front door to the precinct, and they walked in, all the animals eagerly striding forward. When Mugs saw Chester, he raced forward to give him a big greeting. Goliath had been Goliath, first wandering through Chester's legs, then went off to stroll around to see who else was around.

"It's pretty sad," she said, "but the animals are really very comfortable here."

"Why is that sad?" Chester asked.

"It makes it seem like they're on a bad pathway, being this much at home at the police station," she muttered. "They are really good animals, you know?"

He looked at her in surprise, and immediately Mack said, "Don't even worry about it. She's had a rough weekend."

Chester looked at her sympathetically. "How is the head?"

"Just fine," she said, beaming at him. "And thanks for asking. Not everybody does." Then she turned to glare at Mack.

He glared right back. "I did ask you."

"Sure, but that's when you were stealing the coffee out of my house."

"Oh, for the love of Pete." He just shook his head, walked into the back, and called out, "Chester, did you have those pictures for her to look at?"

"Sure do," he said, huffing, as he set off after Mack. "They're in here." He looked at Doreen. "You can come on back here." She shooed the animals ahead of her, and they walked into the small room, where Chester had a bunch of photos laid out.

"These are really grainy," she complained.

"Sorry, they are from the cemetery cameras," he apologized. "So it's not like they are the highest quality."

"Nobody really has much in the way of high-quality security equipment around here, do they?"

"Well, we're all gradually getting more," he said. "Unfortunately that seems to be the way the world is working."

"Isn't that sad?" She sat down, looked at the first picture and studied it for a long moment, then shrugged. "I don't think I've seen this guy before."

"You don't *think* you have?" Mack pounced.

So she looked at it again and said, "No, I don't think so."

He stopped, looked at her, and said, "But?"

"No buts," she replied, and then she shrugged. "Well, maybe there's a but." Both Chester and Mack looked at her, as she put the picture off to the side. "Something is a little bit familiar about him, but it's not like it's telling me who he is and where I may have seen him."

"Okay," Mack said. "We'll keep that one close and see what we can come up with in the other photos."

They went through them all, and unfortunately she didn't identify anybody. Another one was familiar, which was just enough to set their nerves on edge because she couldn't give them any more information than that. The very last photo she looked at for a long moment, then gasped.

"What is it?" Mack asked.

"I think this guy used to work for my ex."

He stared at her in shock. "Seriously?"

She nodded slowly. "That means the work your brother is doing puts Nick in danger," she whispered, feeling fear in her heart. "You need to stop him."

"We can't stop him," he said. "It's already started, if this guy has been in town," he said, tapping the photo.

"Hang on a minute," Chester said. "You need to fill me in on this."

She shook her head rapidly, sending hair flying all around her face. "No, Chester. I don't want you to get hurt," she said gently. "The less you know, the better."

He stared at her nonplussed, as Mack sighed. "Don't

even try to figure out that logic. It seems she is getting worse."

"I'm not getting worse at all," she said. "I just don't want my friends to get hurt. Chester is a friend, and I don't want him involved."

"He's a cop first," Mack said, exasperated. "It doesn't matter what you want because this is what we do."

"But what if he gets hurt because of this?" she asked in a reasonable tone of voice. "Then I'll feel responsible, and I can't have that."

"And why can't you have that?" Chester asked, fascinated.

"Because I'll feel guilty," she said by way of explanation. "I don't need or want any more guilt in my life," she said. "I'm really working hard to be stress-free."

Chester looked from Mack to her and back, as if trying to figure it out, and Mack just shook his head. "I told you. There's no working it out."

"What's to figure out?" she wailed. "He's a friend, and I don't want to put anybody in danger."

Mack leaned over the table, the cords in his forearms pulsing with tension as he glared at her. "We're cops. This is what we do."

"Fine," she said, "but, if Chester gets hurt, that's on you."

Chester immediately sided with her and said, "Yep, if I get hurt, this one's on you." He shot Mack a big grin. "So now what will you do?"

Mack glared at him. "I'll put you to work, that's what. See if you can find out who this guy is and where he's located." He looked at Doreen. "Do you have a name for him?"

She shrugged. "Snoz." Both men stared at her.

"Snoz?" Chester asked, in surprise.

"Well, I don't know what his real name is," she said, "but that's what I called him."

"Why would you call him Snoz?"

"Good Lord, look at the size of his nose," she said. "Isn't it obvious? It's huge."

"Oh, great," Mack said. "Do you have a real name for him?"

"Nope," she said cheerfully. "So looks like Chester can't track him down, so he won't get hurt after all."

"Oh boy," Mack muttered. "Chester will track him down, and he won't get hurt."

"Okay," she said, "but I really don't want anybody else getting hurt."

"Anybody else?" Chester asked. "Has somebody else been hurt?"

She looked at him in surprise. "Well, there's me," she said.

Chester flushed. "Well, I know that," he said. "I thought you meant somebody else."

"Nope, nobody else. Just me." Then she looked at him sideways. "Isn't that enough?"

Chester immediately looked to Mack for help. Mack looked at her and said, "That's enough."

"Fine," she snapped, with a wave of her hand. "We're wasting time. You need to track down Snoz." She frowned.

"What now?" Mack asked.

"You know what? I'm not positive, but his real name might be Bill."

Pinching the bridge of his nose, he calmly looked at her. "Do you happen to have a last name?"

She shook her head. "No, but he definitely works or worked for my ex."

"Well, that we might be able to do some good with." Mack looked at her and smiled and said, "And now we have a reason to contact your ex."

She looked at him in horror. "Oh, no. No, no, no, you can't do that."

"Why not?" he asked.

"Because he'll get really angry," she said, clearly worried.

"So I suppose now you're worried I'll get hurt."

She looked at him in surprise. "Actually I'm not," she said. "I'm worried Chester will get hurt."

At that, Mack raised his hands. "I don't get it. Why aren't you worried about me getting hurt?"

"Because your head is too thick, and you're too stubborn," she said, "but Chester here is much smaller, and he could really get hurt."

Chester immediately nodded. "She's right. I could. I definitely could." But even he couldn't hold back his chuckle.

Mack glared at him. "Don't you start," he said. "Go contact her ex and see if he has this person working for him."

"He used to work for him," she said. "I didn't see him much in the last year I was there."

"Did you see him at all?"

She frowned and said, "He was off doing jobs for him, so I don't know what he was doing, but I didn't see much of him."

"Do you know what kind of jobs he was doing?"

"No, I don't, and he told me that I wouldn't understand it."

"Well, that could very well be true. Who knows what he

was into. And, if you didn't know, you couldn't be asked to explain it to anybody," he said.

"Maybe so." She shrugged. "In the end, asking too many questions of my ex had proven to be problematic for me more than once, so I stopped and didn't pursue it."

"Which is probably smart," he said in understanding. "This Snoz guy could actually be somebody who does jobs, like attacking people."

Her eyes grew round. "That would not be very much fun," she said. "I hate to think of my ex-husband involved in all that stuff, but the evidence does seem to be fairly over-whelming."

"The bottom line is," Mack said, "that we need to find out who this guy is, and maybe this other one as well, so we can figure out what they were doing at the cemetery."

She looked at the first one again and tapped the photo. "He still looks familiar, but I just don't remember where I've seen him."

"Well, that's a start," Mack said. "We'll flash these photos around town and see what else we can come up with."

She smiled. "Good. Then we can go after that little boy."

"What do you mean, go after that little boy?" Chester asked.

She faced him. "Thaddeus was kidnapped, and that little boy seemed—" She stopped. "I can't say *suspicious*, but definitely something was off about him."

"I heard about that," he said. "Arnold was working on tracking down the people there. We don't have many problems in that corner at all," he said, "even though it is a known lower-income area."

"Interesting," she muttered. "Any idea why?"

"Doesn't matter, we're just grateful."

She had to admit he had a point. Because any problem-free areas benefited everybody. "I'll walk back up there again," she said. "I'll take the animals with me."

"And just how will you get there?" Mack asked her curiously.

Frowning, she realized that she hadn't driven her own vehicle here. Suddenly smiling, she asked, "Could you give me a ride, pretty please?"

When Mack hesitated, Chester said, "Considering she's been recently injured, why don't you just take her home?"

"Because Mack knows that I'd leave again as soon as he dropped me off," she said, with a bright smile. "That little boy is on my mind, and I'm worried about him."

"Well, I guess we could always try to find his family," Mack said.

"Good." She hopped to her feet and said, "Chester and Arnold can check out these photos around town."

"That too," he said. "Run me off a copy of those pictures, and we'll take them with us."

At that, Chester nodded and left to make the copies.

She smiled. "See, Mack? That's a really good thought."

"Yes, it is," he said. "We're not idiots, you know?"

"No," she said, "you're not. But you guys miss things."

"Unfortunately we miss way too much," he muttered. "You're starting to make the whole department look like idiots."

"You're not idiots, but sometimes it takes fresh eyes to see what's really been under your nose the whole time."

"We don't want to hear about that," he said with a laugh. "Nobody wants to think that you've overlooked all this stuff." When Chester returned with the copies for him, Mack got up and said, "Come on. Let's go take a look."

Chapter 13

I N MACK'S TRUCK they drove up and down the street and several other streets nearby but saw no sign of the little boy. Doreen frowned. "You know what? I think I'll walk around here on my own," she said. "I suspect that driving around in this big truck that they don't recognize is what's keeping us from finding anything."

"But that would imply that somebody out here is always watching and keeping track to make sure that nothing is going on that they don't know about," he said.

"That's not all that far off the realm of possibility either," she said.

He looked at her in surprise, studying the area around them. "Chester was right," he said. "I've hardly been into this area at all. We haven't had any trouble here."

"Doesn't that strike you as unusual?"

He nodded. "Yes, but not criminally unusual."

"Sure, but, if they do it right, there's no criminality in it."

"Meaning?"

"I don't know," she said, "it just feels odd."

"Well, I've learned to trust your instincts in many ways,"

he said, "so keep talking and tell me what's odd."

"You would expect to see something here," she said. "It's obviously a low-income area, and the people here are clean but not well dressed. They look like they're hardworking, and maybe they've formed together to have like a neighborhood watch to keep the area safe."

"They also don't like cops so they could have a criminal element, or just a distaste for authority."

"Which isn't unexpected. In theory, we should also be able to knock on a door to find out where Isaac lives."

"But not if nobody is willing to share that information. And then the question becomes *why?*" he added. "Why won't they share that information?" He tapped the steering wheel and nodded.

"See? It's easy."

"Not so easy," he said. "It's also getting later."

"Right," she said. "Then nobody will answer doors."

"It's not late, but it's a Sunday afternoon," he said. "So in theory …"

"Right," she said. "In theory, we should probably head back." She was reluctant though.

"Why don't you go home and then maybe, instead of sitting there and fussing about everything, you could have tea with Nan?"

She looked at him in delight. "That is a perfect idea," she said. "I should have called her earlier." She immediately pulled out her phone and called Nan, while Mack drove. "Hi, Nan."

"There you are," her grandmother cried out in relief. "I was expecting to hear from you, but I didn't want to call and wake you up."

"I'm so sorry," she said, hating that feeling of knowing

her grandmother had been waiting for her. "I'm driving with Mack right now."

"Lovely," she said.

"I was thinking about coming for a visit," she muttered.

"Why don't you come for tea now?" she said.

At that, Doreen looked at her watch and said, "No, I don't want to do that," she said. "I'll disrupt you at dinner."

"Hush," Nan said. "We had a big lunch today. It was a big birthday celebration for one of our older people here," she said. "I ate way too much and wasn't planning on going down for dinner anyway."

Impulsively Doreen looked at Mack. "Could you drop us there?"

He nodded. "That's a good idea," he said.

"Is that okay with you, Nan?"

"Okay with me?" she chirped. "I'm delighted."

And, with that, Doreen put away her phone and watched as Mack changed direction. Minutes later, Nan's place came into view. Even as they neared Rosemoor, Mugs and Goliath got all excited. Mack looked at them in surprise. "Wow, they recognize this place, don't they?"

She laughed. "Everybody loves Nan," she said, "even these guys."

"With good reason," he said, with a smile. "She's a super person. You're lucky to have her."

"So lucky," she said, hating the tears that automatically came to her eyes.

"Hey, don't get upset. She's still got a lot of years in her."

"I hope so," she muttered. "It would be terrible to lose her now. I mean, I know I haven't been here very long, but it seems like we've finally gotten to a relationship worth keeping."

"Hold that thought," he said, as he parked. "Now go and enjoy an hour or so with your grandmother."

"Will do," she said, with a bright smile. She remained seated, looked at him, and said, "Keep an eye on your brother now."

He looked at her in surprise. "Why?"

"Because he came to town to help me, and this person from my husband's employment is also in town," she said. "So I'm a little worried it's all connected. There's no other reason for Snoz to be here, and, if you think I'm in danger, it's also quite likely that your brother is in danger as well."

A frown formed on Mack's forehead as he studied her face. "I guess that's possible," he said, "but certainly not something we were thinking about."

"No, but if somebody can stop Nick from putting in that paperwork," she said, "it just won't go in then, will it?"

He nodded. "I'll give him a shout."

"You do that," she said, "and make sure he understands to stay safe."

He looked over at her, smiled, and said, "You can't protect the whole world, you know?"

"No," she said, "I can't. But I can certainly work at protecting the world close to me." And, with that, she opened up the truck and stepped out. Mugs jumped to the ground, barking excitedly, and even Goliath jumped out with alacrity and looked around at the world in joy. "They do love coming here."

"Does Nan give them treats?" he asked.

She laughed. "Absolutely. I think that's half the joy for her."

"Then they were her animals first, weren't they?"

"Not Mugs," she said. "And, if anybody asks, he owns Goliath," she said, with a roll of her eye. There was a call from the corner, and she looked over to see Nan out on her little patio area, now standing at the edge and waving at her.

"There's Nan," she said in delight. She looked at Mack. "Stay safe." He went to say something to her, but she slammed the door shut and turned to leave.

He opened the window on his side and called out, "You stay safe."

Smiling, she said, "I'm fine. I'm always fine."

"Says the woman who was just attacked yesterday, right?"

She gave him a smirk. "Maybe you should figure out who did that," she said, raising her eyebrows at him. "It's not like you've got anything else to do."

"No, looking after you is my full-time job these days," he muttered.

She turned, smiled, and said, "That's okay. So far you're keeping me alive, and that's a lot."

"Yeah, but for how much longer?" he muttered.

Ignoring him, she kept on walking to see Nan.

Chapter 14

IT WAS ABSOLUTELY lovely to see Nan again. And, since she'd calmed down somewhat since Doreen's latest accident, it made for the same kind of visit they'd always enjoyed, full of warm love and companionship. With the animals getting double the treats from Nan today for some reason, and a tray of what looked like warm chocolate chip cookies and a hot pot of tea, the two women sat and commiserated with each other. When Doreen explained more about her theories as to what had happened with Thaddeus disappearing and then coming back with that message, Nan clapped her hands together in delight. "Another mystery," she said. "You do have such luck."

"I already have plenty of mysteries sitting at home." At Nan's frown, Doreen explained, "Remember all those files from Solomon? I could probably pick out any one of them, and Mack would have a matching cold file for it, just waiting for me to solve it."

Nan nodded, patting her hand. "You do have a way with dead bodies."

Doreen shrugged. "Speaking of dead bodies, there's that Bob Small stuff, all those articles on the murders he's supposedly committed."

"Well," Nan said wisely, "when things slow down, you can always check out your boxes. But, for now, what are you doing about the message tied to Thaddeus?"

"Mack is checking out some things. I just hope we can find whoever wrote the *help* note," Doreen murmured. She cast her gaze at her tea. "Do you know any little boys named Isaac?"

Nan looked at her and shook her head. "No, I don't know anybody with that name. I already told you that." She tilted her head to the side. "Are you feeling okay after that head injury?"

She rolled her eyes at her grandmother. "I just thought, maybe if I asked you again, something different might rattle around in your head."

Nan chuckled. "All kinds of things are rattling around in my head," she said, "but none about a little boy named Isaac."

"What about anybody else here? Could you ask them?"

"Sure, I can definitely do that," Nan said, with a beaming smile. "Anything to help out with one of your latest escapades."

"Well, let's hope it's not an escapade," she said. "Let's hope that it's nothing."

"But you do want to find out more about this little boy, right?"

"I want to know that he's okay, at least," Doreen said. "I hate to think of anybody like that suffering."

Immediately Nan nodded. "And you're such a sweetheart to be so concerned."

Doreen shrugged. "I don't know about that, but he struck a chord in my heart somehow."

"Exactly, and that's what people do," she said. "And once you start to care, it's hard to not care."

Doreen leaned forward and said, "Precisely why I don't care very often. A lot of pain can follow."

"Well, you know all about that from your marriage."

At that Doreen winced, but the topic reminded her, so she launched into a recital of what had happened with Mack's brother.

Nan listened, fascinated. "Wow," she said, "so he really thinks he can do something?"

Doreen nodded but said, "I'm a little doubtful though."

"Don't be. Maybe you've actually found somebody who'll help."

"Maybe," she said, "and I have to trust Mack. He hasn't let me down yet."

"You're very blessed to have that friendship," Nan murmured. "He has been so good to you."

"He has been very good to me, even though he drives me crazy."

Nan grinned at her. "That's just part of having a relationship."

"Not that kind of relationship," she warned.

"If you say so, dear," Nan said, but she had that secret smile in her voice that made Doreen eye her sideways. "Don't worry about it," Nan said. "If it's meant to be, it'll happen on its own."

"I'm not ready," she said, "and may never be."

"I know, and I'm so sorry I didn't realize your marriage and your husband had been that hard on you."

"Only because I hate to even talk about it. It was very hard to discuss even the little bit that I had to with Nick, especially with Mack sitting there too. I would never want to go to court, where I had to actually stand up to my ex and to fight somebody like my former divorce lawyer or just to answer questions publicly about the mess that was my marriage."

"No," Nan murmured. "Nobody wants to do that. Let's hope it doesn't come to it."

"Let's hope," she muttered. Soon afterward she stood and said, "It's time for me to head home. I've got to make sure I get to bed early tonight," she said slowly, twisting her neck. "That darn headache is starting to come back."

Immediately Nan was concerned. "You run along, dearie," she said, as she packed up a little baggie of chocolate chip cookies. "Here. Have these for breakfast."

She looked at her grandmother and smiled. "There's a certain amount of freedom in being able to have cookies as my breakfast," she muttered. "Intellectually I do know that it's not what I should be having, but my heart says it wants it."

"A little cookie or two will never hurt," Nan said, shaking a finger at her. "Don't get so fanatical that you forget about the joys in life. And cookies count as one of those joys."

She gave Nan a horrified look. "They better," she said. "They've always counted pretty highly in my world." At that, she burst out laughing, then leaned over, gave her grandmother a big hug, and said, "I'll see you tomorrow. Or at least we'll talk."

Calling the animals to her side, Mugs, who didn't seem to leave her alone very much these days, hurried over, and Goliath moved at his typical pace, but Thaddeus sat on the table and just looked up at her.

"What's the matter, baby?" Doreen asked. "Are you

tired?" She scooped him up, and he hopped onto her arm willingly enough, but she sensed something was wrong.

"He does seem off, doesn't he?" Nan said softly.

"Yes," she said. "I'm a little worried about him."

"Of course you are. Remember what I said about relationships and love?"

"I know it'll be awfully hard when it's time for these guys to go."

"It's hard when anybody's turn comes around, and it happens to the best of us." At the odd look on Nan's face, Doreen sat down with a hard *plunk*. "Nan, are you healthy?" she demanded.

Nan looked at her in surprise. "Oh my, yes, dear. I'm perfectly healthy," she said. "Don't you worry about me."

"Well, of course I'll worry about you," she said in exasperation. "You're all I've got."

"True," she said, "but I was thinking about all the people here at Rosemoor. We've just lost Rosie and several others. There's just been so many of them."

"I know," she said, "and I'm so sorry for any part I played in that."

"You didn't kill them, my dear, and, in most cases, they either committed suicide or were taken by disease."

"Well, not the other ones who were murdered," she said.

"Yes, but you didn't murder them, dear. So again, it's not your fault."

"But sometimes, you know, it feels like it is."

"That's just no way to look at it," Nan said, looking concerned.

"Maybe not, but it's still one of those things that you have to stop and think about and wonder at the way things worked out."

"True, but it's not your fault regardless, and you've got to remember that."

She smiled, tucked Thaddeus up on her shoulder, and said, "I'll try. Love you, Nan. Come on, guys. We've got to walk the long way around."

And she headed over a block, the river was just high enough that she didn't want to end up getting soaking wet again. Besides, one of these days she would get carried right down to the lake, and it would be one heck of a job getting back home again. Walking slowly and now feeling the fatigue settle in as it hadn't all day, she slowly made her way back toward the house. By the time she got there, she was really quite sore and tired. As she started up the driveway, Richard opened his door and called out.

"Are you okay?"

She looked at her neighbor in surprise. "Sure, I'm okay," she said. "Why do you ask?"

He frowned. "I heard you got hurt."

She smiled at him. "Oh, I did," she said. "I got attacked at the cemetery."

He shook his head. "So now even the dead are pissed off at you."

She glared at him. "They are not."

"Well, if they attacked you, they are."

She glared. "They didn't attack me. Somebody else did." He just stared at her in disbelief. "A ghost did not jump out of a grave and get me," she said in exasperation. "Somebody came up from behind and hit me over the head."

"Good thing you've got a hard head."

"Isn't that the truth?" she said as she trudged her way up the driveway.

"Well, take care of yourself," he said. "I've gotten used to having you around."

"Well, that's the nicest thing you've said to me yet."

"But you're damn noisy. I hope you're done with all that construction now." And, with that, he stormed back inside and slammed the door.

Chapter 15

Monday Midmorning …

THE NEXT MORNING, Doreen woke up feeling sore and groggy. While the previous morning had been awesome, this one was starting out a whole lot worse. She rolled over, slowly sat up, then realized it was already past nine. It shouldn't matter, but it did, when she woke and the better part of the morning was already gone. She got up, got dressed, and realized that even the animals were slow to move. As she headed downstairs, she looked back to see Thaddeus dragging his tail feathers on the ground. Immediately she bent down, scooped him up, and asked, "What's the matter, baby?"

He looked at her and whispered, "Big guy, big guy."

She sat on the edge of the stairs and looked down at him in her lap. "Is a big guy involved in this?"

He nodded his head up and down.

She wished she could trust that he knew what that was. "Would you recognize him?" And then she realized how silly it was to even ask him. She cuddled him close and said, "I'm so sorry I don't speak *Thaddeus-talk*," she said against his ear.

Leaning closer, he whispered, "Thaddeus loves Doreen."

Her heart breaking, she whispered back, "Thaddeus loves Doreen, and Doreen loves Thaddeus." He crooned gently against her. She hated to see him depressed like this. She'd never seen anything like this before. She cared so much for this little guy. "I wish I could help you, Thaddeus. I wish I could figure out what to do." Then she looked at him and said, "How about, after coffee, we go for a walk, and we'll go back and see if we can find the big guy."

He immediately flapped his wings. "Big guy, big guy, big guy."

She sighed. "We'll go soon. I just don't know which big guy we're looking for. Or why we'll be looking for him." But she knew there had to be something to this. Instinctively she also wanted to go check on Isaac. There was no guarantee that Isaac was even related to this mess, but something was going on with that little guy. And, if she could help him too, that would be fine. It could just be that he didn't have any friends or that he was scared of people.

Maybe he was coming out of an abusive family situation. She didn't want to push his buttons and make him even more upset either. Sad, and not exactly sure what to do, but having promised the bird a walk, she headed to the kitchen and made coffee. She opened the wooden back door to the kitchen, pulling it inward. When she tried to push the screen door outward, it wouldn't budge. She frowned as she tried again, but something was blocking it.

Calling the animals to her, she headed out the front door and walked around the fence until she got in the backyard, where she saw a big rock against the screen door, stopping her from pushing it open. She frowned because, again, it brought up all kinds of nasty thoughts as to why somebody was doing this. But when she got there, she realized something was written on the rock.

Leave town.

She read it aloud a second and then a third time and looked around. She yelled out to the neighborhood, "That's not very original. And I'm not leaving!" She stared down at the big rock, wondering just why on earth somebody would have thought to do that. Immediately she pulled out her phone, took a photo of it, and sent it to Mack. When her phone rang a moment later, she knew who it was.

"Where's that from?" he asked, his tone preemptory.

"It was outside the kitchen screen door," she said. "Blocking me from opening it."

"You didn't open it?"

"I doubt I can even lift it," she said. "Or maybe I could, but it would take a fair bit of effort. I think the rock is from my garden too."

"Interesting," he said. "I'm on the way."

"Don't bother," she said, "I'll head out for a walk."

"No," he said. "Wait. I'll be right there."

She glared down at the dead connection.

She looked over at Thaddeus and said, "Well, we're in trouble. Now we have to wait for him again." She didn't have to wait long and hadn't even finished her first cup of coffee before he pulled up to the front of the house and came straight back to look at the rock.

He stared at it for a long moment, then studied the garden and saw the spot where it had been picked up from. "It's not that big."

"No, it probably isn't for you," she said, "but it's big enough for me."

"It is, indeed," he muttered. He took several more photographs of it and said, "I doubt there are any fingerprints."

"Probably not," she said, with a shrug, "but take it if you want."

He frowned, then made a phone call.

"Listen," she said. "Before all that forensic stuff starts, I'll go for a walk. I just want to get away for a little bit." He opened his mouth to protest, but she shook her head. "No," she said. "I promised Thaddeus that we would get out. He's quite depressed too. Look at him."

Mack studied Thaddeus, who was sitting on Doreen's shoulder, his wings down, and realized the bird hadn't even greeted him.

"You're right," he said, sounding surprised. "He does look quite upset."

"I think it has to do with whoever it was he saw earlier on Saturday," she said, "so I'm doing this for him." Mack gave her a sideways look, and she shrugged. "Okay, so I want to go back and see Isaac too."

"And you know that he may have nothing to do with this rock message. Or the paper one Thaddeus brought home."

"I know that. Did you guys find any sign of anything strange going on in Isaac's neighborhood?"

"They've mapped out all the families that they know of on several blocks that were close to the cemetery, which is in the same area where we saw Isaac," he said. "A couple trouble spots are there, including a registered pedophile who lives there." She stared at him in shock. He shook his head. "Just because they're out of jail doesn't mean that they're guilty of something new."

"No, but it's a place to start."

"It is, but you won't be starting there," he muttered. "We'll talk to him ourselves."

"Fine," she said. "See that you do." He rolled his eyes at that. Then she nodded and said, "I have to look after Thaddeus. If this is upsetting him, you know I have to make it right."

"Because it upsets the bird?" he asked.

"That and other reasons. But that's good enough for now," she said. "When you guys are done, lock up, will you?" And, with that, she patted Thaddeus on her shoulder. "Come on, guys."

"You're not going up the river, are you?" he asked.

She stopped as she headed down and contemplated the water. "It rose again last night, didn't it?"

"It sure did," he said. "Better take the street."

She nodded. "I guess I can do that much." And, with Mugs and Goliath, she started around to the front of the house and up, going past the cul-de-sac and heading toward the bridge. They crossed over to the other side and back down again.

She muttered to Thaddeus, "It's so much easier when the river path is passable. Much faster too."

He didn't appear to perk up at all. They kept on walking, until they were within about a block of where she had seen the little boy. She stopped, then looked at Thaddeus and said, "You tell me where to go now. Where's big guy, big guy?"

Thaddeus immediately looked at her, flapped his wings, and said, "Big guy, big guy."

"Which direction?" she asked. She pointed down one way and took a step, but immediately Thaddeus pulled back. She pointed in another direction and got no reaction. Then she went to step in the direction of Isaac's, and immediately Thaddeus leaned forward, as if he were showing her the way.

Or at least more interested in that direction. "Okay, I'll take that as a yes on this direction," she said, with a smile, and set off with a jaunty step.

Chapter 16

DOREEN WALKED CASUALLY, as if they were out for a stroll, letting Mugs inspect bushes, Goliath racing forward, then stopping and throwing himself down on the sidewalk, waiting for her. She laughed, bent over, and tickled his belly, then kept on going. They passed the area where the kids had been playing and moved on toward where she'd seen Isaac at the small house. She walked up the block and around because that was the path he had disappeared on, and she was thinking that maybe he went to another area from the backside. As she headed around the block, she realized it was a cul-de-sac and what appeared to be a lot of town-homes.

As she walked, she whispered, "Anything yet on big guy?" Thaddeus leaned forward and stared avidly ahead of her. But she saw nothing in terms of a different reaction. She sighed. "I'll need a bit more than this."

But he wasn't giving her very much to go on. Still, she kept going. She walked up the cul-de-sac, all the way around the corner. She kept a smile on her face, seemingly enjoying the beautiful Monday morning. There didn't appear to be any action outside, which wasn't unusual, not if the kiddos were in school. But were they now? Doreen shook her head. It was hard to say what was going on, but nothing odd was here.

As she headed down and around the corner again, she caught sight of the path that Isaac had disappeared into. She walked up to it, and, with Mugs at her side, they followed it. There were several offshoots, which made it confusing, but just meant that the local kids had made their own routes to their various houses. She followed a couple that led to dead ends. When she got back to the main path, a big man stood there. "Oh, sorry," she said, as she almost ran into him.

He glared at her. "What are you doing here?"

"We came out for a walk," she said with a bright, cheerful smile.

He studied the dog and the cat. "Nobody walks their cat."

"Well, mine likes to go for walks," she said defensively.

He snorted at that. Then he looked at the bird, and his eyebrows shot up. "What's with the bird?"

"He likes to go for walks too," she said defiantly, not liking anything about his attitude at all.

"Right," he said in a slow, drawn-out voice. "Sure he does."

"He does," she said, then looked over at Thaddeus. "Don't you, buddy?"

Thaddeus just stared at the big man in front of him, and his eyeballs circled a little bit wildly.

"What's wrong with him?" the big man asked.

"I'm not sure," she said, studying Thaddeus. She shifted him so he was on her forearm. "You okay, Thaddeus?" She reached out and gently stroked him and felt a little shiver working through his body. "Well, he's obviously upset about something," she said, studying the man carefully.

He put his hands on his hips and towered over them. "He's probably not used to big men," he said.

"Maybe not," she said, "and he does have specific people he likes and dislikes." And then bravely she added, "Particularly people who abuse others." He stopped and stared. She shrugged. "Not that I'm saying you do or you don't."

Shoving his face forward, he said, "Lady, you need to get the hell out of here."

"And why is that?" she asked, aiming for a bravado she did not feel.

"Because busybodies like you can get into trouble when they open their mouths at the wrong time."

She smiled. "Isn't that funny. You're not the first person to tell me that."

"Gee, what a surprise," he said. "Now get the hell out of here. This isn't your place."

"It's not your place either," she said. "This is public property."

"But my place backs onto it," he said, "and you're bugging me."

"Call the cops then," she said in a sunny tone of voice. "Because I'm allowed here, just as much as you are."

He took a step forward, and she refused to budge. Immediately Mugs backed up and started barking at him.

"Shut the dog up, or I'll kick him," he said.

"Kick him, and you'll have all of us to worry about," she snapped. "And then, when the cops come, you can bet I'll have something to say about a man who threatened me when I was on public property."

"You get the hell out of here," he said. "We don't need troublemakers around here."

"Yeah, and who's *we?*" she asked, looking around. "It looks to me like there's no *we* here at all. Just you. So take your bad attitude and go back home, where you belong."

He stared at her in astonishment. "Now you're ordering me around?"

"Why not?" she said. "You just ordered me around."

"Fat lot of good it did me," he said, growling.

"Yep, you're right," she said. "But, if you treat me nice, I might just leave. I might not though, and I'll probably come back. I like little Isaac."

Immediately he stopped, and his face went stiff. "What do you know about Isaac?"

"He's a beautiful little boy," she said, with a bright smile. "I'll come back and visit him often."

"You leave that little boy alone. He's been through enough."

"Well, I wasn't planning on hurting him," she said carefully, trying to figure out his reaction. She wasn't sure if he was being protective, like it sounded. If so, why would that be?

"I told you to stay away from him," he said, shoving his face forward again. "If you come back here, I'll call the cops."

"Call them now then," she said. "I'll even give you the number." And she recited Mack's number immediately.

He shook his head. "I don't know what's wrong with you," he said. "You're either a dumbass or just crazy, but, either way, get the hell out of here." And, with that, he gave her a shove. Immediately Mugs jumped at him and bit him hard in the thigh; then all hell broke loose.

Chapter 17

W ITH Mugs barking and jumping up against the huge man in front of her, and Goliath clawing up his legs, the big man yelped and jumped back. "Call them off, call them off," he cried out.

She glared at him. "They're only protecting me."

He backed up several more steps and forcefully brushed Mugs off to the side.

The dog yelped as he tumbled to the ground, and she immediately stepped forward to rescue Mugs. "Hey, keep your hands off him."

He glared at her. "You're nuts, lady."

"I've been called that a time or two." She pulled Mugs back off the stranger and several feet away, calming him, checking him over.

"Now get this damn cat too," he said, trying to kick at Goliath.

"If you don't stop kicking Goliath," she snarled, "I'll let Mugs back at you too."

He stopped and stared. "You're all nuts."

"Maybe a little nutty," she said, "but we're nice normal people. We don't threaten others on public property, and we don't keep little boys hidden like they're captives."

At that, he froze and stared at her in astonishment, and then a really ugly look came into his eyes. "You stay away from Isaac," he said, his voice low. "Or I will find out where you live, and I'll make sure you never come back here again." And with that, he took off at a run into the woods.

Shaky, she stopped and stared at him. She knew there would be consequences when Mack found out what she'd done. Not only had she gotten into a confrontation that she was bound and determined to avoid but now she'd riled up somebody, and that threat of his had been real. But she wasn't so sure if it was a threat against her as much as it was a threat in order to protect little Isaac.

She didn't know what was going on here, but she was more certain than ever that something was. She was also more than a little shaky as she slowly walked back the way she'd come. She felt gazes all around her, people watching from the bushes and from behind their curtains and doors. But nobody came out and said anything. She didn't know if that man had been a problem for everybody or if he was their protector. A weird sense of togetherness was here.

It wasn't a very large residential section, was more like an overrun pocket of several houses together with this pathway along them connecting one cul-de-sac to another. As she finally made it to the more open cul-de-sac, she held out her hand and saw the tremors visibly shaking her arm. Wrapping her arms around her chest, she quickly walked away.

"Come on, Mugs," she called out. He raced toward her, more than happy with his encounter that had left her shaken, that amazing bravado of hers now gone. She wondered where it came from and didn't want it to be based on the animals defending her. They shouldn't be put in the position of having to. They could have been hurt. She didn't know how she always ended up in these scenarios. She'd just gone for a walk, for crying out loud.

She wondered why the man was so protective of the area. She didn't know, but it was a question that she felt needed to be answered. As she walked around to the corner of the cul-de-sac, a police car raced in at the corner. She took one look and quickly picked up her pace. She didn't know who had called the police, but, if any of the neighbors had called because of the confrontation she'd just had, she didn't want to be the one who had to explain it all. Not if the cops wouldn't pick up that threatening guy as well.

As it was, she went around the corner, then took another corner on a different block, in order to avoid being out on the main road.

Flustered, she realized she'd gotten herself out of her normal travel routes and didn't immediately know how to get home, where she wanted to be. She was just a little too far away for comfort, which was another concern.

When she finally worked her way back to familiar territory and got home, she was a little more stressed than she had realized. She headed straight into the kitchen, put on a pot of coffee, and, as soon as it was done, she went out onto the deck and just sat on the steps, leaning against one of the railings. She was hot; she was tired, and she was still shaky on the inside. Her phone had rung a couple times, but she'd ignored it.

Now as she sat here, trying to ease back the stress and to calm down, she realized *not* answering would potentially cause her more trouble, depending on who it was. She pulled her phone from her pocket, just as it rang again. It was Mack.

"Hey, Mack," she said, trying to keep her tone jovial.

"Where have you been?" he asked.

"Out walking," she said. "I told you that I was taking a walk."

"Where?" he barked.

"Over where Isaac was."

"Dammit to hell, Doreen," Mack said. "Were you involved in a confrontation a little while ago?"

She winced as she stared at her little creek that had turned into a rolling river at the end of her property. Of course somebody had tattled. "I don't know how much of a confrontation it was," she said cautiously. "How did you hear about it?"

"The cops were called."

"And why does everything come back to you?" she asked. "It's not like everybody in the department reports to you."

"I wish they wouldn't report at all, but anytime it involves a nosy woman with a whole pile of animals, everybody automatically directs their inquiries to me," he said in exasperation.

"Ah," she said, "I guess I'm a little too visible now, huh?"

"You think? You're just avoiding the question."

"Okay, yes, it was me," she admitted.

"So, what happened?"

With a sigh, she quietly told him and said, "When he finally took off and left, I just came home."

"That is not a threat we're prepared to ignore."

"No," she said softly, knowing that Mack was genuinely worried and upset. "The thing is, I don't know if he was threatening me as much as he was protecting his people."

"And that's quite possible," he said, his voice hard. "But he shouldn't be going around ordering people off public property, and he can't threaten you, not with your animals there."

"Well, I think he knows that by now," she said with a laugh, then, out of nowhere, she choked back a sob.

His voice immediately softened. "Are you okay?"

"Yeah, I'm okay," she said, hating that weakness shivering through her again. "It's just frustrating."

"Frustrating, why?"

"Because I didn't necessarily get the feeling that he was a bad guy. More that he was trying to be protective, and I just don't know what's going on in that neighborhood."

"Well, we'll have to find out," he said, "and this still has nothing to do with that message Thaddeus brought home or with whoever attacked you, and that's frustrating to me," he said, "because, once again, we have way too much happening all at one time."

"That's just it. Since so much is happening and seemingly unrelated, it could very well be related," she said. "It's all got to be linked somewhere. Surely not that many people can hate me."

He snorted. "When you keep pissing people off like this at such an alarming rate, you can easily get that many to hate you."

"That's not fair," she cried out. "I'm just trying to help people."

"But not everybody appreciates that kind of help. I keep telling you that you have to watch out because not everybody is nice out there."

"Not anyone apparently," she muttered. "Not lately anyway." She took a long slow deep breath. "So, I'm sitting on the deck having coffee," she said, "almost defiantly."

"Not surprised. Are you feeling okay after my brother's visit?"

She hesitated at that. "I am," she said, "but—"

"But what?"

"I don't know. It just feels like we're opening another can of worms. It's bad news."

"Of course it's bad news, but it was bad news already, before we ever opened it. It existed as bad news," he said, "but you were bearing all the brunt of it, as it festered inside you. Now that you've finally spoken out about your ex, we'll excise all the pus and the infection out of it."

She burst out laughing at that. "That's gross. I now see my ex as this big shiny pimple that needs to be popped," she said.

"Good," he said. "Keep thinking of him that way. It'll make things a little easier as we go forward."

"I really don't want to go to court and defend myself against him," she worried out loud.

"You've got to remember that divorce court is a very different thing than criminal court."

"It still feels like it's me who'll be on trial, not him."

"Forget about the whole trial thing," he said. "That's not what this is about at all. I can promise you that the last place he wants to be is in court. Let Nick work for a while. You'll see."

"Says you," she muttered. She reached out her free hand, checking for tremors. "I just need a couple days to get over the last attack."

"Which one was that? Today's or Saturday's?" he asked, with a note of humor in his voice.

"Both," she admitted. "Maybe I'll just stay home for the

next two days."

"Please do," he said. "Why don't you try to make some friends around town? And not the ones you wind up getting arrested," he said quickly.

"There was talk of people wanting to form an amateur sleuth club."

Mack almost growled. "Great. A Doreen fan club. Just more people to get into my business." He sighed loudly. "I mean real friends, the kind you can go have tea with, so you have more people to visit than just Nan."

"I've hardly had a chance yet," she said, looking around her backyard. "I have neighbors, but the only one who talks to me is Richard, and that's not usually in a nice way." She explained what he'd said earlier.

"I'm sure all that construction in your backyard did upset him," Mack admitted. "But he should also realize it's not an ongoing thing."

"No, but we had plenty of people here over the antiques as well," she said.

"Did you ever hear back from them?"

"No. I sent Scott an email a few days ago, so I should probably follow up."

"Yep, you sure should," he said. "And isn't it time for you to get some money from the secondhand store?"

"I think it's still a bit early for that," she said.

"Oh, right. That was supposed to be after three months, wasn't it? So not quite yet then. Are you doing okay for money though? Do you need some? I know you said—even before you were hurt—that you didn't need to do much work in my mother's yard this week and that we should put it off to next week, but you are welcome to work this week and next."

"I still have some of Nan's cash in the bowl. I had to dig into it for some of the pizza for the guys."

"So, you still have some there though, right?"

"I'm not starving," she muttered.

"Well, I'm glad to hear that," he said, "because the last thing I want you to do is not buy groceries because you're afraid that you won't have enough money left."

"Well, it is a valid concern," she said.

"Do I need to come over and cook something?"

"No, no," she said. "I'm fine." She could almost see the frown forming on his face. "Honest," she muttered. "I'm fine. And last night Nan sent me back with some cookies."

"Cookies?" he said in disbelief.

"Yeah. That's about all I feel like eating these days anyhow."

"You can't live on sugar," he said in horror.

She snorted. "It's food, isn't it?"

"Not good-enough food to be eating on a regular basis," he said. "Are you just trying to shock me to divert my attention from your morning walk?"

She burst out laughing. "Well, maybe," she muttered. "Anyway, I'm fine. I still have groceries."

"When I was there making pancakes, you didn't have any groceries," he said. "I was searching through the cupboards and the fridge just to find something to make pancakes with."

"But you succeeded," she said, "so it can't be that bad."

He sighed. "If I bought groceries, would you cook?"

"Are you buying groceries I can cook?" she countered.

"Well, what can you cook?" he asked. "Have you learned to do any other dishes yet?"

"Pasta," she said, "and omelets."

"Right. We were supposed to get you comfortable making a few basic recipes that you could count on, and nachos would be one of them, wasn't it?"

"Yes, but then you ate my salsa," she said in an accusatory note.

"That tiny little jar? And we both ate it, as I recall."

She frowned. "But you ate more than I did."

He groaned. "I'm not getting into that discussion again," he said. "Besides, I'm pretty sure it was half and half."

She thought about it and then gave in grudgingly. "Yeah, you're probably right. And, no, I don't need groceries right now," she said. "I've really not been very hungry." As a matter of fact, her stomach was still a little queasy from the stress.

"Are you okay from that most recent attack?" he asked, his voice sharp.

"I told you that I was," she said.

"Yeah, but then you said you weren't hungry."

"Wow," she said, "I don't get much of a chance to do anything without you picking me apart."

"Uh-oh. Time for you to have a cup of tea and relax," he announced. "You're getting cranky."

"I am," she admitted. "Anyway, I'll talk to you later." She hung up on him, then sat here, smiling, as she thought about the satisfaction of just being able to do that. And maybe it would make him feel better that she had. It was a little more in character for her.

Chapter 18

S HE DIDN'T KNOW why she was so unsettled, but this whole Isaac thing was getting to her. And she didn't even have any proof that anything was wrong, which just added to her frustration. Surely there could be something wrong. But still, nothing popped up that she could do anything about, and that was even more frustrating still. She got up and poured herself another cup of coffee, then walked back outside again.

Just as she sat down, Nan called. Doreen smiled in delight when she saw the number. "Hi, Nan," she muttered.

"Are you okay?" she said.

"Of course I'm okay," she said. "I'm fine."

"You sound a little shaky."

"Yeah, that's okay. I've just had a long visit on the phone with Mack, and now I'm sitting outside with a cup of coffee."

"Maybe it's the coffee," she said. "Maybe you're drinking too much caffeine."

She stopped and stared at the phone. "Please don't try to talk me out of my coffee," she said. "It's the one true joy in my day."

At that, Nan sighed. "You know how sad it is to hear a woman of your age say that?"

Doreen winced. "Let's not go there. We're not talking about relationships."

"We don't even have to talk about relationships. Let's just talk about men."

"How about we don't?" she said, fully aware that Nan had lived a fun and varied life that in no way compared to the life that Doreen currently lived.

"Have you eaten?"

"Not in a while, but I'm fine. I'm not terribly hungry today."

"Oh dear, maybe that head injury is hitting you harder than we thought."

She winced at that. "You and Mack seem to think that, if I'm not hungry, I'm sick."

"Well, honey, you've almost always eaten everything under the sun that was in front of you because you're nearly always starving."

"Well, maybe I'm finally getting full," she said. "Now did you ever find anything out about Isaac?" She was hoping to distract Nan and to change the subject.

"I did, indeed," Nan said, "and the answer is that nobody knows anything about him."

Doreen stopped and stared. "Nobody in that whole place?"

"Nope. Nobody. I've talked to all kinds of folks here, and they all say that it's not a name they know."

"That's unusual."

"It's more than unusual." And the older woman's voice lowered to a whisper. "So, we've started some bets."

"Bets about what?" she asked in surprise.

"Who he is, and how long it'll take you to get to the bottom of it, of course. So you need to keep me in the loop, in case I need some insider information."

"You can't just bet on my success or failure in this," she protested.

"Why not?" Nan asked in surprise. "I've bet on you every time. I mean, I know that, at some point in time, you'll probably fail at something," she said, "but, if you've got your heart set on finding out who this Isaac is, I'm sure you'll figure it out. And I'll be right there to cash in."

Doreen stared at the phone, hating the pressure, yet realizing Nan would never change. "Well, I'm certainly glad you're raking in the dough on my actions," she said. "It's too bad I can't get paid for helping all these people."

"You know what? It is too bad," Nan said thoughtfully. "When you think about it, you're doing a ton for everybody else."

"Well, I don't want any thanks, and we had an awful lot of people here building this beautiful deck," she said, "so I'm certainly not asking for any more help from anyone."

"They've done well by you. That's for sure."

"They have, indeed. I wonder if I can find a secondhand chair and table set to sit on out here one day," she said.

"I could ask around," Nan said. "For all I know, we could find some secondhand stuff close by here."

"Well, if it's there at Rosemoor, you'll need it for yourselves," she said. "You all could certainly use some more outdoor furniture there."

"That's why I love my little deck so much," Nan said. "This little bistro set is lovely, and I have the couch here for sitting long-term."

"And that's why I'm sitting on the steps," Doreen said,

with a laugh. "Because I've got this beautiful deck and this beautiful backyard and garden that I still need to work on," she said, "but I don't have a place to sit."

"That's right. You said the chair broke, didn't you? Also you don't have a barbecue yet either, do you?"

"No, and I know that Mack would absolutely love to have one here, and he would show me how to use it, but I think a table and chairs or at least one chair should come first."

"Well, if you get bored, you can always go down to some of the secondhand stores and see what you come up with. That's a great way to spend an afternoon." Then she stopped and said, "You know what? We still have about two hours left before they close, if you want to go today."

She looked at her phone. "I guess it's only three o'clock, so there's plenty of time."

"Yep, a couple are on Springfield Road, and then a couple are up in the Rutland area."

"I don't even know where they are though."

"I do. So why don't you pick me up, and we'll go?" she said, clapping her hands in delight.

"I think that's a great idea."

"Me too. I'd love to get out for a little bit." Then she stopped and said, "Unless you don't want to spend time with me."

"Of course I do, Nan. Don't be silly." She looked down at her coffee. "I'm just drinking my coffee."

"Well, you have a bit of time yet," she said. "We don't have to race away."

"How late are they open?"

"I don't know for sure," she said. "You've got your phone. You can check and then call me back and let me know when you'd like to go." And, with that, Nan hung up on her.

Doreen stared down at the phone in bemusement. "Not quite the same when somebody does it to you," she muttered. "But at least Nan does it mostly because she's out of conversation." Pouring herself a second cup of coffee, she noted that only one cup was left. She went and sat outside again. A table would be nice, and a chair or two would be lovely. She could actually sit down and not just on the hard surface.

On impulse, she phoned Nan back. "I'm just finishing my second cup," she said. "So I'll pick you up in about fifteen minutes."

"Perfect," Nan said. "I'm really excited."

She laughed and said, "Me too. It'll be fun." When she hung up, she rose and considered leaving the animals behind, but that didn't make much sense to her. She called Nan back. "Do you think we can bring the animals?"

"Oh, I'm sure we could," she said. "We absolutely don't want to leave them behind."

Doreen frowned at what may have been a hint of sarcasm and said, "Well, I just don't know. Maybe it's not a good idea."

"I think it's a perfect idea," she said. "And, if the clerks don't want us to go inside, I'm sure we can go into other stores."

With that, Doreen decided to give it a try. Especially so soon after losing Thaddeus, the last thing she wanted to do right now was lose them or leave them behind. Finishing her coffee, she put her cup in the sink and grabbed her purse. After loading the animals in her car, she slowly drove out of her garage and down to pick up Nan. She hoped this was a good idea and liked the thought of finding a table. If it was cheap enough. She had some of the money from Nan's bowl rolled up in her wallet, just in case.

As she drove closer, she saw Nan standing impatiently outside, waiting for her. She smiled when she saw Doreen drive up and quickly hopped into the car. "This will be fun," she said excitedly.

"I've never really been to a secondhand shop," Doreen said, "though Mack and I went to some garage sales once."

"Well, this is a very different story," she said, and she quickly explained how to get to where they were going. By the time they pulled into the parking lot, they'd been driving for fifteen minutes.

"Is this the farthest one away?"

"Yes, that's why we're starting here," Nan said. "Then we'll work our way toward home."

They went inside the store with the animals, and nobody said a word. Feeling much calmer about the concept, Doreen walked through everything but didn't like much of what was here.

Nan kept shaking her head, as she looked at various things. "There's always the potential to find all kinds of good stuff here," she said, "but unfortunately not today. But not to worry, a couple more are within walking distance here." So they went back outside, and Nan led her across the street, where they went through two more stores, but still found nothing.

"Well, another one's around the corner. Let's try there." By now, Doreen had realized what kind of stuff was to be expected at these stores. Some of it was overpriced, and some of it was decent. She had eyed a couple jackets, but, so far, she didn't really need one and hadn't really figured out what she might need for winters here yet, so didn't want to spend money unnecessarily. Although the jackets appeared to be quite reasonable, every time she looked at something, Nan came over and checked it out for quality, then made her feel bad, thinking she was wasting her time. Finally, at the next stop, Nan said, "Is there anything else you're looking for?"

She shrugged. "I don't know if I need a coat or not," she said, "so I'll keep looking at them, but I don't really want to buy anything yet."

"Do you have any at home?"

"I do, a couple from you actually, but until it's wintertime, it feels weird to wear them, so I don't yet know if I'll like them or not, you know?"

"Well, that's a good point too," she said, "but still, if we find something that's perfect, no reason not to buy it, if it's cheap enough."

"Well, some of this stuff is cheap," she said, "but some of it isn't."

"And that's the trick to buying in a secondhand store. It's like garage sales," Nan said. "You can get a lot of great deals, but you can also get taken too."

"Well, I don't have enough money for that," Doreen said with a smile. When they walked into the next place, she spotted a beautiful rocking chair in the corner, but it wasn't for outdoors. She looked at it and sighed. "Isn't that lovely?"

Nan checked it over and nodded. "It is, though I'm not sure where you'd put it."

"In the living room," she suggested. But, as she wandered around, she sat in it for a moment. "But I don't know what else to put in there, so it seems like buying one piece isn't a good answer."

"You already have a few single chairs, so, no, it isn't a great answer. Better we find you something that rocks for the deck. You'll still have several months of good weather outside, and then we can look for furniture for inside."

They wandered through the store and, at the back, found a little bistro table. She looked at it and said, "This is almost like yours," she muttered.

"It is, indeed," Nan said, looking at it with a critical eye. "And it might be a good answer for you when you're alone," she said. "It's not big enough to have a meal out there, but it is something to set your coffee on."

"Well, it's a table, but nothing goes with it," she joked.

"I wonder if they have more around here, if not we'll keep looking for a small set," Nan muttered as she moved things around. Obviously used to the way the system worked, Nan dug deeper and deeper into the stacks of furniture.

"Is this how you found lots of your antiques?"

"Well, we found some like this," she said, "but estate sales were best for that."

"I can imagine," she said, "but I don't know what's an antique versus what's not."

"No, and it's not something that you necessarily pick up overnight, with so many imitations out there." Just then she said, "Aha," and pulled a chair forward. From the outside, it looked like it wasn't anything special, with a weird brace on the front and the sides. Nan pulled it around, then told Doreen to sit, cautiously, in case it wouldn't hold her weight. Doreen sat down and then made a startled exclamation as it rocked but not in a normal way.

"It's called a glider rocker," Nan said. "And this one is meant for outdoors. Now if it only had the footstool." Her voice trailed off, as she returned to digging into the stash piled up behind her.

Doreen sat and rocked gently in the chair. Mugs sat at

her side, wagging his tail happily, and Goliath hopped up into her lap and made himself comfortable. "I guess you two approve," she said with a smile.

Just then somebody walked toward them. "I could make you a deal on that chair," he said. "We have so much stock, we need to get some of this moving."

"Well, I guess it depends on how much of a deal you can make," Doreen said cautiously. She really was enjoying the chair and was reluctant to get out of it. But then she was sitting in the middle of a store, so that wasn't very normal either.

Just then, Nan popped out from the back, carrying something that looked like a footstool, but not quite. She put it down in front of Doreen. "Here. Put your feet up on this."

And Doreen realized that the footstool rocked as well. She stared at the two pieces in delight. "These would be lovely on the deck." They were a woven material, although she didn't know if it was plastic or some weird rattan.

"They're made with an all-weather material," the store owner said, as if understanding he would make a sale.

Nan nodded. "But they are quite used, definitely in need of a good washing, and some of the material is worn down." At that, the store owner and Nan set to haggling quite heavily.

Doreen still hadn't even seen a price tag on the chair and wasn't sure it would fit in her car for that matter. But, with Goliath curled up in her lap, and now Mugs on the footstool gently rocking, she saw this as a perfect way to sit outside and to enjoy her morning coffee.

Finally Nan turned to look at her and, with a voice of triumph, said, "Sold!"

Chapter 19

Monday Late Afternoon …

NAN INSISTED THEY go straight to Doreen's place. With the help of the store owner, they had jammed the chair halfway into the trunk. Even now, she saw the trunk lid swinging gently as she drove up the last rise to her place. "I'm not sure it's safe to drive like this," she muttered.

"Oh, posh," Nan said, with a wave of her hand. "It's perfectly fine."

Doreen rolled her eyes at that, but, once inside the garage, she hopped out, let the animals out, and then walked around to the back of the car. Together, she and Nan got the footstool out and were reaching deep into the trunk to get the chair, when strong arms leaned between them and pulled it right out. Surprised and startled, Doreen turned to face Mack, his face grim, as he set it down for her.

"Oh my," she said, "perfect timing."

"Well, timing anyway," he said. "I don't know about perfect."

She frowned. "What's the matter?"

He shrugged, then stopped and stepped back, looking at the chair. "That's actually quite nice." He looked at Nan.

"Where did you find this treasure?"

"Up at that Max's secondhand store in Rutland," she said.

He frowned and shook his head. "No, that one closed down about a year ago."

She waved her hand and shrugged. "Well, whatever one moved into that space then. He's got all kinds of stuff in the back, jammed up together. Had to dig through that to find this. Anyway, we made a heck of a deal."

Mack nodded. "How much did you pay for it?" He looked over at Doreen, and she flushed, then looked at Nan and said, "Nan wouldn't let me pay for it."

"It's a sad world, indeed, if I can't pay for a chair for my granddaughter to enjoy on her new deck. That's been my only contribution to the entire process, by the way, and it was surely overdue."

"I'm sure you contributed much more than you think," Mack said drily.

Doreen nodded. "It was some of the money that I found in the house that paid for the pizza and the beer for the deck crew," she said, with a smile.

"Oh, good," Nan said in delight. "I'm glad I managed to do something to help out." She looked at Mack, then patted his big bicep and said, "Now, could you be a dear and carry that chair around back for her?"

"Happy to." He picked up the chair with one hand and the footstool with the other, then easily swung them both out of the garage and around the path. Nan sighed happily. "It does my heart good to see a big strong healthy man like that."

Doreen decided to stay quiet, not wanting to risk sending Nan off into another tirade about her granddaughter's lack of a love life. Nan had plenty of her own memories to muse upon. Closing the garage door, Doreen headed for the kitchen, where she put on the teakettle. Stepping out onto the deck, she stopped to admire the chair and the footstool.

"We should have bought that little table," she said instantly, when she saw the two of them.

"I know," Nan said, frowning. "I was thinking the same thing just now."

"Was it at the same place?" Mack asked.

"Yes. It was just a little bistro table. I couldn't picture it at the time, but now it would be just the thing."

"You just need a little table, right? I might even have one over at my mom's place," he said.

"Oh, I can't take Millicent's," she said. "She will need it."

"I think she has a couple there. I'll ask her." He pulled out his phone and stepped off to the side.

She heard him greet his mother, but the rest of his side of the conversation drained away as he walked toward the river. She sat down on the rocking chair and smiled. "This is beautiful, Nan." She hopped back up and said, "Try it."

Immediately Nan took a seat and smiled. "It's lovely. We should see if we can find you a second one."

"Oh, my gosh. Another one like this would be perfect," she said with a laugh. "Just imagine the two of us sitting here, like a couple little old ladies."

"Well, I'm an old lady," Nan said, raising an eyebrow. "You're just acting like one," she added, then glanced meaningfully over at Mack.

Instantly Doreen felt the heat rise up her cheeks. "Don't go there," she said.

Nan's laughter trilled across the backyard. "I'm not going to," she said. "I'll just have to trust in him to take the necessary steps."

Doreen's jaw dropped as the older woman stood and said, "I'll go make a cup of tea."

Doreen stared at her receding back, wondering if she really meant that. Surely Mack wouldn't make that move toward her, would he? She studied him for a long moment, admiring the stocky hips, the broad shoulders, and the muscle of a strong male in his prime. He carried himself with a grace and a purpose, like somebody who knew what he wanted and was happy to do whatever needed to be done in order to get it. She had to admire that.

Whereas she fell into and out of various phases of her life, it seemed. Just then he finished his call, turned, and walked toward her. "Where's Nan?"

"She went inside to make a cup of tea," she said. "Can I get you something?"

"Tea?" he said, but his tone was doubtful.

She burst out laughing. "Tea won't kill you, you know?"

"Doesn't mean it'll be good for me either," he said, grinning. "Mom said she thought she had a set but wants to think about it first."

"Oh good," she said with a bright smile. "If not that's fine. I'll find something eventually. And you don't get to change the conversation. Tea would be good for you. I could even give you a nice herbal one."

At that, he wrinkled up his nose and said, "Or we could just put on a pot of coffee."

She smiled. "You know that I'll never be against a cup of coffee." She walked into the house.

Nan immediately shook her head when she saw what Doreen was up to. "You drink far too much coffee," she scolded.

"I do not," she said, automatically patting Nan on the shoulder. "Besides, I never know what to do with half of the teas you have here."

"Well, there are reasons for each one of them," she muttered and pulled out several of the boxes. "This is chamomile to help you sleep. This one is raspberry leaf tea for, you know, that time of the month," and she waggled her eyebrows at her. "I mean, you aren't that old yet."

Doreen sighed. "I wish I was."

"Too bad for you. I'm still hoping for a great-grandchild."

At that, Doreen started to laugh. "I don't think that's happening anytime soon."

"Well, I don't know about that," Nan said. "Give it time."

As she put on the coffee, Doreen looked outside to see Mack sitting in the new chair. She nudged Nan. "I think he approves."

Nan burst out laughing, as she walked outside. "I didn't think you'd fit."

"I sit, so I fit," Mack said in a weird voice. He had Goliath in his arms and Thaddeus on his shoulder.

Doreen gasped, as she walked out to join them. "I think you've completely charmed my furry and feathered family away from me."

"Nope, but they're happy to have me visit," he said, with a smile. "And I have to admit that it's nice to have this kind of a welcome."

"But what have you done about finding Isaac?" Nan asked immediately. He looked at her and frowned. She shook her head. "Don't you give me that look, young man. I know perfectly well what's going on with Isaac."

He leaned forward and said, "What do you know about Isaac?"

"Well, not that," she said. "I asked everybody at the home, and nobody knows anything about him."

He frowned at her and stared over at Doreen.

She nodded. "Yes, I asked her because, if anybody knows everything or everyone, it's Nan, and, if she doesn't know, then usually somebody in that place does."

"I could talk to Richie about it," Mack said absently, as he studied the lawn around them.

"I already did," Nan said immediately. "He doesn't know the name either. Everybody's got their thinking caps on now though." She glanced at Doreen. "Besides, a bet's riding on this one."

He sighed. "Nan, you're not supposed to be betting anymore."

"Oh, it's just for fun," she said.

"Pennies?" he asked.

"Cookies," she said immediately. Something tongue-in-cheek about her tone of voice made Doreen look at her skeptically, but her grandmother just beamed her a bright, cheerful smile, so she wasn't sure if Nan meant it or not.

"Well, somebody has to know something about Isaac," Doreen said. "There has to be a birth certificate somewhere."

"But does there?" Nan asked. "Way back when I was born, birth certificates were only issued if you needed to get passports and driver's licenses. Most people didn't care, and, in my mother and my grandmother's day, we certainly didn't. All kinds of folks had babies and didn't worry about paperwork."

"And that could be what we're seeing here," Mack said,

"but that would mean that Isaac wasn't born in a hospital," he said.

"Lots of babies aren't born in hospitals. That's nothing new. When you look at it over the span of my lifetime, actually being born in a hospital is what's new," she muttered. "At least in the last sixty or seventy years."

"Well, it's certainly more common now that home births are making a resurgence," he said.

"I never understood that myself," Doreen said. "You'd think you'd want the best medical support available."

"Sure, but there's also a certain amount of stress and strain from all the noise and irritants involved in a hospital," he said. "So, if you can have the birth, relaxed at home, with good medical care right there, using a midwife or attending nurses, then perfect."

She nodded. "I've never really thought much about it," she said. When she heard the buzzer of the coffeemaker, she went inside, then poured two cups and came back out again. She heard Mack and Nan discussing something else as she returned. "Uh-oh." She frowned because Nan was already glaring at her.

"You didn't tell me that he attacked you," Nan cried out in horror.

She handed Mack his coffee. "Well, it doesn't matter if I did or didn't," she said. "He didn't really attack me, just pushed me and threatened to do worse, and besides, once again, Mugs defended me. Goliath too."

Nan immediately crouched beside Mugs and cuddled him, though the dog didn't know what the fuss was all about and didn't appear to care. He happily rolled onto his back and kicked out his feet, perfectly content to accept the accolades coming his way.

"Do you know who he is though?" Mack asked her.

"He was big," Doreen said, "like bigger than you."

He looked at her in surprise. "Not too many men in town are of that size," he said. "I could name most of them on one hand."

"Well, in that case, you should know him yourself. He did have a scar alongside the jawbone here."

He stared at her and said, "Randy?"

"I don't know," she said. "Big, and he had a brush cut. Looks like he's just past his prime, like he used to be a fitness buff or in the military or something, but carrying a little bit extra around the middle."

"That would be Randy too," he said, staring at her in amazement.

"Is that good or bad?"

"I'd say Randy is a good guy," he muttered. "I'll have to think about that."

"Well, if you know him, you can go talk to him."

"Or somebody has already reported it, and it'll filter my way anyhow," he said.

"You said you'd heard about it already. That's why you came to check on me."

He looked at the coffee and said, "I guess you'd be upset if I got up and left right now, wouldn't you?"

She nodded slowly. "Particularly if you won't tell me why."

"Nope. Not telling you anything," he said.

"And the rock?" she asked suddenly.

He shook his head. "Nothing on it."

"Right," she said. "Of course not."

"Rock?" Nan asked curiously. "What are you talking about?"

Mack looked at her and said, "What? You didn't tell her that either?"

She shrugged. "I didn't want to worry her."

"Tell me what, young lady?" Nan glared down her nose at her.

"Somebody just wants me to leave town," she said. "So a large rock from the garden was placed against the screen door to the kitchen, so I couldn't get out."

Nan gasped. "Wow. People really are targeting you, aren't they?"

"Well, I was hoping not," she muttered.

"And after all you've done for this town too," she said.

"But think about it, Nan. A lot of people, like maybe somebody close to Steve, are upset because I put him behind bars."

"Well, I suppose that's possible," she said, "and that neighborhood wouldn't be very far away from here either," she said, looking toward the river. "He's really only a few houses down."

"Well, it's more than a few houses," she said, "but maybe somebody like that is just upset and causing a ruckus. For all I know, Richard put it there, hoping I would stop all this noise and commotion in the neighborhood."

Nan started to laugh. "That's far too much effort for Richard," she said. "But I can see your point. You have stirred things up."

"I have, indeed, but not in a mean-spirited way."

"Putting people behind bars would definitely be seen as mean, if you or yours ended up on the wrong side of the bars," Nan said.

"Maybe, but I'm just trying to be helpful to the families of all these people who have gone missing," she said in defiance. "What am I supposed to do, ignore the clues?"

"No, not necessarily." Nan looked at her and said, "Well, it was the cemetery and that whole kiwi thing that got me thinking," she said, "because of the big garden fair. I'm surprised they haven't asked you to be involved."

Mack grinned. "I don't think they want her anywhere close to the fair. Who knows what else she might unearth."

"Oh, that was just terrible, wasn't it?" Doreen muttered. "All those women, dead." She shook her head. "Actually I'm okay to avoid gardening for a while, now that I think about it."

"Good." He tossed back the last of his coffee, put his cup down, and said, "Now I'm leaving."

"Oh, wait." She jumped to her feet. "You have to tell me about this Randy guy."

"No, I don't," he said, with a big smile. "You stay here and stay out of trouble, and I mean that," he said. "And don't you dare go back looking for Isaac." She gave him a quick frown, and he shook his head. "No, I'm serious. Let me go talk to them and see what's going on."

"As long as you do it," she said, raising a finger at him.

He immediately grabbed the finger and said, "Don't shake that thing at me," and, with that, he quickly disappeared.

She stared down at her nails, then looked at Nan. "Do you know how long it's been since I had a manicure?"

Nan laughed and laughed. "It's a different world for you, honey," she said. "They definitely look like working hands now, but I don't think it's a bad thing."

"Before, I don't think I ever did a day's work in my life," she said. "I don't have to even think about it. I know I didn't."

"No, that's not true," Nan said. "You have to realize that the work you did then was very different, and you were trying to stay calm, to make sure everything appeared to be perfect, and that you yourself were flawless," she said. "That was a major job in itself. How many times a day did you touch up your makeup?"

Doreen wrinkled her face. "Constantly," she said. "He would look at me a certain way, and I would know something wasn't quite right, and I'd have to go freshen up."

"And yet it wasn't that anything wasn't right. It was his way of criticizing you constantly," Nan said.

"Did I ever tell you about all that?" she asked, puzzled.

"No, of course not. It was something I'd seen for myself on a visit."

"He's not a very nice man." Just then her phone rang. She pulled out her phone and said, "Oh, it's Nick."

"Mack's brother?" Nan asked, as she leaned forward.

"Yes, Nan. Hello?" she said into the phone.

"Hey, this is Nick, Mack's brother."

"Yep, I can see that on my phone," she said humorously. "What can I do for you?"

"Well, you haven't hung up, so that's good."

She laughed. "No, but honestly, I've forgotten everything that we were supposed to do."

"I just wanted to let you know that I did file the paperwork today."

"Wow, it's a Monday night, after normal working hours," she said.

"It's all filed online," he said, "so that isn't necessarily an issue."

"Okay, do I start worrying about the boogeyman jumping out behind me from now on then?"

"From what I understand from Mack, that's been an ongoing problem for you already."

"Okay now, that's not fair," she said, "but you could be right. I definitely have some issues with people in town here."

"Well, now you have to keep an eye out for a few who might not be townies."

"I know. Mack was trying to track a couple guys, one who may have worked for my ex already." There was a no surprised exclamation on the phone.

"Is he?"

"Have you talked to your brother today?" she asked in dry tone.

"No, actually I haven't."

"Well, maybe you should. Particularly now that you filed the paperwork."

Not long afterward, Nan excused herself and walked back to Rosemoor.

Later that evening, Doreen went upstairs and sat on her bed, staring out the window. She still had just a mattress on the floor, waiting for that hopeful pot of gold at the end of the auction rainbow. It still hadn't come in yet. She checked her laptop, but she found no email response from any of the auction people. Sad, and yet wondering how long she could keep going, she checked the calendar on the consignment store, but again it wasn't quite time for a check from them either. Although it wasn't *that* far off, so she dashed off a quick email, wondering when she might get a check. She didn't expect an answer right away, but Wendy was apparently working on the books or something because she emailed right back.

In about two weeks. Can you hold out till then?

Doreen replied with a happy answer in the affirmative. She still had a good $670 in the bowl which made her happy. If she were careful, that could last two weeks easily. But she had bills to pay too. One of them was a tax bill that she had sitting here and hadn't even opened. She didn't know what to do with it, but she knew it would be large. Somehow she was supposed to pay it, and she frowned at that reminder. Since the property had become hers, she'd learned there was more to owning property than just having a place to live. There was the maintenance, the things you wanted to change, and things that had to be changed.

Chapter 20

Tuesday Morning …

WHEN SHE WOKE the next morning, Thaddeus was curled up at her shoulder, but his tail feathers looked limp, and his head definitely wasn't nearly as perky and happy as he normally was.

"Oh dear," she said, "what am I to do with you?" Immediately she got dressed, and, with him on her shoulder, she asked him, "Is it all about the big guy again?"

He leaned against her and said, "Big guy, big guy."

"What about Isaac? Are you worried about Isaac?"

A weird sound came from his throat, but he didn't say anything. "Oh, dear, we have to solve this."

She didn't know what to do. Maybe they should put a little camera or some tracking device on his ankle. She almost smiled at that idea. Could they actually track a bird these days? Well, of course they could, but that was for migration, endangered species, and things like that. She didn't think it applied to pets, but she could be wrong. With the coffee dripping, she looked on the internet, somewhat surprised to find that she could even get a collar for cats that had GPS tracking in them.

She looked down at Goliath. "Something tells me that you wouldn't take to that very kindly at all." But she also knew that, if anybody tried to steal him, she would do whatever she could to get him one immediately. These animals were way too precious to her to have anybody else come along and take any of them like that. And, once she thought about it, the thoughts just wouldn't leave her mind. It wasn't that these animal GPS units were hugely expensive, but, when you didn't have an income, any expense was huge.

She and the animals all headed downstairs, where she opened up the kitchen screen door—or tried to. When it wouldn't budge, her heart sank, and she looked at Thaddeus. "Have we got a problem again, Thaddeus?" He just looked at her and peered over at the windows. "I think we have another problem," she said. She couldn't quite see again, even from the kitchen windows. She walked through the house and out the front door, then around the house, with Thaddeus on her shoulder, Mugs bouncing at her side. Goliath hadn't even bothered getting out of bed yet.

At the kitchen door, she looked at another large rock from her garden. As she stared out at the mess of rocks in her garden, she could easily see the footsteps. She walked over to the garden, took a closer look, and realized the footprints were large, most likely a big adult male, and, from the depth of the prints, he was probably quite heavy. She placed her own foot close to the side of one footprint and deliberately stepped beside it, as if walking, but she didn't sink anywhere near as much.

"Large and heavy," she said. Immediately she took a photo of the footprint and sent it to Mack, then returned to the kitchen door and took another picture of the rock itself. She added a text message. **For the second night in a row.**

She didn't get an immediate answer but decided to move the rock. Carefully using a paper towel and her foot, she nudged it away from the door and opened it up, so they could at least have their coffee outside. She sat in the new glider, with Mugs settled beside her, and Goliath, who finally decided to get up, in her lap. Thaddeus sat on her shoulder. She glanced over at him.

"I don't know what to do for you, Thaddeus." He just sat slumped on her shoulder, and she worried and fretted over his behavior. "Maybe I should take you to a vet," she said, then winced, because, if one thing was guaranteed to kill her bank account, it would be vet bills. But still, Thaddeus was worth everything to her. She'd even ask Nan for help, if it came to that. She knew Nan would immediately assist financially for something like that, just because Thaddeus had been hers first.

Thinking about that, she picked up the phone and called Nan. When her grandmother answered, she said, "Nan, have you ever seen Thaddeus really depressed? He is acting very odd these days, ever since he disappeared and came back with that message."

"I hadn't very often, except when somebody he really liked used to come by and then didn't come visit anymore," she said. "I once had a friend named Larry, but he died. Thaddeus got really depressed that time too."

"Interesting," she muttered. "I was thinking it might be whoever it was who put the message on his leg, but I don't know how to help him."

"No," Nan said. "We'll have to find out who it was that he saw."

"And how do we do that?" Doreen asked.

"Well, I'd say Isaac, but we're not even sure he was involved."

"No, but maybe we should put an ad in the paper," Doreen said suddenly.

"Oh, now that's a great idea," Nan said. "But what would you say?"

Doreen winced. "I know. It sounds foolish. *Hey, folks, my bird is sick. Anybody know why?*"

Nan chuckled. "What if you put something at the cemetery? We haven't found out what happened there either, have we?"

"No, not at all," she said. "Talk to you later, Nan."

With those thoughts on her mind, she said, "Hey, Mugs, why don't we go back to the cemetery and see where you and Thaddeus go?" And, with Thaddeus on her shoulder, she quickly ate some toast, grabbed another cup of coffee, put it in her travel mug, then, with all the animals, she drove out to the cemetery. She walked to the area where she had been attacked, groaning when she saw the spot where the lilies were and the added disturbance from all the footprints flattening the ground around it.

"Not exactly a good memory here, is it, guys?" Mugs barked and jumped around, sniffing underneath the plants and heading from one gravestone to the next. Goliath just lay in the middle of the lilies, looking like he was some kind of a diva. Doreen smiled, then took a photo and sent it to Mack. At least he'd appreciate it, or she hoped he would. With Thaddeus looking a little bit better, she put him down on the grass and said, "So, show me where you went, Thaddeus. Show me where you went."

Thaddeus looked at her, cocked his head, and strode off.

She had no idea what direction he was going, but she was willing to follow. She also knew that anybody listening to her right now would think she was absolutely off her rocker, but she gave Thaddeus credit for an awful lot more brainpower than most people had. And for good reason. He had been a huge help in solving all kinds of issues, and she wouldn't knock him if he needed a little bit of help on this one.

He did stop and get sidetracked by a few things but eventually kept wandering. It was more of an aimless wandering now instead of a directed stride, and that did worry her. Still, she kept watch and stayed behind, just sipping her coffee. It was a Tuesday, so everybody was at work, and this place should be more or less empty, at least of the casual family visits and funerals that occurred on the weekends.

And, true enough, she couldn't see anybody around, except for in the distance, somebody mowing the lawn. She ignored him and kept following Thaddeus. When he came to the intersection, she stopped and watched to see what he would do. They had managed to get out of the cemetery through a side gate, and now they were on a street with a big intersection.

"I can't imagine you crossed here on your own," she said out loud.

He turned to look up at her and said, "Thaddeus helped. Thaddeus helped." She looked at him in surprise, then bent down and gave him a lift onto her shoulder. "Is this help, big guy?"

"Big guy, big guy," he said, throwing up his wings and making a weird cackling sound.

With the animals at her side, she pushed the button at the crosswalk. All the Tuesday morning rush-hour traffic stopped, which she imagined they weren't terribly impressed with, but she crossed to the other side, animals in tow. She quickly realized they weren't very far from Isaac, just approaching from a different perspective because they'd come at it from the cemetery.

She nodded. "If nothing else, that connects you and Isaac," she muttered. As they kept moving in that direction, Thaddeus got progressively more anxious. She watched him carefully. "So tell me what's going on, Thaddeus. Did you meet Isaac?"

He didn't say a word about Isaac. In fact, he didn't say anything, and that worried her too. "Did you make new friends, Thaddeus?" She wandered down blocks aimlessly, keeping track of the fact that the cemetery was at her back, so she could find her way home again. Plus, there was enough traffic noise from Spall Road, which turned into Glenmore Drive, to keep her oriented. She wandered up and down the blocks, looking for any reaction from Thaddeus.

When she stumbled upon one of the paths that looked like it led into a darker area, she studied it from all angles. "You know something? I think this is the same path we were at yesterday. Just a different entrance." Mugs barked several times and woofed his way forward several feet.

"Mugs, come back here." But then he caught sight of something, and, with his nose nearly dragging across the ground, he surged forward, Goliath on his heels. Doreen raced behind him.

"Come back! Mugs, come back!" She called out, again and again, but he wasn't having anything to do with it. She passed a squalid-looking house, then realized the backyard area was lined with shack after shack, with sheds in the back, and lots of them were like that in here. She didn't quite understand how that was allowed within the city, but it happened. She'd seen lots of places in her lifetime that looked this way, but they were in slumlike areas—not what she expected to see in Kelowna.

Something was sad and forlorn about them. She heard rustling in the bushes, as if maybe people were there, but it was more likely dogs or squirrels even. She kept walking through until they were at the same spot where she had met the rude protective stranger. Mugs immediately bristled. She reached out a hand and said, "It's okay, buddy. It's okay."

At least she hoped it was. She hadn't told Mack where she was going. She hadn't told anybody. She kept walking, checking out several of the small pathways, and thankfully met no one. Only as she walked down the last one did Thaddeus immediately perk up and cried out, "Big guy, big guy, big guy."

She stopped, looked at him, and said, "Is this important here?"

She looked around and found another one of those backyards full of what looked like shack upon shack upon shack. Some had plywood connecting these shacks, all different sizes, shapes, and colors—all kind of a mess. But somebody had tried to make it painstakingly neat. She looked at the fence, which was also dilapidated, and odd pieces of wood were screwed together against railings that had long since given up the ghost. So it was patchwork upon patchwork, but at least what was there was secure enough to hold something in.

She took several photos, trying to keep calm and quiet, in case anybody happened to be looking her way. She took photos of all of the houses along that pathway and kept walking forward. Even as they went past, Thaddeus twisted to look backward. On the opposite side of the path was another home with a mowed backyard; along one side was a shed, and on the other was what looked like a tiny toy house or a playhouse. She smiled at that because, even though the playhouse looked like it could use a good coat of paint, it also looked like it had served somebody well for many years. And that was worth a lot.

She kept walking until she came back out to another cul-de-sac. She stopped, reoriented herself, and used her phone to find out exactly where she was. Then realized that she had just come around the circle and was only a block away from where she'd started. Taking photos of the houses along these blocks as she went forward, she sent them to Mack along with a text. **Thaddeus only perked up when we got here.** She sent him photos of the houses on both sides.

He immediately called her. "What are you doing there?" he asked. "That's where you had the confrontation. Are you telling me that you went back?"

"Yes," she said. "I did. But there's no sign of him today."

He groaned. "Are you just asking to get into trouble?"

"Of course not," she said, "but I woke up, and Thaddeus was really depressed. His tail feathers were hanging. He didn't want to eat, and he didn't do anything. It was just terrible."

"Ah," he said. "That makes more sense."

"Mack, I just thought that if I could let him lead me to where he was when he went missing, it would help. I actually started from the cemetery. I'm sending you a photo of the corner of the cul-de-sac, the streets here," she said, "so you can see where it is."

"And I care why?"

She could tell from his tone of voice that he hadn't had a great morning. "I'm sorry. I know it's Tuesday, and you are at work, and I don't want to bother you," she said. "I just know that Thaddeus did disappear, and we did get that little message around his leg. I can't guarantee it has anything to do with this corner. I just know that he perked up when we got here and only here."

"Fine," he said grudgingly. "I'll take a look later today. I'm booked all morning, and I have to show up in court just before lunch."

She winced at that. "Better you than me," she muttered. "And, by the way, your brother phoned last night. I forgot to tell you."

"He did? Why?"

"To tell me all the papers have been filed," she said. She stood at the corner of the cul-de-sac, watching as the cars went up and down the streets. "He also didn't know about the photos that you found. You know? The ones of the guy I identified, Snoz. Were you able to track down him or the other familiar-looking guy?"

"No luck yet. The one guy was seen in a gas station, but apparently the vehicle was leaving town."

"Ha! I'll believe that when I see it," she muttered. "He could say anything you wanted him to, and you wouldn't know for sure."

"Believe me. We're aware of that," he said. "Now, would you go home and stay safe?"

She smiled and said, "Well, we'll go home," she said, looking down at the guys.

"Stay safe."

"I'm not sure that's possible."

Chapter 21

DOREEN HEADED DOWN the cul-de-sac but kept looking behind her. When she finally got to the corner and was ready to go around the block, she caught sight of eyes staring at her—and a small brown face and towhead.

She smiled and said, "Hi, Isaac. How are you doing?" At that, the face disappeared behind the tree. She backed up a bit, casually calling Mugs and Goliath to her.

"Isaac, do you want to come say hello to the animals?" His head popped around the corner again. "Hi, little guy," she said. "Come say hi to Mugs and Goliath."

He hesitated, looking at the dog and cat, but, when Mugs caught sight of Isaac, he barreled forward, woofing excitedly, his tail wagging. The little boy laughed.

"See? He likes you," she said, with a bright smile. He looked up at her hopefully. She nodded. "It's true. He doesn't do this with everybody."

Isaac looked down and wrapped his arms around Mugs, as she smiled. "See? He definitely doesn't do that with everybody."

The little boy laughed again. Goliath, not wanting to be

left out, moved closer to get some of the attention. Immediately Isaac wrapped his arms around the cat and hugged him close.

Doreen smiled. "We're so glad we saw you this morning, Isaac," she said. "Are you doing okay? Did you get lots of sleep last night?"

He just nodded.

She studied him, noticing he wore the same clothes he'd been in before. As she glanced down the pathway behind them, no one was in sight. "What about your mom?" she asked. "Is your mom doing okay?"

Immediately the little boy stopped and looked up at her.

Doreen nodded. "I hope so," she said.

He just nodded and didn't say anything, but it was obvious that the mention of his mom had affected him in some way. She continued to smile and to talk gently to him. "Mugs really likes to have his belly scratched," she said.

Isaac immediately reached for Mugs and scratched his belly. Mugs obliged by throwing himself onto the sidewalk.

She chuckled. "See? He is always happy to get lots of love and attention." The little guy looked up and seemed to relax a bit more. She glanced around. "Are you allowed to be out here on your own?"

He shook his head.

She nodded. "I don't want you to get in trouble." He didn't say anything but continued to pet Mugs. She wished he would talk, but she knew he wasn't impaired; he was obviously just insecure, scared even. Doreen waited and gave him some time to play with the animals. Then she said, "Shall we walk you back home again?"

He hopped to his feet and started to walk up the pathway. She followed behind. When he realized that she was following him, he looked a little surprised, but Mugs immediately raced up to his side again. Isaac laughed and led the way forward. When he got to the place where she had been taking photos, he hesitated, gave Mugs a great big hug, then instantly disappeared. Doreen immediately raced forward, trying to see where he disappeared to.

She discovered a gap in a nearby chain-link fence that she hadn't seen before. And with the thick bushes on the inside of the fence, she couldn't see into this particular backyard. She didn't dare go inside herself, and there was no reason to, since this is obviously where Isaac belonged. Now she just had to get Mack to do something about checking things out further. She had to ensure the child was safe. It really bothered her to think that something negative could be going on in his life.

Happy that she had at least found out where he lived, she took a quick photo, and, with the animals at her side, she headed back down to where the pathway opened up to the cul-de-sac. As soon as she did, she found several men standing there, hands on their hips, glaring at her. She sighed. "Good morning, guys," she said in a cheerful voice.

"You were told to stay away," one man said.

She looked at him in surprise. "Who said that?"

He didn't say another word and just crossed his arms over his chest.

"So you'll call the police then?" she asked him gently. "I'm just concerned that little boy is okay."

"He's fine," the man said.

"If that were the case ..." she muttered, eyeing the three of them closely and realizing that this could get ugly very quickly. "If that were the case," she repeated, "why are you so worried about me being here?"

"Because we don't want you to bug him."

"But we're not bugging him at all," she said. "He really loves my animals, and they really love him as well. Is that wrong?"

"Leave and don't come back," said the man who had been quiet until now.

"Well, I live here in town," she said gently, "and obviously you have a reason for not wanting me around. It's just making me mighty curious."

At that, the smiles—or at least the somewhat genial look on the third man's face—fell away. "Don't come back," he warned. "You're not welcome here."

"Why is that?" she asked. "Are you keeping Isaac a prisoner?"

He looked at her in surprise. "Hell no."

"Well then, why are you so worried about me finding out more about him?" she asked slowly. "Because, if you're not involved in something that's hurting him, why do you care?"

He just shook his head. "You don't know anything."

"No," she said, "I don't know everything, but I do know a lot, and that little boy could use a little more love and attention."

"He's getting it," they said, almost in unison.

She frowned. "I'm not convinced. And, if I'm not convinced," she said, "I'm not leaving."

They just stared at her, looked at each other, and one said, "Why are you being so difficult?"

"Because you've threatened me," she said, "and that makes me worried about Isaac's care. Anybody who will neglect a little boy like that doesn't deserve anything but jail time." At that, one of the men got extremely angry, and she shook her head. "Don't bother trying to threaten me," she said, glaring at him. "I would much prefer to champion the underdog and see that little boy gets a decent life than listen to you guys threaten me."

At that, the third man, who had been studying her, spoke up. "I think I recognize you," he said.

"You don't know me from shit," she said. Then she clapped her hand over her mouth because she swore. She dropped her hand away, hoping they hadn't noticed. They were looking at her curiously now.

"What do you mean, you recognize her?" one of the guys asked the third guy.

"She's that crazy lady with the animals."

She gasped. "I'm not crazy," she said.

He sneered at her. "You're the one who's been digging around into all the cold cases," he said. "You're definitely crazy for doing that."

"Well, it might not be for everyone," she said, with a shrug, "but that doesn't make me crazy."

"Yeah, it does," he said with a sneer. "You're always sticking your nose where you're not wanted."

"Well, that depends," she said. "If you're on the side of the family who never had a chance to find out what happened to your loved ones," she said, "you'd see it differently. But if you're the crook or somebody who got away with murder all these years, then, yeah, you're probably not too happy to see me." She glared at him, crossed her arms over her chest, and tapped her foot, as she studied him. He was stocky and reminded her of the gardening brothers who had been involved in the deaths of their parents and sisters. "Is that what you're up to?" she asked. "Are you one of those guys who does the dirty work and waits for somebody else to pay the price for your crimes?"

He stared at her. "Shut up," he said. "You don't know nothing."

"And again we're back to that," she said. "I'm just here to make sure that little boy is okay."

"We told you that he's fine."

"Yeah? So where is his mother?" she asked.

Immediately one of the guys stiffened. "You think his mother will make a difference?"

"Maybe," she said. "I don't know what's going on here, but you can bet I'll find out."

"You get out of here and stay away," he said in a low tone.

"Yeah, and what will you do about it?"

"Well, maybe you'll get a visitor in the night," he said in a dark tone of voice.

Immediately she felt the presence of fear slide down her back, but she stuck her neck out even farther. "Oh, so maybe I do have a reason to call the cops on you then."

"You got no reason to call the cops on us at all," he said. "You're the one who's trespassing."

"Nope," she said, "this is all public land, so I'm not trespassing at all. But, if you've been coming into my yard and causing all kinds of chaos at my place, you can bet that will be a different story for you." She said, "Now that I know it's you, I'll call the cops right now." She pulled out her phone.

Immediately he tried to grab it from her hand.

She backed up, and Mugs barked like crazy to keep him back. She glared, "If you're the one breaking and entering and trespassing on my property, you're darn right I'm calling the cops. I've been looking for you, and so have they."

"I don't know what you're talking about," he said.

"You're a crazy person."

"We already went through the fact that I'm not crazy," she growled, "so stop saying that." She crossed her arms over her chest again and said, "Either you're the one who's causing all the chaos at my house or you're not."

"I'm not," he said, glaring.

"You just threatened to visit me in the night," she said, "and I've already had somebody do just that."

"Yeah, I wonder why," he said. "It's because you keep sticking your nose in other people's business."

"You better look after that little boy," she said, "because mistreatment of a child is everybody's business."

He stopped, stared at her, and said, "Do you really think he's being abused?"

"I don't know what the deal is, but something's going on here, and he doesn't look like he's very well cared for."

"Well, he's a hell of a lot better off now than he was before," he snapped.

"Prove it then," she said, staring at him.

He shook his head, nudged one of the other guys, and said, "Let's go."

"Yeah, sure. Run away," she said. "Remember. You treat him well … or else."

He stopped, looked at her, and said, "Lady, did you just threaten me?"

She smiled. "I don't have to. The law is enough to take you down, if you're abusing that child."

"I'm not abusing the child," he roared.

She patted her arm and said, "Well, you haven't convinced me of that. Every time I come around to make sure he's okay, one of you guys are standing in the path, making life difficult for me."

He stared at her. "Who else was here?"

She shrugged. "That huge guy with the scar."

Some of the color left his face. "Randy?"

"I think that's who it is. Yeah," she said, remembering the name that Mack had used. "What about Randy?" They looked at each other, and she saw that something had shifted. Something about the name Randy had set them off. "Is he a friend of yours?" she asked.

Immediately he shook his head. "No, he's nobody's friend."

"Oh, I met a few of those guys too," she said, nodding her head wisely.

He looked at her and said, "Don't be such a wiseass," he said. "If Randy told you to get the hell away from here, you should have listened."

"He did tell me that," she said, "which is why the three of you aren't doing much to scare me."

"Well, you should have respected Randy because that's one scary dude."

"Yeah, I got that part," she said, "but you're still not making things any better for yourselves though."

He shook his head. "You're playing with fire here. You don't know what the hell's going on, so just go home before you get hurt."

"Oh, so now you're concerned about my well-being?" she said, with a snort.

Frustrated, the first man turned and looked at her and said, "Lady, just leave before Randy finds out you came back."

In that, she recognized some truth. "You're scared of him," she said.

Immediately he shook his head. "Hell, no," he muttered.

"I'm not scared of him."

She nodded. "You are. It's obvious."

"No, I'm not," he yelled.

She looked at him, then over at the others and said, "I don't believe him."

"Would you just get lost?" One of the men hissed the words and raised his hands.

"Sure," she said, "but I don't know why I should have to."

"Because," he said. "Just because."

As she went to walk forward, one of the men noticed Thaddeus.

"What the hell is that on your shoulder?"

She looked at him in surprise. "Why, it's Thaddeus." Immediately the bird sat up.

"Thaddeus is here. Thaddeus is here."

The man looked at him in surprise. "I remember him," he said. "He came through here a few days ago."

"It's one of the reasons I'm back in this quarter," she admitted. "I think he connected with Isaac."

He looked at her and frowned. "I don't think so."

"Do you know where Thaddeus was then?" she asked eagerly. "We're trying to figure out what happened. He disappeared and then all of a sudden reappeared."

Frowning, the man said, "He was here, but I don't know how he got here." He shook his head, looked around, and said, "Did you guys see him?"

Both of the men looked at him like he was crazy. "We've got better things to do than watch what a parrot does."

"No, it wasn't that," he said. "Somehow he flew in here, but I think he came from the cul-de-sac."

"Was he trying to get away from somebody?" she asked

in horror.

He frowned. "I think he was getting out of a vehicle, but I'm not sure where and what. He could have just hitched a ride."

"Unfortunately, with him, that's quite possible," she said, with an eye roll. "He does get into trouble sometimes. He's curious, and then he gets into the back of various vehicles and sometimes goes for a ride where he didn't expect to go."

He nodded. "I think that's exactly it," he said. "I don't remember what truck it was, but it might have been one of the gardeners who works at the cemetery." Frowning, he looked around and said, "But I don't think he knew the bird was even there."

She thought about that and nodded. "You know what? That's quite likely. And then he flew in here?" she asked, pointing out the pathway.

He nodded, then changed his mind. "I'm not sure. I saw him getting in the truck, and I didn't really realize what I was seeing because it didn't make any sense," he admitted. "Next thing I knew, I saw him in the pathway here, but I don't know if he flew, walked, or hitched another ride," he said, looking at the bird. "Does he fly?"

"Not well," she said. "Not well at all."

"Interesting," he muttered.

"I figured that maybe Isaac saw him," she said, "because look at Thaddeus. He's been much happier since I came down here again." He looked at her in surprise. She shrugged. "Thaddeus is very people-oriented."

"Interesting," he muttered. He looked at the others and shrugged. "It's possible."

The other guys shook their heads. "We don't need her

interfering."

"Maybe not," she said, "but you never know. I might be able to help."

"There is nothing to help with," the first man said harshly.

She frowned at him. "You're hiding something that involves Isaac, and my bird here got involved somehow," she said, "so that means I'm involved."

"And you can just get uninvolved," he said, shaking his finger at her.

"Hey, I want to see that little boy doing well," she muttered.

"Then stay away," he said in exaggeration, but at least now the same threatening edge to his voice was gone that had been there before.

She frowned, as she looked at him. "I guess it depends on what's going on."

"Nothing's going on."

"Is he in school?" she asked.

He just glared at her.

"So he's not, and there's no birth certificate for him either."

At that, all the men stiffened and looked at her.

She shrugged. "I checked, of course."

Chapter 22

"YOU CHECKED A little too much," the first guy said in a dark voice. "Now get lost." And, with that, he turned and strode away. The other two turned and raced to catch up.

She frowned as she thought about what could possibly be going on here. "If it's a cold case," she called out, "I can help."

The men stopped, looked at her, and said, "No cold case here."

She frowned. "I think there is. Or, if there were one here, I could help."

"There isn't," the first guy said in defiance.

"Unless, of course, there's been a murder or kidnapping or something else here that was never solved," she said in a crafty voice. They stopped again, turned, and glared at her, as she raised her palms. "Fine," she said. "So there isn't anything I can do here."

"No," the one guy said, "you're finally getting the right message. Go home."

She nodded, and, calling the animals to her, she slowly moved off to the side. When she got around the corner of the cul-de-sac, a little old lady called from her porch.

Doreen looked over and asked, "Are you talking to me?" The woman nodded and motioned for her to come quickly. Doreen raced up the steps, animals in tow.

The woman looked at the dog in delight. "This is the famous Mugs, isn't it?"

"Well, I don't know how famous he is," Doreen said, with a grin, "but yes. Was there something you wanted to say?"

"It is a cold case," she said.

"What are you talking about?"

"It's a cold case."

Doreen studied the older woman. "Okay, what is a cold case?"

"That little boy," she muttered. "He just appeared one day."

Doreen stopped and stared at her in shock. "He just appeared one day out of the blue?"

The old woman nodded. "Yes, and we don't know where he came from."

"What about his mom?" she said.

"We're not sure. We don't know exactly what happened."

"Well, how long has he been here?"

"It's been a couple years now," she said. "Isaac is a sweetheart."

"So, who looks after him?"

"Well, a man looks after him, but I don't think they're related."

"Ah," she said, "that's what they're afraid of then. That somebody will take him away."

She nodded.

"Of course, but if Isaac has a family out there somewhere," Doreen said, "then we need to find them." The lady just shrugged. "So, what is the case about?" Doreen asked, looking at her in surprise.

"I just told you. It's a cold case."

"Oh, you mean because it happened a few years ago."

The woman nodded. "Yes, yes, of course."

That wasn't quite Mack's definition of a cold case, but Doreen might be able to work with it. "Do you know anything else? Do you know where Isaac came from? Like what corner of town, or was he from out of town?"

"I heard rumors," she said, leaning forward, speaking in a really low raspy voice. "Something about him coming from Vancouver."

"And he just stayed? There should have been other people with him, right?"

The old lady shrugged. "I don't know," she said.

At that, Doreen nodded. "You know where he lives?"

The woman nodded again. "You were there," she said. "I saw you somewhere on the pathways. I'm sure you saw him."

"I saw him disappear behind a fence."

"Exactly," she said.

"Is he related to the other man who's looking after him?"

The old lady shrugged. "We don't argue with him."

"Ah. Is it Randy?"

She nodded.

"So, Randy is looking after Isaac then?" It was like pulling teeth to get information out of this woman. But still, she was providing valuable information.

The stranger hesitated, then decided that she should retreat, as if she'd already spoken too much.

Doreen immediately reached out again. "Is there anything else you can tell me?"

The old lady shook her head. "No, and I shouldn't be telling you any of it. Randy will get mad."

"But why would he get mad?"

The old lady looked at her, and she said, "You were right. Because he doesn't want to lose Isaac."

"Exactly," she said.

"But if he is allowed to keep him, then that would make life easier on him."

"Maybe," she said, "but I don't think he'd be allowed to keep him."

Just then came a loud raspy cough and the stomping of feet. The woman's face turned pale, and she raced inside, slamming the door on Doreen.

Doreen turned, but nobody was in sight; yet she heard voices coming down the pathway. She looked down at Mugs and Goliath. "Now we'll get in trouble."

But, as she looked around the corner, she thought maybe she could slip across the property and disappear from sight. Picking up Goliath in her arms, she softly called Mugs to her and raced around the old lady's steps. She hid in the bushes between there and the next property. Sure enough, Randy came storming out, as if looking for her. He stood at the cul-de-sac, his hands on his hips, muttering out loud, something about *Stay away.*

She figured that message was for her, even though he hadn't actually seen her this time. Still, it was a close call, and she decided it was time to go home. She needed to contact Mack and to give him the details. She waited until Randy disappeared, and then she and her animals hurried back to the cemetery. When she got there, she noticed that Thaddeus was still looking behind her.

"It's okay. We'll take care of it, buddy. We'll find out what's going on." He seemed to be in better spirits, and she was thankful for that. In no time they were all in her car and heading for home. When she got there, she had no sooner stepped out of the garage and went to close the door when she saw Mack pulling up behind her.

He glared at her. "You were supposed to come home."

"I know I was." She went on to explain about the three men and what she'd found out from the old lady.

"What?" he said, frowning. "I've known Randy for a while," he said cautiously. "I didn't know there was a little boy in his life."

"Well, apparently he's been looking after him for a while," she said. "As in a couple years. Nobody really knows where he came from—maybe Vancouver."

Mack jumped in. "Nobody is talking about where he came from, and that's a whole different story."

She had to admit he was right there. "Fine," she said. "Nobody is saying much, let's put it that way."

He nodded slowly. "Maybe I need to have a talk with Randy."

"Yeah, you do that," she said. "I think he spends a lot of his time threatening people."

"Well, that's partly because of his size," he said. "He was also a prison guard down at Abbotsford for a few years, and that intimidation just comes naturally to him."

"And yet you're not intimidated," she said.

He looked at her in surprise. "Of course not. Why would I be?"

"Well, he's huge for one," she said with a chuckle.

"Not for me, he isn't."

"Yeah, that's true enough," she muttered. "There's some

advantage to you guys being the size you are."

"A lot of advantages to it," he said, "also disadvantages."

"Yeah, name one," she said in a challenging voice.

"Well, I need a lot more food than you do for one thing," he said, motioning at her front door. "Will you ever open this door so we can go in?"

"Are you depleting my coffee supply again?"

"Maybe," he said, "but I also brought groceries." He pointed to his truck.

Immediately she gave him a fat smile. "I guess you can come in then."

He rolled his eyes. "Gee, thanks." He grabbed the bags and followed her to the door.

She opened up the front door to let the animals in, then took one last look around the front of the house. She couldn't see anything suspicious, but, feeling like she had maybe stirred up some trouble that she would regret, she carefully closed and locked the door. He watched her curiously. She shrugged. "One of the three guys threatened me. He said he would come in the middle of the night."

"Wow," he said, glaring at her. "You really know how to stir up trouble, don't you?"

"I do," she said. "The problem was, I accused him of doing it already. You know? Locking me in with the rocks."

He stared at her in surprise. "I don't know how much of a *locking in* that was," he said, "since it was more of an inconvenience than anything. I was thinking it might have been kids. Like maybe the kids who saw you rescue Thaddeus."

She stopped and stared and then said, "Oh, I didn't even think of that."

"That's why I'm the detective, and you're not," he said,

waggling his eyebrows at her.

She snorted. "In that case, you better have a talk with Randy and figure out what is going on with that little boy."

"Maybe I will," he said, with a smile, "but obviously other things need to be done first. Part of that involves food," he said, walking through to the kitchen.

"What are you making?" she asked excitedly.

He looked at her, smiled. "Nachos."

She almost jumped up and down for joy. "And that means we can eat pretty fast, right?"

"Well, it doesn't take all that long to prepare, if that's what you mean," he said. "Why? Are you hungry?"

"Yeah," she said, "I didn't eat much today." He stopped, slowly turned, and glared at her. She shrugged. "I didn't really feel like it. When Thaddeus gets all upset, it's hard to eat."

He nodded. "Well, that's true," he said, "and I know you're very close to Thaddeus, and we don't want anything to go wrong with him."

"Nope, we sure don't," she said, "so I just headed out after some toast."

"And you haven't eaten since?"

She shook her head. "Nope, we've been gone."

"Good, I was hoping we could have lunch," he said, "instead of dinner. Nachos aren't necessarily a huge meal."

"Well, it can be," she said in surprise. "I've seen it as a big meal."

"Maybe so," he said. "I just figured that, if we had a good lunch, then I would go to work afterward."

"Interesting," she said, "and that works for me because I'm hungry."

He snorted. "You know how I said you're always hungry? Yet this last time apparently you weren't so hungry."

"Well, I wasn't," she said. "It's one of those *anxious and I don't know what I'm doing* kind of things."

"If you say so," he said, looking at her. "Let's get some nachos made up, and then we'll see."

"Did you say you have to go to work afterward?"

He nodded. "I was up late last night working," he said, "so I'm going in late today, and I'll do a late shift again."

"Why were you working late?" she asked in surprise.

He just looked at her and then said, "Because somebody dumped an awful lot of paperwork on us."

"Sure," she said, "but that you could do during the week."

"And today is Tuesday," he reminded her. Then he turned and unpacked the groceries. As he pulled out a bag of corn chips, she walked up to see more.

"So, what will we do?"

He brought out a block of cheese, handed her the grater, and said, "Start grating." As she grated, he fried up ground beef and put some interesting sauces and green chilies in it.

"Is this your version of nachos?"

"Yep, it's a family favorite," he said.

"And you're using it to distract me from the conversation."

He laughed. "Yeah. I absolutely am."

"Wow," she said, "that's not fair."

"Is it working?"

"Well, you're making me hungry, that's for sure," she said. "But I still want to know what you were doing working so late on a Monday night."

"Fine. We were trying to figure out this Isaac thing," he said.

"Well, I just figured it out for you. Talk to Randy, since he's looking after him."

"Yeah, but at the same time I need to have a little bit of knowledge before I go storming in there. Like, why this little boy has no birth certificate, and why he's not in school."

"Because I don't think he is Randy's kid, Randy is just looking after him. This one old lady also said it was a cold case," she said. She gave him a bright smile. "Which means it's part of my domain."

"News flash, Doreen. You have no domain," he said in exasperation. "There's the law, which I am employed to fight for and to uphold," he said, "and then there's you."

"What about me?" she said, her brows drawing together.

"You and your job seem to be all about getting into trouble," he said, as he gave her a fat smile. "So, you just keep grating cheese."

Chapter 23

NOT MUCH LATER, when Doreen was presented with a delicious-looking nacho mess, she was absolutely enthralled. Melted cheese, corn chips, diced tomatoes, guacamole, onions, and even ground meat sprinkled over the top. It was beyond her imagination to have considered he could make something like this. Not only had he done it but it seemed simple and without any fuss. She realized that, if she prepared a slight variation of it, she could make something even simpler and faster for herself. They sat down at the kitchen table; then Mack looked outside and frowned.

"Now what?" she asked, in exasperation, as she reached for her first chip.

"We should be eating outside."

"We should be," she said, "but that puts one of us in a chair and one of us on the footstool, or both of us sitting on the steps."

He nodded. "Not ideal for a dish like this. We need to get you a table."

"Well, that's why I went out to the secondhand stores with Nan," she said. "We went to lots of places, but there just wasn't anything right for the space and really affordable."

"No," he said, "you have to go to the right places at the right time to get the deals."

"And how are you supposed to know what the right places are at the right time?" she asked, looking at him in surprise. "Because Nan is a pretty smart shopper."

"She is," he said, "and I'm sure she got you a heck of a good price on that chair, but you know there are deals that can be had at other places too, like estate sales."

"Which we would have done, if we'd known about any," she said.

"True, plus there are other secondhand stores. I'm sure we can roust up something."

"It would be nice," she said, looking out the kitchen window. "To have that beautiful deck and not be able to sit out there is kind of criminal."

"Don't even mention that word," he said.

She frowned. "I don't do it on purpose, you know?"

"I know," he said, slowly lowering his head to look at her. "That almost makes it worse when you just seem to be a magnet for trouble."

"Well, I didn't attack myself, and I just went looking to see what I could do about Thaddeus and the little boy."

"I get that," he said, "but you walked right in where angels fear to tread."

"That's because they need to be worried about not getting back to heaven," she said blissfully. He stopped and stared, but she just shrugged. "I don't know what that means either," she said. "Look. I'm just trying to help. If you could find out what was going on with little Isaac, then I wouldn't have to."

"We're on it," he said. "Somebody should be going out

there to talk to Randy now."

"Why not you?"

"Because I know Randy, and they didn't want that to be an issue."

She slowly popped another melty cheese-laden nacho chip into her mouth, loving the flavors that burst through her taste buds. "I get that," she said, "but sometimes isn't it better if you do know people?"

"Sometimes, but not always."

"Besides," she said, "it's not as if I have anything else to do."

"Yes, you do," he said. "Recover from that last injury."

"Another crime you have yet to solve. A current crime at that, so it's definitely on your docket."

He nodded. "And we have managed to track down various people we found who were at the cemetery, but nobody can place them where you were found."

"Of course not," she said. "I was deliberately walking away from everybody because I was emotional."

"You were emotional? Never," he said.

She glared at him.

"Oh, come on," he said. "I didn't mean it in a bad way."

"Of course not," she said. "But the thing is, I just wanted to be away from people for a bit. There had been a lot of deaths, and I wanted these poor little old ladies to have some respect as they headed off on whatever journey comes after this."

"When somebody saw you and took advantage of that," he said. "You appear to have amassed a few enemies."

"Maybe. I also wonder, though I don't have any reason for thinking this," she said, "but I do wonder if it could have been my ex."

He stared and said, "I thought you were pretty adamant it wasn't him."

"I was, but then I started thinking about it, and, if Nick had already started an investigation of my ex and reported his bimbo lawyer's improprieties, it is quite possible that my ex would have done what he could to shut me up."

"To include killing you?"

She stopped and stared. "Well, he didn't kill me though, did he?"

"No," he said, "but that doesn't mean it wasn't on his mind."

"No, or it was just a warning."

"Warnings are usually clearly warnings," he said. "In this case, somebody literally attacked you, and you didn't even get a chance to defend yourself."

She frowned. "It could also have been any one of the other cold cases I worked on."

"Yeah, like I said, we have a plethora of suspects in this case regarding your attacker."

"I guess maybe I have amassed my share of enemies." She sat back in her chair and stared at him in dismay. "I so wanted to make friends here, you know? I just wanted to be in a community where I felt wanted and where I belonged," she muttered. "Instead it seems like I've gone about this the wrong way."

"It's not that you went about it the wrong way," he said, "but your need to do something to help, that curiosity, and the way your mind works," he said, "has gotten you into a fair amount of trouble, time and time again. And, with that, we have disgruntled people."

"Do you really think they're after me?" she asked, staring out the kitchen window. "I didn't think I made that many enemies."

"You only need to make one," he reminded her.

"Well, I certainly have that, haven't I?" She groaned.

"And maybe it's somebody completely unrelated," he said, looking at her.

"Which would be even worse because we would have no idea where to start. That would be a stranger-danger deal, and we would have no way to track down anything."

"And, yes, before you ask, we did look at the vehicles coming in and out of the cemetery."

"Anything?"

"A rental," he muttered. "We tracked it back and found it was rented to a John Smith."

She laughed at that. "Wow, they're not even trying to be original."

"No, they aren't, which leads us to thinking it was deliberate. Deliberate to rent a vehicle. Deliberate to go to the cemetery. But was it deliberate to attack you? That's the part we can't ascertain for sure."

Chapter 24

DOREEN AND MACK continued with their meal, and, when they were done, Mack said, "Come on. Let's take our coffee outside and sit on the deck."

"Even if it's not on a chair?"

"You can have the chair," he said. "I'll sit on the steps."

"Do you think we could find a table and some chairs for it?" she asked. "It really would be so lovely to eat out here."

"I'm sure we can, and I don't think it'll be all that much money," he said. "Even brand-new, the cheap sets are a couple hundred bucks, so we should be able to get something better than that."

She nodded, smiling. "That would really be nice." They quickly cleaned up the dishes and made some coffee. Then, when she pushed open the screen door, it wouldn't easily budge. She started to chuckle. "Has he struck again?"

Mack stared at her in outrage, then peered through the glass window. "Seriously?"

"I wouldn't be at all surprised," she said. "But I didn't hear a thing."

"Neither did I," he said, glaring at the door. "I'll sneak around the side," he said. "I've been looking out here the whole time, so it must have just happened when I put on the coffee." He turned and raced out the front door.

She thought he would go around the right-hand side, but instead he went around Richard's side, and, next thing she knew, there was a squawk outside, and she cried out in joy. "It looks like he got him!"

Mugs started barking, and Thaddeus called out, "Big guy, big guy."

"Well, Mack's our big guy," she said, looking at Thaddeus. "Surely you're not confused on who big guy is?"

He just bobbed his head up and down and flapped his wings, "Big guy, big guy."

Suddenly the rock was removed, and the door was flung open. And there was Mack, with a glare on his face, holding a skinny kid by the upper arm. "Do you know this guy?" he asked.

She looked at the boy, frowned, and said, "He was one of the kids chasing Thaddeus down the river," she said slowly. She looked back at Thaddeus. "That's why you're crying out big guy, isn't it?"

"Big guy, big guy, big guy."

Mack looked at Thaddeus, looked at the kid, and said, "What do you want with this bird?"

"I don't know anything about the bird," he protested.

Mack released his grip on him, and the kid shrugged his shirt back into place and glared at both of them. "I wasn't doing nothing."

"Well, you were trespassing," she said, calmly studying him. "He looks like he came from that same corner," she muttered to Mack.

"He's a long way from home then."

"Could have come by bike without any trouble," she

said. "It's not all that far as the crow flies. Especially considering he's in the other side of the eco center."

Mack frowned, as he stared at the kid. "What's your name?"

But the kid's face turned sullen, and he shoved his hands in his pockets.

"Take him down to the station and lock him up for the night," she said. "Maybe come morning, he'd be more willing to talk."

The kid started to sputter.

"What do you expect?" she asked the boy. "You leave threatening messages on people's doorsteps. You trespass on people's properties, and you're here, trying to steal my bird," she said, the outrage in her voice growing. "Do you think you'll get a warm welcome?"

"I'm not trying to steal him," he said, looking at Thaddeus. Then his shoulders slumped. "But I sure wouldn't mind having him."

"Well, you're not going to," she said. "He's mine."

He glared at her. "You didn't look after him though, did you?"

"Meaning?"

"I saw him around the cemetery," he said, "and he was all alone, and nobody was there to look after him."

She turned and glared at Mack, who at least had the good graces to look apologetic. "Actually," she said, flipping back to look at the kid, "I was attacked and unconscious at the cemetery. You don't happen to know anything about that, do you?"

He looked at her in surprise, then the bird, finally at Mack. "What? Why would I? I wasn't even on the grounds."

"The detective here picked up my animals because he

came to find out why I wasn't at home. In fact, my animals found me unconscious in the cemetery. Mack knew that I'd gone to a funeral there, so he came by and grabbed them, as they are well-known for searching out trouble," she said, for lack of a better term. "And they did find me, but, when I woke up, with the paramedics and police all around me, Thaddeus had disappeared."

The kid just looked at her, his mouth open.

She nodded. "So, you took off with my bird, stealing him from where he belonged."

He shook his head. "I didn't know he was with you though. He was just a little ways from my house."

"Maybe not," Mack said, crossing his arms over his chest. "But it's obvious he's not some animal that you just get to pick up and take away," he said. "Since when is that a thing? Do you do that with squirrels? Do you do that with crows? Do you do that with somebody else's dog?"

The kid shuffled in place. "Well, no," he said. "I just thought ..." And then he stopped and let the words fall away.

"And what connection does Thaddeus have to you making those threats and leaving them at my back door?" she asked, glaring at him. "And why with rocks out of my own garden?" He just looked at her. "Did you think I would leave, that I wouldn't take my bird with me or something?"

He shrugged. "I thought maybe, if you left, you would leave the animals behind for a weekend or something, and I could come in and get them."

"Okay, so now you're planning a breaking-and-entering scenario so you could steal my pets?" she said, her outrage growing even more. She glared at Mack. "Surely there's charges we can file on him for that alone."

The boy protested. "That's not fair," he said. "It's just he's kind of sweet."

At that, Thaddeus strode up and down her shoulder. "Sweet. Thaddeus is sweet. Thaddeus is sweet."

She looked at Thaddeus. "Don't let it go to your head, big guy."

He immediately started in. "Big guy, big guy, big guy."

She rolled her eyes at Mack. "He's apparently quite confused over the *big guy* thing."

"No, he said that when he was with me," the kid said.

"Speaking of that, where did you take him?" she asked, studying his face closely.

He shrugged. "I took him to my room."

"And where is your room?" Mack asked.

At that, he pinched his lips together.

"Well, you'll tell me, or I'll find out anyway," Mack said. "The difference is, I will be pissed after having to do the work myself."

Finally the kid gave up his address, which put them right in the same area they had been looking at.

"It's good to know that we were in the right corner of the neighborhood at least," she said, studying the kid. "What's your name?" And again he clammed up. She shrugged. "Do you think we won't find out?"

"Abner," he said quietly.

"Well, Abner. Do you realize that there is some severity to these actions of yours?"

He shrugged. "I don't have much," he said. "I was really hoping to have the bird." His gaze locked on Thaddeus. "He's really unique."

"He is, but he's not just a bird," she said, "he's part of my family."

At that, the kid's eyes flew wide open. "What do you mean?"

"He's like a child to me," she said. "They all are. They sleep in my room. They walk with me everywhere. They're even involved in all my cold case investigations," she said. "Thaddeus isn't something I would just hand over to you, like a rock. He has feelings and affections and loyalties … to me."

"But if he stayed with me long enough," Abner said, "he would become my family."

There was such a note of wanting in his voice that she stopped and looked at him. "Do you live with your mom?" He shook his head. "Where do you live?" He looked a little confused. "Ah," she said, "you live in a foster home, don't you?"

He nodded slowly. "But I'm almost eighteen," he said, "and I'll move out then."

"It's almost impossible to find a place that will take a bird like this," she said. "And you can't share him because he wouldn't become yours. He would become everybody's then." He frowned and stared off in the distance. "Besides, it's not an option," she said firmly. "Thaddeus is mine. He's part of my family. He was my grandmother's before me and is still an important part of my family."

His shoulders slumped again, and he slowly nodded.

"Did you show him to anybody else in your foster home?"

He shook his head. "No, not at all," he said, then he stopped. "But you know something? He did disappear on me."

"What do you mean?" Mack pounced.

"I lost him for a little bit," he said. "I know I had locked him up in my room, but, when I went back, he wasn't there."

"That's interesting. Where did you find him again?"

He shrugged. "I saw him in the yard, and then, when I went after him, he disappeared."

"That's because he was coming home," she said.

"I don't even know how he got back here," he said.

"He was floating on a branch coming home," she said, pointing to the river behind him, "and I did see a bunch of boys chasing him."

He frowned at that. "Was one of them a redhead?" he asked angrily.

She nodded slowly. "Yes, but you were one of them too, weren't you?"

"Well, I was farther down the river, so I didn't see him."

"I thought it was you," she said in confusion.

"No," he said, "it was probably my cousin. He looks just like me."

"That's possible," she said, her face clearing, and she realized that he'd been just far enough away that she couldn't have done a positive ID on him anyway. "The problem is," she said, "because they were chasing him, I don't know who to trust when it comes to kids. Not everybody will look after him."

Immediately Abner nodded. "I know."

Mack stepped in. "And what's your beef with the red-headed kid?"

"He's another foster kid," he said, "but he's really mean."

"So, did he see you with the bird then?"

"I tried hard not to let him, but he must have. Then he probably let him out of my room."

"Is anybody else in that foster home?"

He shook his head. "No, just the two of us. Although they have other kids who come and go sometimes."

"Is there a mother?"

Again he shook his head.

"Interesting. What about Isaac?"

For a moment, the kid looked confused, and he stared at them, his brows furrowed. "Isaac?"

"That little neighborhood kid."

His gaze cleared. "Oh. He's just another kid from around the corner," he said, shrugging his shoulders. "He's always around but not really there. He gets in trouble if he plays with us."

"And do you have any idea who he belongs to?"

"Well, another house," he said. "I don't know about his parents though."

"Are there any parents?"

"I'm not sure. Everybody takes it easy on him." He stopped and then said with a shrug, "He's different."

"So, you're saying he's got some issues? Maybe some mental challenges?" she asked.

"Maybe," he said, "I don't really know. I don't think he goes to school."

"That's interesting," she murmured. Studying Mack, she looked back at the kid. "I think you need to show us where you live. We'll give you a ride back home, and you can show us."

"No," he cried out. "Don't do that. Please. My foster family will get really mad at me."

"And when they get upset with you, what do they do?" Mack asked.

"They get mad," he said. "Randy doesn't like it if we get

in trouble."

At that, Mack froze. She looked up at him and said, "Your friend, Randy?"

"Acquaintance," he corrected.

She nodded, looking over at Abner, who was now studying Mack with uncertainty. As if to say he was now less trustworthy because he knew Randy.

"Listen, Abner. Does Randy ever hurt you?" she asked.

He shook his head. "Nah, he's okay. It's just, it's not the same as having a home-home."

"I get that," she said. "I just want to make sure Randy isn't hitting you or locking you up." She used the term on purpose because of the note that she had seen. The note that Thaddeus brought home on his leg.

"Nah," he said. "Randy is okay."

She saw some of the tension in Mack's shoulders ease. "What about the rest of people around there?"

"It's like any place. A couple drug dealers, a few drunks," he said. "Everybody else's okay."

"You okay there?"

"Yes. Randy makes sure we have lots to eat. We did talk to Randy about Isaac. He was pretty protective. Everybody is," he said.

"Maybe because he is special," she said. "That often brings out the protectiveness in people."

"Maybe," he muttered. He turned, and he looked down to kick a rock, and then realized it was the rock he had placed there. He cringed at the memory.

"Did you put the first one there, Abner?"

"Well, I saw somebody do it," he said. "So I just thought, maybe that's what they were trying to do."

"What do you mean?" Mack pounced.

Abner looked at him in surprise and took a half step backward. "Well, I just put this one here," he said.

Doreen bent down, picked up the rock, noting it was a lot smaller and the lettering was quite different. "When did you see somebody doing this?"

"Two nights ago," he said.

"Can you describe him?"

"Well, it was pretty dark already," he muttered. His hands went right back into his pockets, as he shifted nervously.

"Would you recognize him?"

Immediately Abner shook his head. "I don't think so. I've never seen him before."

"Tall or short?" As if on impulse, Mack made a sudden noise and pulled out his phone. He scanned through several photographs and then held up a phone. "Was it this guy?"

The kid looked at the picture, looked at Mack in surprise, and said, "Yeah! That's him. How did you know?"

Immediately Mack turned the phone around to show her.

She recognized it as taken off the cemetery's video camera. It was the one guy she'd recognized who they had been trying to track down. The one who used to work for her ex. Snoz. "Look at that, John Smith, or Snoz as I called him in my head," she said. "What a surprise."

"John Smith? Is that his name?" the kid said doubtfully.

"Well, that's the name he's using on his rental car," she said.

He shrugged. "I didn't see a car. He came out the side of the house though, and he left that way."

"And why were you here?"

"I often come to the river," he said. "Just to get away.

My life is not all that great sometimes."

"Uh-oh," she said out loud.

He looked at her in surprise. "What do you mean?"

"Are you like seriously depressed?" she asked.

His shoulders hunched.

"Abner," she said, speaking gently. "What happened to your family that you ended up in foster care?"

A few long moments went by. "My dad killed himself," he said quietly.

"I'm so sorry, Abner. How long ago?"

"About six months or so." He turned around to look at the river.

"Is that why you're sitting at the river?"

He shifted uneasily.

"Are you thinking about doing something to yourself?" she asked gently.

His shoulders stiffened. "No," he snapped.

"Well, I would understand if you had those thoughts sometimes," she said quietly. "I've thought about it myself before."

His gaze flew to hers. "Seriously?"

She nodded, crossing her arms over her chest. "Life can be pretty rough, and sometimes we can get to a point where we think maybe that's the best answer."

He nodded. "I did think about it," he said. "Maybe that's why I found the river originally. Normally I sit up higher at the eco center," he said, "but it's really nice down here. It's just so much farther away for me to have to get home."

"Where's your bike?" Mack asked.

He looked at him in surprise, then pointed to the other side of the river.

"You know you could fall in any time, right?"

"I have actually. Several times," he said. "Maybe that's why I don't think about it so much anymore."

She knew there was more to the story, but he wasn't being very forthcoming. And then she got it. "Because you had a scare and came close to drowning, and it made you rethink the options?"

"Yeah," he said quietly. "I just have a little bit further to go to get through foster care."

"And then what?" Mack asked.

"I'm not sure. I was hoping for college, but you need money for that."

"It depends," Mack said quietly. "It depends on what you're looking at and if there's grant money available. There are all kinds of options."

"Not when you're a kid like me," he said.

"What about your cousin? Does he have family?"

"Yeah, that's one of the reasons I'm in that foster home to begin with. My uncle is right around the corner."

"And yet he wouldn't take you in?"

"No, but I wouldn't want to live there anyway. He's a drunk."

"A mean one?"

"Yeah, a mean one," he said, "is there any other kind?"

She smiled. "The weepy kind, the life-of-the-party kind," she said, "but it seems like the mean drunks are the more prevalent."

"Yeah," he said, as he started to back up. "I need to get going," he said, looking around.

"Maybe," she said, "but we'll drive you home."

"I've got my bike," he said, taking steps down off the deck. "I need to go."

She looked at him, and she looked at Mack, then asked, "Do you need any other information from him?"

"No," he said, "I got it all."

Chapter 25

DOREEN DIDN'T GIVE Mack a chance to say anymore and just nodded and said, "We know where you live."

Abner grimaced at that. "Does that mean you're coming after me?" he asked, turning to look boldly at Mack.

She immediately shook her head. "Not at the moment," she said. Mack glared at her. She shrugged. "I'm the homeowner. And besides, Abner, you helped us identify the person you saw putting the rock behind the door," she said quietly. "We do appreciate the help."

Mack just glared from one to the other.

The kid shrugged and said, "Like you said, you know where I live." And then he bolted.

Mack made a movement, as if to follow, but she grabbed his arm and said, "There's no point."

He nodded, as he relaxed. "It's instinctive," he admitted.

"I know," she said, "but think about it. We do know where he lives. And now? I don't know. We'll have to digest it all. I do think we need to check further as to what's going on in that corner," she said, staring out at her property and beyond.

"And yet, if you're not charging him for trespassing," he

said, "not a whole lot we can do."

"No, but obviously something odd is going on with Isaac."

"But that doesn't mean anything to you," he muttered.

"But somebody sent that message with Thaddeus."

"But you never asked Isaac about it, did you?"

She shook her head. "No," she said. "It still feels like something else is going on there."

"I'm sure there is," he said, "but I need to head out."

And, within just a few minutes, he was long gone, and she had promised to lock up. But, even as she went to lock the front door, a vehicle pulled into her driveway. She stopped and frowned. The last thing she wanted was strangers here right now, and, of course, Mack had already left. Not that it should make any difference, but somehow it felt like it did.

She watched and waited for whoever it was to get out of the Jaguar. She snorted. Her days of driving around in fancy sports cars and high luxury vehicles like this one were long gone. Remembering all the antiques, she brightened. Maybe her visitor was somebody who had a connection to the antique world. She raced down the front porch steps and stopped, almost bouncing in place. The door of the car opened, and a woman stepped out into the bright sunlight.

Doreen gasped and stood there, staring. Horrified, she cried out, "What are you doing here?"

Her ex-lawyer turned and glared at her. "Well, I wouldn't even be here if it wasn't for you and all your stupid troublemaking."

Instinctively Doreen backed up several steps. She had left the front door open, relieved to see Mugs and Goliath sitting there on the top step. Neither of them were being aggressive, but, at the same time, they weren't exactly wagging their tails in welcome. "Well, I don't want anything to do with you," she said, "so you can leave."

"I'm not going anywhere until I talk to you," she snarled.

"Well, I'm not talking to you," she said. "If you want to talk to me, you talk to my lawyer."

"Oh, a fine lot of good that'll do," she snapped. "Your lawyer has already caused me enough trouble."

"Not my fault," she muttered, as she backed up even farther, meeting Mugs and Goliath. Just then, Thaddeus hopped up onto her shoulder from behind, making her start.

The woman started to cackle like a witch and, "What the hell is that thing? That's gross and disgusting. Why do you have it on your shoulder?"

Doreen's back stiffened at the insult. "Thaddeus is an African grey. He happens to be a friend of mine, and I'll not take it kindly if you continue to insult him."

"What will you do about it?" she said, with a sneer in her tone.

"I don't have to do anything," she said. "Everything is already in motion."

At that, the lawyer frowned. "That's what I'm here for," she said. "You need to call off your dogs."

"Why on earth would I do that?" she said.

"Money."

Doreen hated that, for a moment, she actually considered what money would mean to her. "Nope," she said. "Not interested."

"You have to be interested. God almighty, look at this hell you're living in now. And this after moving from house to house as a charity case for months."

"Well, that should have made you very happy, since you were sleeping in my bed," she said. "Ah, but it's not a very comfortable bed, is it?" she said. "Especially considering the one you have to share it with."

At that, the lawyer snorted. "That's quite true," she said. "But it's still better than being alone and broke."

"Nope, not in my case," she said. "I'm quite happy where I am, thanks. Now you can take off. You're not welcome here, and, if you continue to stay on my property," she said, "I'll call the police."

"Do you think the police will really give a shit what you say? You're just a nobody here."

"Maybe, maybe not," she said, pulling out her phone. "Are you ready to take that chance and have your name sullied with an arrest for trespassing and harassment?"

"You've already done that," she cried out. "How dare you try to ruin what I've got."

"Oh, like you ruined what I had?" Doreen asked.

"You didn't have anything. You were too stupid to even see what you were signing, and it's not like you can go back on it now."

"Well, that remains to be seen," she said, "but I'm not getting into it with you now. As I said, if you have business with me, please contact my lawyer."

"The hell I will. I'm not contacting your damn lawyer. You can talk to me now."

"Goodbye," Doreen said, and she and the animals stepped back into the house and slammed the screen door shut. She waited breathlessly to see what the lawyer would do. Sure enough, the woman raced up the porch steps. Doreen backed up immediately and closed the wooden door too. With her heart pounding, she stood in the living room and listened to the lawyer pound on the door, screaming. At one point it seemed she was using her purse to batter the door. She quickly turned on the Record function on her phone and recorded the noise, catching Robin roaring in outrage. Just then Doreen's phone rang.

"What's going on?" Mack asked.

"Yeah, that's my ex-lawyer," she cried out. "She's here attacking my door. She wants to talk to me, and I've referred her to my attorney several times, which has rubbed her the wrong way."

"The woman who cheated you?" he asked.

"Yeah. She pulled in right after you left, which makes me wonder if she wasn't waiting for you to leave."

"I'm on my way," he said. "Man, have I got a thing or two to say to her."

"And you'll be too late," she said. "This woman planned it very carefully."

"That's all right," he said. "I'm already in the truck, heading your way."

"Well, as you can hear, she's still screaming. I told her that I would call the cops, but she didn't believe me and said I was just a nobody around here."

He laughed. "Well, you might have arrived as a nobody, but you've sure made yourself known in a hurry." And, with that, he hung up.

Doreen stuck her head against the living room window. "You better get out of here," she said. "I've called the cops."

Robin looked at her uncertainly; then she shrugged and said, "That's hardly becoming behavior."

"You're a bit of a shrew, aren't you?" Doreen said. "I suppose my ex found that out already and is dumping you."

"No, he is dumping me because of your damn lawyer."

"Oh my, that's too funny," she said and started to laugh. And, once she started, she just couldn't stop. The irate lawyer outside her door gave one last agonizing scream of rage, then raced down the steps.

Doreen stepped outside and looked just in time to see her backing out of the driveway, whipping around the cul-de-sac, then disappearing around the corner at a high speed.

And, sure enough, just thirty seconds behind her, Mack came barreling up the driveway and parked. He hopped out and glared at her. "Where is she?" he roared.

Doreen pointed the direction she left in. "She's driving a dark-green Jaguar." Nodding, he jumped back into his truck and took off. As she stood here, wondering at this latest turn of events, she started to giggle. It was too funny that her ex had already dropped this woman like a hot potato as a result of the pressure that Nick had applied. And all of it had happened so fast. But her ex was not somebody who wanted anybody causing a fuss and dragging his name through the mud.

As she thought about that, she wondered, for the first time, *Why?* Was there really some criminal activity he was trying to keep under the table? She was pretty sure there was, but it just wasn't a world she walked in. Even though she had lived it and breathed it, everything was done without her knowledge, and that just made her even sadder.

As she walked back into the living room and on into the kitchen, waiting for Mack to return—if he did—she put on the teakettle and sat out on the deck in her one chair. As soon as she'd gotten settled with a hot cup of tea, her phone rang. Thinking it was Mack, she immediately asked, "Hey, did you catch her?" There was silence on the other end for a moment; then she heard Nan's cheerful voice.

"Catch who? What have you gotten into now?" she asked in excitement. "Did you get a new case?"

Immediately Doreen groaned, kicking herself. "No," she said. "Sorry, Nan. I thought you were Mack. No, there's no new case."

"Tell me more. Tell me more," she said. "Life was so boring before you came."

Doreen groaned again. "You know what? It can go right back to being boring too."

"No, no, that won't do. This is so much more interesting," she said. "So, who are we after now?"

Shaking her head, Doreen just laughed and said, "The lady divorce lawyer who screwed me over," she muttered. "She came here, pounding on the door, wanting me to call off Nick."

"Nick, Nick, Nick," Nan said, as if ruminating on where she'd heard the name before.

"Mack's brother, the lawyer. Remember?"

"Oh, of course," she cried out. "And she wants you to call off the dogs, huh? Well, that's good news, indeed. Nick must be barking up the right tree, … so to speak."

"Good one, Nan. Apparently my ex has turned her out because of something that Nick did."

Nan started to laugh and laugh, clapping her hands and giggling. "Oh, I love it," she said. "The mighty one has fallen off her throne."

"Well, I don't know that she has fallen, but she's definitely pissy and angry at the moment."

"Oh dear," Nan said, very businesslike all of a sudden. "I'm not sure you should be alone right now, dear. A scorned and angry female lawyer could be nothing to laugh at. Add in the fact that you've interrupted what was a pretty cushy and lucrative scenario for her, and I see potential danger at every turn."

"Well, she was here, yelling and screaming, and then tore off just ahead of Mack, so he is chasing her down, as we speak," she said, with a level of smugness that was probably just wrong. But what the heck? At times in life, when one could take a moment and appreciate what was happening, she would darn well enjoy seeing that woman turned out on her butt. At that, she started to giggle. "I'm actually pretty happy to hear that he turned her out, I must say."

"My yes," Nan said. "That man was insufferable, but to think that, after compromising her very career to save him some of his precious money, only to have him give her the boot, just makes it all so much more delightful. Did she threaten you?"

"Nope, not at all," Doreen said. "Well, not directly at least."

"Do you think that she will do anything stupid?"

"Well, she already has. She came here and pounded on the door, ranting and screaming. Mack heard her over the phone, and I even recorded some of it. So I should probably listen to that before I hand it over. But I don't think she is a serious threat."

"No, well, I hope not," Nan said. "What we don't want is for her to bring your ex down on you. That man is three shades of crazy."

"At least three shades," she replied, with feeling. "But I don't think we need to worry about that," she said, not wanting Nan to worry. "He's probably already washed his hands of her in the same way he washed them of me. I'm sure he's got the next little chickie in his sights already."

"Good for him," Nan said. "They're all poisonous, and

one of these snakes will turn around one day, and he'll be the one who gets bit."

"I can't wait," Doreen said cheerfully. And, with that, she hung up from the call and sat here to enjoy her tea, a smug smile on her face.

Then the doorbell rang, with yet another unexpected visitor.

Chapter 26

DOREEN GROANED BUT got up and walked to the front door. Instead of opening it, she waited. This time Mugs barked like crazy at the door, and Goliath was upset as well. Mugs's barking held just enough menace in its tone that she decided to peer around the curtain instead. And she saw the man who had been in Mack's photo. *Snoz.*

The one who the kid had identified as having put the rocks at her back door. The one she had identified as having worked for her ex. She hesitated and then let the curtain fall quietly back in place. Quickly she texted Mack. She knew he wouldn't read the text right away, depending on what he'd gotten into while chasing the woman in the Jaguar, but this guy scared her. She put her phone on Silent, as she watched what he did. He rang the doorbell again and again. Then there was silence, except for the animals' response, but he didn't move.

She heard a funny sound, and she realized he was trying to pick the lock. She raced back to the kitchen, locked the backdoor, and set the little bit of security system that Mack had originally put in for her. It had yet to be replaced with something better, and now she realized she needed to—and soon. Once she had that set up, she breathed a little bit easier and quickly texted Mack again. But Snoz was still working at the front door, and, with any luck, as soon as he managed to break through the lock, the dreaded sirens would go off. But she couldn't count on it. Because she had never yet put it to the test like this.

She had enjoyed that little sense of security, knowing she had a security system, but what if it didn't work? She couldn't believe how this afternoon had gone downhill so quickly, and she didn't even know why. She wanted to just open the door and ask Snoz why he'd done what he had done and what he was here for. She wanted to ask if he was the one who had attacked her at the cemetery.

But, if he was here now, was this connected to her ex or was it connected to her divorce lawyer? Or both? All of it made a little bit of sense, yet, at the same time, it made no sense at all. She thought about it long and hard, and, knowing Mack would hate her for it, she made a decision. It was still early enough in the day that, if she went outside, screaming bloody murder, somebody would come to her aid. Wouldn't they? At least Richard should. But then again, she hadn't been exactly the neighbor he wanted, so maybe he'd be perfectly happy to let somebody knock her out again.

Frowning, she watched as Snoz continued to work on the lock. And then she stepped forward, opened the door immediately to set off the sirens, then slammed the screen door outward. But there was no alarm. She stared in shock, as the man glared at her. Not knowing what else to do, she went on the offensive. "So, are you back for another chance to hit me over the head. I mean, that's what you do, isn't it? Attack vulnerable women?"

His glare changed into an ugly scowl, as he reached out

with a fist, intent on decking her. But she saw it coming and moved her head ever-so-slightly at the last second, and his fist pounded into the wooden door frame behind her.

Mugs had already been trying to get around both doors so he could attack this guy, and, when Mugs did, the guy kicked him hard, and Mugs dropped to the ground.

"Mugs! Mugs!"

Snoz sneered at her. "You think a dog will keep me out of there?"

"I don't care what keeps you out of here," she cried out, "but you're not getting in without a fight." She pushed him hard and then pushed him again and again.

He backed up ever-so-slightly, and she took advantage of that and pushed him down the porch steps. He stumbled and fell onto his butt, but he bounced up in one motion. "You are a menace," he said.

"Is that why you tried to kill me?" she cried out, frightened to see that Mugs wasn't moving. She started screaming, "Richard! Richard! Help!"

Almost immediately her neighbor's door popped open, and he stepped out, looking at what was going on.

"Call the police! Call the police! This guy is the one who tried to kill me in the graveyard!"

He stared at her in shock and immediately slammed the door as he raced inside.

Her attacker laughed. "Do you really think anybody cares?"

"Yeah, they care," she said. "You're working for my ex, I suppose." He looked at her in surprise. She shrugged. "It's the kind of thing he'd do. He is the weaselly type who wouldn't take on his own dirty work."

"Maybe," he said, studying her with interest. "He did say

that you were quite a piece of work."

"He just wants me to quietly disappear and to leave him alone."

"Yet you won't take the smart route and do that, huh? Too bad," he said, "but I'm not here on his behalf."

"Then why are you here? Is it my bimbo ex-lawyer? Because she was just here ranting and raving too."

He looked at her in surprise. "She was just here?"

She nodded. "What? Are you looking for her too?"

He just smiled and said, "This could be a lucky trip."

"Not if you're planning on taking me out," she said. "I've got nothing to do with anything."

"Maybe," he said, "but I do jobs for a lot of clients, local and far away. You've pissed off some interesting people."

She stared at him. "Are you actually saying you're not here because of my ex?" He slowly shook his head, and that nasty grin made her heart freeze. "So who hired you then?" She asked the question slowly and was afraid of the answer.

"Somebody who will go to jail for a very long time—unless you're not around."

"No, no, no," she said. "Everybody going to jail deserves to because they've done some terrible things."

"But, if you're the only one who has anything to say," he said, "then maybe not."

She stared at him, her mind ripping through the cold cases, trying to figure it out. "No," she said. "Everybody has been found with bodies or some evidence like that," she said. "Look at Steve. How many dead bodies were buried in his yard?"

"I don't know anything about him," he said, with added interest. "Maybe I should contact him though. He might have something he needs done to make his life a little easier."

She stared at him. "Is that all you do? You go around and help all these criminals?"

"Why not?" he said. "Somebody needs to, and a lot of these criminals have money. A lot of money."

"That's true," she said as she stared at him. "I certainly don't."

"That's because you didn't know how to play the game," he said, with a flick of his wrist.

"So, what will you do, just shoot me?"

"Well, it's supposed to look like an accident," he said.

"That means that nobody would know that it's you."

"Well, nobody will know it was me anyway," he said.

"It sure didn't look like an accident when you knocked me out in the cemetery the other day."

"Yeah, that was a hasty attempt," he said. "A couple homeless people were there, and I figured they would get blamed."

"I didn't even see them there," she said in surprise.

"No, they left at the same time and went the wrong direction," he muttered. "So what should have been a simple plan just failed."

"Yeah, and instead you were picked up on the cameras," she said, with a smile. He stared at her in shock, and she nodded. "So you're not so good at what you do either."

"I'm plenty good enough to take care of you," he said.

"And they really intended on you killing me?" she asked sadly. "Am I so bad as all that?"

"Well, she'll spend the rest of her life in jail because of you."

She froze. "It's a woman?"

"Person," he corrected immediately.

She shook her head. "No, no, no," she muttered. "You

said *she*, plain as day." She gasped. "Penny! Oh, my God, Penny is behind this." She stared at him in shock.

In a move that she couldn't believe had been so fast, Snoz slapped a hand over her mouth and pushed her back into her house. She tried to scream, but no sound came out, and his grip was like a clamp. Almost at the same time, Goliath clawed at his legs. He roared, then grabbed the cat by the scruff of the neck and threw him across the room.

Doreen tore her mouth free and screamed at him. "Don't you touch my cat like that!"

He slapped her hard across the side of her face. Her head hit the door, and she slowly slid to the floor. Goliath came racing back, and now Mugs was up and barking and growling like crazy. Even Thaddeus flew up at the man, throwing his wings at him and climbing up him.

Her attacker roared. "This place is a zoo," he said, and he brought out his gun and fired it in the air. Almost instantly the house went dead quiet. She looked around, frantic, but saw no sign of Goliath, Mugs, or Thaddeus.

He looked around too. "Where are they? Where are those damn critters?" he yelled. "I'll shoot them first and then you."

"And how does that make it look like an accident?" she asked quietly.

Immediately the gun barrel was pointed right between her eyes. "I'll take your body and deep-six you in the lake," he cried out. "I don't give a shit anymore, and I'll kill those stupid animals of yours." He had a great big scratch down his face, and his hand was bleeding. "Where are they?"

"What are you talking about?" she said.

"The animals. Where are they?"

"I'm sure they're in hiding by now," she said, reaching

up a hand to her throbbing head.

"Well, get up. You're coming with me," he muttered, and he forced her to her feet.

Shaky, she moved with him, then stopped. "You could just leave me here, you know?"

"That won't do me any good, and it certainly won't get me paid."

"Penny can't pay you anything. She's too broke."

"Well, she's apparently not that broke," he muttered. "It's already sitting in escrow."

Doreen didn't even know what that meant, but he seemed confident he'd get paid somehow. "She can't hate me that much."

"What did you think?" he sneered. "That you'll still be best buds after this? You're putting her in jail for life."

"She killed people," she replied.

"So what? So have I."

"Are you sure it's not my ex who's doing this?"

He stopped, looked at her, and said, "What are you, just stupid?"

She shrugged. "No, I'm not stupid," she said, "but I'm definitely not terribly happy."

He looked out the front window, as if wondering if he could get her into the vehicle without a fight.

Just then, with all her might, she jerked free and raced toward the kitchen. When she heard the gun fire and felt her shoulder burn, she knew she was in trouble. She hit the kitchen back door at a flat-out run and tumbled out to the deck, where she rolled and rolled.

He came out behind her, swearing and cussing.

Her shoulder was on fire; the pain was excruciating, and there was absolutely nothing she could do to stop it. She lay flat on the deck, her hands up, as if to ward him off. "Stop," she said. "You don't have to do this."

"No, I don't have to," he said, "but believe me. Now I want to." He lifted the gun, aimed it at her, and pulled the trigger.

Chapter 27

D OREEN CRIED OUT, her arms over her face, knowing the bullet would hit her. Instead, it seemed to go wild. When she peered up at him, he was grinning down at her, like a madman. "Right," she said, "this won't make it look like an accident."

"Exactly," he said, "now get up."

Wincing at the pain in her shoulder, she managed to get to her feet. None of the animals were in sight. But then she caught a glimpse of Goliath, sneaking through the bushes behind Snoz. She smiled with relief, hoping the cat would stay out of sight and be safe. She never wanted them to get hurt because of her. That would never be an acceptable end to any of this.

She didn't want to get hurt either, but she just hoped that Richard had actually made the 9-1-1 call and that help was on the way. It occurred to her that people might be of the opinion that it served her right. How many times had she been told to stay out of trouble? Still, even now, under threat of death, she couldn't stop fighting for justice. While there wasn't a whole lot she could do to save herself now, she would do anything and everything she could to slow down her imminent demise. So, now that she was upright, she moved ever-so-slowly over to the deck steps.

"I suppose you'll take me down to the river and drown me," she said, trying to keep her voice calm and even, yet still appear cowed and fearful. The last thing she wanted was for him to think that the river was somewhere she wanted to go, but, at least there, she thought she might have a chance to get away.

"It's a hell of a good idea," he said, "since everybody knows that you're crazy about the river."

"Yeah, that doesn't mean I'm crazy though," she said, "and I'm certainly not one to commit suicide."

"I don't know about that," he said. "It sounds good to me." He stared at her, then down at the river and nodded. "And, given the circumstances, that's probably the best I can do right now."

She frowned and, at his orders, headed toward the river—slowly. The last thing she wanted to do was go for a swim, but she'd take that over a bullet any day. At the river's edge, she looked around. The evening was settling in. It was darker now but not quite dusk. "Almost out of daylight," she said in a conversational tone.

"I know," he said. "So it's perfect. Nobody will find you until morning."

She twisted around to look at him. "But, if I'm shot up with bullet holes, you can bet they'll be coming after you."

"Nah," he said. "Nobody knows I'm here."

"You're wrong there," she said. "You've already been identified as the person who left the threatening notes on rocks at my kitchen door, though I still don't understand why you did that. And then there's my neighbor ..."

"I did it to distract you," he said. "As for the neighbor,

he's a problem I can take care of easily enough. Besides, you have so damn many enemies, it was just fun to mix it up a bit. To get you rattled, so you wouldn't be expecting me when I popped in one day."

"Well, I wasn't expecting you today. That's for sure," she muttered. Down at the river, she stopped and said, "Now what?"

"Get in," he said, almost lethally.

She looked up and down at the river, and, as she did, she thought she caught sight of somebody in the trees up ahead. It was Abner. She frowned and slightly shook her head at him, hoping that he didn't come to her rescue and get himself hurt. She looked back at her vindictive attacker. "Well, I hope Penny rots in jail for this," she said.

"There won't be a case without you," he said cheerfully. "So she won't."

"Great," she said, "all the more reason to survive." And, with that, she dove into the water, gasping at the cold, then staying under.

Chapter 28

Tuesday Evening, Dusk …

DOREEN POPPED UP to the surface, gasping for air, Snoz racing along the washed-out path, trying to find her. He fired into the water, close to where she was. Mugs came downriver after her. Doreen stared in horror as Snoz lined up for a shot at Mugs, when another shot fired out. Snoz turned, took one look, and saw other people coming. He roared in anger and headed down the riverbank route that she always took to see Nan. She was in the water, swept along in the current. She could barely see what was happening upriver, but it looked like Mack had finally arrived.

"Yay for the cavalry," she muttered, desperate to stay on the surface while fully dressed was a challenge. In the growing darkness, the roar of the river overwhelmed her senses, as the current carried her farther down. She had no clue where Mugs was now, but, as Doreen watched, Goliath raced along the top of the fences all the way down to where the block turned to go to Nan's. Doreen swam toward Mugs and managed to meet up with him, only his head above water. And perched on top, of course, was Thaddeus.

She wanted to laugh, and she wanted to cry, but instead

she did a combination of both and ended up taking on more water than she should have and started coughing. With the dog in one hand, she caught hold of a root sticking out from the bank, and hung on for life, while she pushed Mugs and Thaddeus onto the riverbank. And saw legs racing toward her.

There was Abner, with a big branch and a rope in his hand. When he threw it toward her, she managed to grab it, but lost her grip on both branches and started going down-river again. Mugs barked, Thaddeus crowed and cawed, and she heard howling from the fence post, as Goliath sat on top at the safest and driest part and watched as she floated past.

In her mind she knew this was ridiculous. She had so many people on both sides now trying to reach out to her, but the way the high water sent her bouncing from rock to rock, she knew she would look like hamburger soon. Not to mention her arm was killing her, which was why she couldn't grab or hold on to the branches for long.

Finally Abner threw the rope again, and she managed to grab it with her good hand. But, just as she did, a big wave ripped her away, and the rope was torn from her grip. She groaned as she floated back down the river again. She was almost to the mouth of the river, which was not the worst place to be, she thought, depending on how far out this current carried her.

She was miserable, had never been in so much pain. She was now freezing cold, in shock from the bullet burn, and felt the weight of all the clothing she wore pulling her down. She stayed above water, tried to direct herself to the shallow-er water near the bank, only now realizing somebody else was in the water, swimming, arms cutting through the river at a strong pace. She waited until he got closer, then realized with relief it was Mack. She tried to speak, and he just shook his head and said, "Shut up."

"How can you be mad at me for this?" she cried out. But she was quickly flipped on her back, and he held her with her head up, in a lifeguard hold, as he moved strongly toward the far side. She heard people on both sides of the river shouting encouragement, screaming at her. Finally he dragged her onto the shore, where she was quickly picked up by several other men and carried up higher. She cried out, "Mugs! Thaddeus!"

"I've got them," Mack called out, standing up, soaking wet and fully dressed, but holding Mugs, with Thaddeus, who was now squawking loudly from his shoulder.

"Big guy. Big guy."

She groaned. "Now, if only I knew what *big guy* he was referring to."

One of the paramedics said, "I thought he meant *the* big guy."

"What big guy?" she asked, her teeth starting to chatter.

"He's one of the guys who does a lot of the events in town here, and he lives over by the cemetery," he said. "He's a really big guy."

"Maybe that's it. Does he know animals?"

"Absolutely, he's got all kinds, including birds."

She looked at Mack triumphantly. "Do you know him?"

Mack slowly shook his head. He looked at the paramedic and asked, "Who is this guy?"

"I think his name is Jerry or something," the guy said. "If you go to his website, which has something to do with animals for kids parties and hospitals and whatnot," he said, "you should be able to contact him."

At that, Mack nodded. "You take care of her," he said.

"I'll take care of that."

She cried out, "I need the animals."

"And that's just too bad," he said, with a big fat glare. "You can't have them in the ambulance, and you can't have them in the hospital."

She glared. "Look at you. You're enjoying this."

"What I'm enjoying," he said, "is knowing that, at least over the next four hours, you'll be stuck at the hospital, but you'll be out of trouble."

Chapter 29

Wednesday Evening, Dusk …

FOUR HOURS ACTUALLY turned into twenty-four, and, only after convincing the doctor to let her convalesce at home, she contacted Nan to let her know that she would get a cab ride home. Her Nan was against the idea of Doreen leaving the hospital, but she was adamant.

"I'm not sick, so I shouldn't be taking up a bed. My shoulder isn't badly hurt. The bullet did go through the top of the shoulder, but it didn't hit bone. Yes, I'm sore certainly, but I want to be at home. I don't want to leave the animals alone."

Finally Nan groaned. "Fine. I'll meet you at the house." And she hung up.

With that, Doreen turned to the receptionist at the front of the hospital and asked, "Is there a way to call for a cab?"

The woman nodded and pointed to a yellow phone on the wall. "That's the cab company," she said. "If you have the app for one of those ride programs, you can also call them."

But her cell phone was at home, so the yellow cab phone it was.

Minutes later, she stood outside, trying not to shiver, trying not to look like she was in as much pain as she was. Because the last thing she wanted was for somebody to send her back inside again. Soon, a cab pulled up, and she got into the back seat, grateful, as she gave the driver her address.

All the way she worried about the cost, how long it would take her to get into the house, to grab money out of Nan's bowl, and to bring it back. But, when she got home, she was pleasantly surprised to find that the charges were low. Thanking him profusely, telling him that she would just be another minute or two, she slowly slid out and walked up the driveway. At the door, she rapped hard to let Mugs and Goliath know she was here.

Immediately she heard barking from inside, and she smiled and pulled out her key hidden on top of the door frame, mentally noting she'd have to change that place now, pushed open the door and stepped in. She grabbed the money and walked back outside to pay the cab driver, then returned to her house.

She was greeted by all three animals, barking and meowing and crowing at her side. With tears in her eyes, she bent down and sat on the floor, Thaddeus on her good shoulder thankfully, as her arms wrapped around both Goliath and Mugs as much as she could, while one wove over and around her, and the other wiggled so hard it was difficult to even hold on to him. Laughing and crying, with Thaddeus rubbing up against her cheek, Doreen felt her heart swelling with joy. "I'm home, guys. I'm home."

Mugs barked, and she laughed, then kissed the top of his head and gave the side of his face a good scratch. "I'm so sorry. I would have been home last night, if I could have."

She looked around the house, wondering how the animals had fared in her absence. But she was surprised that everything appeared to be normal, at least from this point. "Did Mack look after you?"

She knew she could trust him with it, but she had never left the animals yet, and she didn't want to be in a position where she had to again. Speaking of which, her shoulder was giving her some pretty hefty pain. The doctor had given her a shot before letting her leave the hospital, and she was grateful for that, but now just the movements and holding it unnaturally and the jarring from hugging Mugs and Goliath made it really hurt.

Using her good arm, she pushed herself up onto her knees and then slowly stood. She walked through to the kitchen, smiling when she saw the coffeemaker. "They gave me coffee there," she muttered, "but it's not the same as being at home."

She put on coffee, while she went to feed the animals. She didn't know if they had eaten at all, but food remained in their bowls. Was that from last night? "Did you guys not eat because I wasn't home, or is this new food from tonight?"

She expected them to be upset because of the change in their routine. Also they had been frantic when she'd gotten into the ambulance. She felt a little rougher than she'd expected to. She took her coffee out onto the deck and sat down in the chair, closing her eyes.

"There you are," Nan said, as she came around the bend on the river and up the pathway. "You don't look so good."

"Well, I was hoping to feel better."

"You should have stayed in the hospital."

"Nope, I'm not that bad. This is nothing that I can't stay at home and heal from. Besides, sick people are in there. Plus, people die there all the time."

Nan laughed. "That's where they're supposed to die."

"I hope not," Doreen said simply. "I'd much rather die in my bed."

"You and me both," Nan said, with a quick, bright grin. She looked at Doreen's coffee. "Is there a second cup?"

"Of course," Doreen said. "Do you mind getting it yourself?"

"Of course not." Nan walked in and returned with a cup of coffee, and Doreen immediately stood from the one chair on the deck.

Nan looked at her in shock and said, "Oh no, you don't," she said. "You're injured."

"Not that bad," she said. "The nightmares were the worst."

"About getting shot?" Nan asked, with a wise nod.

"Oddly enough, no. About losing Mugs in the water."

Nan stared at her, chuckled, and said, "I'm pretty sure Mugs would have fared much better than you out there."

"It wasn't so bad," she said, "but I was trying to keep him up, while the weight of my clothing was pulling me down. Thaddeus was cheering me on all the while, and screeching when water hit him." she shook her head in bemusement. "I'm a good swimmer but—"

"Being a good swimmer is one thing. Being an uninjured swimmer who's been swimming on a regular basis and able to combat the force of that water is another. Add in the chaos and concern of the animals ..."

"Why was the water so high?" she wailed.

"There was a storm up in the mountains and the last of the snow came barreling down."

"Right," she said. "That does happen, doesn't it?"

"It sure does, dear. It had been settling down, and then

it rose up," she said. "It should be back to normal again by tomorrow."

"How nice that my attacker got it at just the right size," she said sarcastically.

"Maybe not."

She looked at Nan. "Did they catch him?"

Nan shrugged. "I don't know," she said. "Have you managed to talk to Mack at all?"

At that, Doreen winced and frowned, looking out of sorts. "Nope. I'm not calling Mack," she said in a hard voice.

Nan looked at her granddaughter in surprise, and then Nan started to chuckle. "Is that because you're upset with him because he forced you to go to the hospital or because he doesn't know that you're out yet?"

Wrinkling her nose, she contemplated the options presented and then shrugged. "Either. Or maybe both. He'll be livid when he finds out."

"No, he won't. I bet he already suspects this is where you are."

"But does he understand it?" she asked.

"I would think so," she said. "He's been looking after the animals well enough."

"Not really," she said. "If he did feed them last night, nobody ate."

"Of course not. You weren't here, and they were upset because of you," she said quietly. "Anytime I would get ill and not feel too good, they would go off their food too."

It made sense in a way. Doreen knew that, when she was upset and stressed, she barely ate either. The two women sat in the sun and enjoyed the early evening weather.

"Are you going to bed after this?" Nan asked.

"I don't know," she said. "I can't have any more painkillers for a few hours."

"Then be still and rest."

"What about that gunman?" she muttered.

"I'm not sure about his whereabouts, but, if Mack knew you were home, he might send security to keep an eye out."

"He can't spend his life looking after me, and law enforcement doesn't have the budget to have someone else sitting here looking after me either," she muttered.

"Maybe not, but neither can they afford to lose you."

Doreen snorted at that. "In many ways I think they would be happy if something happened to me." She felt Nan's sharp gaze and gave her a wan smile. "Don't worry about me," she said. "It's just been a pretty rough week."

"I totally understand—between the attack at the cemetery and that stupid divorce lawyer of yours and now this," she said. "And then to think that you ended up shot and swept downstream."

"Well, we both know it's hardly the first time I've been in the river," she said, laughing.

"You could have died," Nan said in a serious tone.

Doreen reached across and gripped her grandmother's hand. "I was thinking about you," she said, "and how I really wanted to spend years with you before it was your turn."

"And here you're the one who almost kicked the bucket," Nan whispered. Holding on to each other, they took a moment to just reconnect to all the important things in life and how neither wanted to go too soon.

"All the years we lost," Doreen said, shaking her head. "Such a shame."

"Not your fault," Nan said. "Maybe you had to get to this point to be able to appreciate it. I'm just glad that we're here together now."

"Me too. When I saw my former divorce lawyer, and I realized that she'd been turned out by my ex too, I wasn't jealous and had not a single thought about going back there or even taking her bribe. All I felt was so grateful to be here, so grateful to have the life that I have now. The life," she said, turning to look at Nan, "that you gave me."

"No," Nan said, with a shake of her head. "I gave you a house. You're the one who turned it into a home and then found a hobby, a calling really," she said. "This community loves you, and this nice deck is just proof of that."

"Well, apparently an awful lot of people don't love me." She looked at Nan, frowned, and said, "And I didn't even get a chance to tell Mack about it."

"What are you talking about, dear?"

"The person who hired this guy to attack me wasn't my ex at all."

Nan looked at her, eyebrows raised. "Did he tell you that?"

Hating that she would have to, she pulled out her phone, while Nan watched, and called Mack.

"You know that you could just rest," he said, his voice brisk.

"Did you catch him?"

"Ah," his voice gentled. "Of course, you'd be worried about that."

"That and something else," she said. "He was hired to do this."

"Right, that's what we figured," he said.

"But, Mack, it wasn't my ex," she added.

"What? Did he say who it was?"

"Not in so many words but kind of." There was a silence on the other end. She sighed and said, "I think it was

Penny."

"What?" he cried out. Even Nan gasped.

"He said that, if I were gone, there's a good chance that *she* could get off completely. But, if I'm correct, and I'm around to testify and to explain everything that happened, then she's likely to go away for a long time. But, other than that, the lawyers would probably get her off with something quite minor."

"Well, in a way that may be true," he said, his voice thoughtful. "I didn't think she had the money for something like this though."

"Neither did I, but Snoz said that she had enough, and he didn't sound like he was at all concerned about collecting. Something about the money already somewhere in escrow."

"That would make sense too. And he actually told you that?"

"Yes, because I kept saying it was my ex, my ex, and finally Snoz got mad at me and said it had nothing to do with him."

"Oh, he got mad at you? Gee, what a surprise. Some guy is holding a gun on you, and you go out of your way to make him mad? Go figure."

His voice was deceptively smooth, and she knew he was quite pissed. "Thanks for looking after the animals," she said hurriedly. "I appreciate it."

"Wish I wouldn't have had to," he said in that deliciously smooth tone, hiding the simmering anger beneath.

"No," she muttered, "me too." She sighed. "Okay, fine. But I did get away."

"You did, but you also got shot in the meantime," he said, his voice rising.

"Barely, but I also got away again," she said. "So there's

got to be some benefit to all this."

"Well, at least we may have a good idea who hired him now, but we still have to prove it."

"Well, if you had him in your grasp," she said, "I'm sure you could check his phone records and where he's been, tracking him around town here and all."

"Maybe," he said, with an edge in the voice, "but I was busy."

She wisely chose to be silent for a moment.

"Did you get him to explain why he attacked you in the cemetery?"

"Yes," she said and quickly told him what Snoz had said.

"So that would have been an opportunity that he took advantage of, but, when that didn't succeed, he had to try something else."

"It was supposed to look like an accident," she muttered. "How does he think shooting me would make it look like an accident? Even you would figure that out."

Silence. "Even me?"

She grimaced and looked at Nan, who had a horrified look on her face. "I didn't mean it that way," she said. "I'm tired and not feeling good. I'm hurting more than I expected, and I'm just cranky and not thinking about what's coming out of my mouth."

"Well, I'll give you a pass on that one today," he said quietly, but that edge to his tone definitely remained. "And, no, we didn't get him. We were all more focused on saving you."

She sighed. "So, once again, I'm at fault. I get it."

"No, not necessarily," he said, "at least everything ended up okay."

"Well, I'm not sure how *okay* it all ended up," she muttered. "You don't have him, and you could go talk to that little minx of a divorce lawyer until you're blue in the face, but she won't help you at all."

"We'll figure it out," he said, his tone turning brisk. "You're in the hospital safe and sound, so I don't have to worry about you, and I can turn my attention to resolving some of this."

She looked over to find Nan glaring at her. Doreen shrugged, as if to say, *What do I do?*

"You tell him," Nan said in no uncertain terms.

"Is that Nan there?" Mack asked.

"Yes, she's here," she said, staring down at the phone. "And you won't like this—"

"Won't like what?" he said in a sharp voice, before she even finished. And then he groaned, having figured it out. "Damn it, you're not in the hospital anymore, are you?"

"No," she said. "I came home this evening and wanted to get back to the animals. So I caught a cab."

"The animals were fine, you know?"

"Maybe," she said, "but I wasn't fine without them."

He sighed. "You could just look after yourself for once."

"And I am," she said. "I'm just sitting here on the deck, having coffee. Nan is here visiting."

"And she was actually in favor of you leaving the hospital? I'll be right over," he said and promptly hung up.

She put the phone down beside her. "Yeah, he is definitely angry."

"Which part of that conversation gave you that impression?" Nan said, staring at Doreen in fascination. "He'd let you get away with murder."

Doreen looked at her in surprise. "What are you talking about?"

"The way you talk to him, the things that you do and say. The times that he looks after you." She shook her head. "The man is clearly in love with you."

Laughter rose up in the back of her throat, and, when it finally burst free, Nan just stared at her with her hands on her hips.

"You see? That's the problem with you. Now you don't think anybody could possibly be interested in you."

"Well, being abandoned is one thing," Doreen said. "And being abandoned or tossed out and replaced by your ex does give one a poor sense of self-confidence," she admitted. "But you're wrong, Nan. I think Mack likes me. We're definitely friends, and he seems to feel obligated to help get me back on my feet. But any more than that, I'm not sure."

"That's because you're blind and deaf."

She glared at her grandmother. "That's not fair," she protested.

"Maybe not, but it's the truth," she said. "I'll be on my way. I'm sure you two have a lot to discuss. You think about my words," she said, with a shake of her finger, "and don't waste this opportunity."

"Waste what opportunity?" Doreen asked, raising both hands. "I'm not even legally divorced yet. I think it takes a whole year of separation first, and I'm only about nine months into that process, if we count from when I was first tossed out of his house."

"And you don't have to wait until you are divorced to start considering Mack," Nan muttered. "Goodness," she said, "I always kept it one at a time, but nobody said I had to let the seat grow cold beside me." Muttering to herself, she shook her head and walked back down to the river.

"Are you sure you should go walking down the river

path at dusk?"

Nan lifted a hand. "It's dropped quite a lot already," she said. "The path is there. It's a bit slippery, but I'll be fine." Doreen didn't like to hear that, and she gingerly hopped to her feet and moved down the pathway.

"I'm coming with you then," she said. "I can't stand the thought of you having an accident on the way."

Nan stopped, then looked at her and said, "You're the one who almost drowned."

"And what? You'll go down the same road? What if I don't hear from you when you get home again?"

"Fine, you stand here and watch," she said. "You'll be able to see that I get all the way down to the end without a problem." And that's what they did.

Doreen sat at the edge of the river and watched as her grandmother slowly made her way down the pathway. And, indeed, it was surprising just how much the water had dropped. The fact that it was river-fed meant that a ton of water came down in one big cascade, but then would easily disappear into the lake because nothing continuously fed it.

She heard a bright whistle and saw Nan waving at her as she went around at the far side and onto the street. With a happy sigh of relief, Doreen stood and slowly walked toward her deck. As she got there, she looked up to see Mack standing there, his hands on his hips, glaring at her.

She shrugged. "I was just watching to make sure Nan got home safe. She insisted on walking down by the river."

Mack's eyebrows shot up. "She went down the river pathway?"

Doreen nodded. "And I didn't want her to, so I insisted on at least watching to make sure she got there okay."

"Good," he said, staring down at the river. "The water

has dropped a lot, hasn't it?"

"It has." She made her way up the few steps to the deck and sat down in the chair. "How come I'm so tired?" she muttered.

"Well, maybe because you're injured," he said, his voice calm. He walked over and stood in front of her and studied her face.

She smiled up at him. "I know. I'm pasty and pale and look tired. On the other hand, I'm home. So I'm happy, and things are looking up."

"Looking up?"

"Well, I'm not almost drowning in the river anymore," she said. "And I have no bleeding or otherwise untended wounds."

"But what I see is a woman who doesn't seem to know when to stop or to even want to take care of herself," he muttered.

"Snoz attacked me and my animals in my own home," she said, staring up at him. "You know I would not back down. You know I would put up a fight. What else was I supposed to do?"

"I'd like you to go over exactly what he did do," he said, sitting down on the footstool in front of her. "Right from the beginning." It took a moment to collect her thoughts, and, when she did, she went over the scenario as best she could recall.

"He was so mean to the animals. I thought he'd really hurt Mugs with that vicious kick," she said. "But then he threw Goliath across the room. So, when he shot me, I knew it would get even worse."

"You think?"

"Well, what was I supposed to do?" she said again. "I

texted you as soon as I realized there was trouble." He looked at her in surprise. She pulled out her phone to show him and then frowned. "Well, I thought I was sending them to you," she said.

He reached out a hand for her phone, and he looked at it and said, "You sent them to someone else," he said.

"Oh, great," she said, as she looked closer at her phone. "Oh, jeez, that woman wouldn't give a darn if I was shot or not."

"It would have been nice if you'd reached me though," he said. Then he stopped and said, "Okay, this message I recognize."

She nodded. "I thought I was sending all of them to you."

"Well, you got one sent to me anyway. I made it here in time, but the gunman did get away. We've got everybody out looking for him now though."

"Maybe," she said. "You've got his picture and his rental car to John Smith," she said in a sarcastic tone. "But you know he can sneak his way around town without any trouble."

"Everybody is out looking for him," he said firmly.

"So he can double back around and get me here?"

"Well, you were supposed to be in the hospital."

She looked at him and said, "Did you think that maybe he is at the hospital, looking for me?"

His eyebrows shot up as he studied her. "That wouldn't be very smart of him."

"It *would* be very smart of him," she said, "because all kinds of things happen in hospitals." She leaned forward and said, "People die there all the time, you know?"

He rolled his eyes at her. "Yeah, I think I do know that."

He pulled out his phone though and said, "I'll call security at the hospital and make sure."

"Maybe they should check the feeds to make sure they don't have anybody like him coming through."

He just glared at her and said, "I'm the law enforcement professional. Remember?"

She shrugged. "I'm just a sidekick. Got it."

He groaned. "No," he said, "you're more than that. You've been a huge help. But you're the one under attack right now, so you have to give us a little bit of room to help."

"How about a lot of room?" she said, with a wan smile. "Thanks for the save, by the way."

Chapter 30

D OREEN SAT BACK and watched as Mack called the hospital. He had gotten in the habit of walking away from her when he was on the phone, probably so she couldn't hear everything. She looked down at Mugs at her side. Thaddeus was wobbling around the garden but seemed to be more perturbed than ever. She groaned as she stood and walked over. "Thaddeus, what's the matter?"

"Big guy, big guy," he said, in a hoarse voice, no longer his big crying voice.

"Fine," she said. "We'll ask Mack as soon as he gets off the phone."

At that, Mack spoke from behind her. "Ask me what?"

"What was that about the animal guy?"

He nodded. "I did talk to him. He did see Thaddeus. In fact, Thaddeus was at his place for a while."

"Oh, good," she said in delight. "At least we know where he was."

"As far as he knows, he didn't do anything to bring him to his place, but he admitted that he did have a vehicle with animals in cages and stuff, so it's possible Thaddeus hitched a ride."

Immediately her smile fell away. "Do you believe him?" she demanded. "Does that match what Abner said?"

"I'm not sure that I believe him," he said. "I'll go talk to him again."

Immediately she smiled and said, "That's perfect. Because, as you can see, Thaddeus is still pretty upset." She looked at him and said, "What kind of animals?"

"A lot of species that he takes to schools apparently."

"Was there another African grey, by any chance?"

"Oh," he said, a puzzled look on his face, then he glanced back to Thaddeus. "I wonder if that's what he saw."

"It doesn't explain the message on his leg though."

"No ..." Mack's voice trailed off. He shocked her and said, "I guess it might be easier to keep you with me and out of trouble that way."

She nodded. "Definitely."

"Then let's go. We'll come back later and get you some rest."

She was determined to appear as normal and as healthy as possible. She called Thaddeus to her shoulder, picked up her cup, walked back into the kitchen, placing it in the sink and filling it with water.

As Mack came through, he locked up the kitchen door. "Are you feeling okay in the house?"

"If you mean because I was attacked here, yes," she said quietly. "Although I did have a few questions about the security system, wondering if I had set it correctly and if I opened the door when he was here, would that have set off an alarm that anybody would have heard?"

"It would have set off an alarm, yes. As it is, Richard called it in, when he realized you were in trouble."

She looked at him in surprise. "Wow," she said. "I was

hoping he would do that, but I really wasn't sure. I'll need another lesson on this alarm system."

"Okay. Actually several others called it in as well," he muttered. He led the way through the front door with all the animals and helped her up into his truck.

"It would be really nice to solve this," she said. "I'm pretty upset about Thaddeus here. That's why I keep trying to track things down."

"I know you are," he said. "Let's go see if we can at least solve one problem."

She smiled. "You really are a good man."

"Hey, what brought that on?" he said in alarm.

She looked at him in surprise.

He backed up the vehicle in the driveway and drove off and around the corner.

"Well, you've been chasing people all over the place right now," she said. "Whatever happened with that horrible little bimbo lawyer?"

He frowned. "We caught her, and she was brought in for questioning. She did confess to threatening you but said it was an emotional breakdown and that it wouldn't happen again."

"Do you believe her?"

"No, not at all," he said, "so we're tracking her to see what's going on."

"Good," she said. "I don't really care to see her again."

"You shouldn't have to," he said. "I don't expect her to face any real consequences at this point."

"Because she can do that legal-speak stuff or because it wasn't that severe?"

"Unfortunately because it wasn't that severe," he admitted.

"Right," she said, with a groan. "You really do have to get hurt before anything really happens, don't you?"

"Not necessarily," he said, but she didn't believe him.

As they kept driving, she said, "Did you look up this guy's website?"

"I did, and I spoke to him on the phone. I told him that I would come by and take a look, and he seemed quite amenable to it."

"Good," she said. "I still need to get to the bottom of why Thaddeus and *the big guy* are so important." Surprisingly, Thaddeus remained silent at this mention.

"Oh, and I thought it was Isaac you had to get to the bottom of."

"I suspect it's both," she said. He looked at her in surprise. She shrugged. "You know Thaddeus has a nose for trouble," she said.

"You're the one with a nose for trouble," he muttered.

She grinned. "I learned everything from Thaddeus."

"Great," he said, "that'll go down well."

"Don't knock it," she said. "My animals have done a lot to help you out."

"I'm not knocking it," he protested. "I'm just trying to understand it."

"Some things in life are just not meant to be understood."

"That may well be true," he said, as they pulled into the area that she recognized well by now.

"Did you talk to Randy?"

"I did. He said that it's a fairly tight-knit community, but a few oddballs live there. Some people they just generally avoid. Others are good to work with, so they do more community stuff together," he said. "As far as Isaac goes, he said he belongs to the neighbors, and everybody is quite happy to let him join in, but he's a little bit off, and they let him be. Randy said he wasn't sure quite what was going on, but that Isaac had experienced some bullying recently. Randy was just trying to be protective."

"Poor Isaac," she said immediately. "It's just not fair that anybody would bully him."

"But that's the world around us."

"Doesn't mean it *has* to be the world around us," she snapped.

"Oh, I agree," he said. "But that explains that."

"Maybe," she said. "So if the note wasn't anything to do with Isaac, who's it got to do with?"

"Well, for that, you may have to just keep talking to Thaddeus here."

At that, he cawed and called out, "Big guy, big guy."

Doreen stared and looked all around. "What is he talking about?" They pulled into the driveway of what seemed to be a normal-looking house, but it had high fences all the way around. "I suppose that tall fence is for the animals?"

"Yes, and he does have a license, and he is fairly well-known in the community."

"Great," she said, "so no crime?"

"There was never a crime," he said. "The crime occurred when somebody attacked you."

"Yeah, somebody you didn't catch."

"Nope, I sure haven't," he said. "Go ahead. Rub it in. It really helps."

She winced at the sarcasm. "I'm sorry. I know how hard it is to find these guys once they take off."

"Everybody is out looking." Hopping out, he walked around his truck, opened up her door, and said, "Come on."

And, with that, they walked up to the front door. The knock was answered almost immediately, and the guy was a decent size, actually bigger than Mack. The two shook hands, as he looked over at Doreen and smiled. She introduced Thaddeus.

"And there is Thaddeus," he said. "I didn't know his name before though."

"I'm really surprised," she said, "not too many people know this bird."

"No, not at all," he said, "but he's the one who came to visit us before."

"I'm not sure how he got here," she admitted.

"I'm not either, but he was quite busy following whatever trail he was following."

"You didn't see how he got here?"

He shook his head. "No, and I just saw him on my fence the one day. Then he hopped in to say hi."

"Say hi to who?"

He looked at her in surprise and said, "Oh, you don't know?" Walking around, he said, "Let's go meet him."

"Meet who?" Mack asked quietly.

"Big Guy," he said, with a smile.

At that, Thaddeus started crowing, "Big guy, big guy, big guy."

She looked over at Mack and said, "Well, that's one mystery solved."

"Maybe," he said, following Jerry out to the backyard, where they saw huge cages and pens all around.

"Wow," she said, "I wasn't expecting to see something like this inside the city limits."

"Oh, I have a license for it," Jerry said, "and these are all rescue animals."

"Wow," she said, completely flabbergasted. "And where's 'big guy?'" she asked.

He motioned to a large cage on the far side. "This guy." He opened the cage and out came a huge parrot, not the same type as Thaddeus. He looked like a macaw maybe.

When it flapped its wings and squawked, Thaddeus instantly imitated him and cried out, "Big guy, big guy."

The other parrot shrieked and squawked several times, thrilling Thaddeus to no end.

"Oh my," she said, laughing. Thaddeus was clearly starstruck.

"This guy has been around for quite a few years. I take him on a lot of trips with me," he said. "He loves to go to the beach and to see people."

"Wow," she muttered. "I don't even know what to say." She looked up at Thaddeus. "Now are you happy?" Indeed, he had perked up beautifully. "Thaddeus seemed to be quite different when I got him home," she said, "and he kept talking about *big guy*."

Jerry chuckled. "And that would be this guy," he said.

When she reached out her left, uninjured arm, the macaw immediately hopped on and walked up, so he was stood on her other shoulder. He was a lot heavier than Thaddeus and a lot bigger.

Mack looked at the two of them, then shook his head. "That's not what I expected. Thaddeus has made a friend and apparently was a little lost without this one."

"I didn't think that was even possible," she muttered.

"They're quite social," the trainer said. He reached out a hand and said, "I'm Jerry, by the way." She shook his hand.

"I'm Doreen. Sorry, I should have introduced myself before," she said. "This is Mugs and Goliath." He looked at her and at the animals, and then his face lit up.

"Oh, my gosh. You're the amateur sleuth!"

She winced at that. "Mack here wouldn't appreciate you calling me that," she said, "but, if you mean I'm the person who's been involved in working some cold cases," she said, "yes, I am."

"Pleased to meet you," he said. "Very pleased to meet you." He looked at the big macaw and said, "Aren't you, King?"

"Is it King or Big Guy?"

"Well, his name is King, but, because of his size, we tease him about being a big guy."

"Right," she said, "and here I thought there was a mystery to be solved."

"Nope, no mystery here," he said, "at least none that I know about."

"What about Isaac?" she asked him.

"Isaac? He's quite a cutie. A real nice kid."

"Do you know anything about his history?"

"No, I sure don't. One of the things that we try to do here is just accept people and not dig too much into their backgrounds."

"I get that," she said, "but something seems quite sad about him."

"Well, his dad, I think, separated from his mom a long time ago, so I'm not exactly sure what the deal is."

"We don't ever see him with anybody though. What about the man or whoever is looking after Isaac?" she asked. "Do you ever see him?"

"No, he's one of the guys who is kind of a loner. We tend to stay away from him."

She nodded. "Do you mind showing me where he lives?"

"You don't know that either?" Mack asked.

"I saw where he left, but, from the path side, so I don't know which house it is."

"It's the one with all those buildings on the property," Jerry said, motioning to the left. "But I don't know that anybody will answer the door, even if you knock."

"We'll go see," she said, then looked at Thaddeus. "We'll have to say goodbye to King. Say, *Goodbye, King.*"

Immediately Thaddeus said, "Goodbye, King. Goodbye, King." The macaw squawked a few times and flapped his wings. With King now on Jerry's shoulder, they walked back out to the front yard. "Any time you want to bring Thaddeus by for a visit, I'm sure King would be happy to see you," Jerry said.

She smiled at him. "You know what? That might not be a bad idea, and it might keep Thaddeus happy."

"Anytime," he said. He pulled a card from his back pocket and said, "You can reach me here."

She accepted the card and said, "Look at that, Thaddeus. You might come for a play day."

Back in the front yard, rather than getting into the vehicle, they walked over to the neighbor's place. Mack walked up and knocked on the front door. There was no answer. He knocked again.

Finally a man opened the door, looked at Mack, then looked at her and frowned. "What's the matter?"

It sounded like an odd greeting to her. She just smiled and asked, "Are you Isaac's father?"

He frowned and nodded. "Why? What's that little kid done now?"

She rushed to reassure him. "Oh, no, he hasn't done anything," she said. "I just wondered," and she stopped, hesitating. Mack moved closer to her, one eyebrow raised. "I just wondered if he's okay," she said in a rush. The father looked at her, but there didn't appear to be anything in that gaze that helped her figure out if he was happy at her concern or pissed off.

"He's fine," he said, leaning against the doorjamb, crossing his arms over his chest. "Why? What's this all about?"

"Nothing really," she said. "I just saw him out in the pathway, and I worried because he was all alone."

He frowned at her. "And he got in trouble for that too," he said. "He knows better than to go over there. But what can you do? You can't watch him every minute of the day."

"No, of course not," she said, "but he's okay, right?"

"He is very okay," he said, then hesitated to say anything else. "Look. I know you're just one of those do-gooder types. Rest assured he is fine."

She nodded slowly. "Does he go to school?"

"Not yet," he said, "but he is due to go next year."

"And he will go?"

He shrugged. "No reason not to send him. He's not slow or anything," he said, "just quiet." Straightening up, he glared at her.

"And I didn't mean to imply that either," she said immediately. "I've just been concerned, that's all."

He waved at her. "And now you can take that concern and look after somebody else," he said. "Isaac is just fine." And, with that, he stepped back and slammed the door in her face.

Mack looked at her. "And now what do you want to do?"

"I guess there's no law enforcement angle to this, is there?"

"Nope, none at all."

She hesitated. He walked down the steps, and she frowned that she couldn't just follow him.

He looked back at her. "So what is it you want to do?"

"What'll it take to get into his backyard?"

"It'll take a warrant," he said, "and a warrant will require justifiable cause, which we do not have."

She sighed and slowly moved down the steps beside him. "That bad?"

"Yeah. It just feels like something's wrong," she said, "and I can't toss off that feeling about the message."

"I noticed you didn't mention that to either of them."

"No," she said, "I wouldn't dare."

"Why is that?"

"Because I think somebody is in trouble," she said. "If we let it out of the bag that they've put out a plea for help, how can we possibly expect them to stay safe?"

He looked at her and looked around at the neighborhood. "You want to walk up the pathway, and you can show me around a bit?"

She nodded cheerfully. "Now that I do want to do." With that, they walked around the corner of the house and headed back to the pathway where she had been before. She came up to where she'd last seen Isaac, and almost immediately his head popped through the bushes.

"Why, hello, Isaac. How are you today?" She smiled broadly, and he smiled back. "This is my friend Mack." Isaac looked at Mack, and his smile fell away. "He's okay," she said. "He's a very good guy." Isaac looked at her, looked at Mack again, then back to her, still not saying a word.

"Hey, Isaac, where's your mom?" Mack asked. "Can we talk to her?"

He slowly shook his head.

"Why is that?" Mack asked. Doreen stayed quiet, expecting Isaac to say she wasn't home.

"She's not allowed to talk to anybody," Isaac said.

At that, she stiffened. "Oh, well, maybe, if we went inside, we could talk to her."

He shook his head. "Nope. Not allowed at all."

"Okay," she said, desperately trying to figure out what to say to him. "Maybe your mommy wants to talk to me."

He looked at her in surprise, and then he looked behind him. "I don't know," he said, chewing on his fingers. Even as she watched, it looked as if he was trying to fit his whole fist inside as well.

She reached out a hand and gently patted him on the shoulder. "It's okay," she said, "not to worry."

He looked at her, looked up at Mack, and then shrugged.

"I'd really like to talk to her."

He nodded slowly.

"Could you take me to her? I'd like Thaddeus to meet her. And maybe Mugs too." At that, he looked down at Mugs and grinned. Mugs walked over and rubbed up against the little boy's legs. Isaac bent down and wrapped an arm around the dog and gave him a big hug.

She looked back at Mack, then spoke to Isaac. "If you take me to talk to your mommy," she said, "Mack will stay right here."

"Will he keep the puppy?"

"No, of course not. I want your mommy to meet my puppy too." At that, Isaac laughed. "Puppy. Bring puppy," he said, then disappeared into the cutout in the chain-link fence. She stared at the fence and sighed. "I don't think that hole is big enough for me," she muttered, but, with Mack's help, she managed to squeeze through and only ripped her shirt once. She looked back at Mack and could tell from the look on his face that he was not at all happy about this development.

"You know it's the only way right now," she said. "I'll be back in a minute." And, with that, she disappeared through the shrubbery.

Chapter 31

DOREEN HEARD MACK in the background, whispering at her to stay hidden, because nobody knew just how the owner of the house would feel. But the little boy was dashing ahead around a shed. She followed the best she could, and, when she came to one, he dashed in behind what looked like a blanket thrown over the top. She stopped, then looked to make sure she was out of sight of the house, then stepped in behind him. There was a surprised gasp, a little shriek, then a muted voice.

"What did you do? What did you do?"

Doreen waited for her eyes to adjust to the darkness, and then very quietly, she said, "Hello, my name is Doreen." There, sitting in the far corner, she saw what looked like a young woman. Doreen smiled and crouched on the floor, so she wouldn't be so imposing, then said, "Hi." She pointed to Thaddeus on her shoulder. "Do you know this guy?"

The woman slowly stood and walked a few steps closer. "How did you get in here?" she whispered. There obvious fear in her voice, and she kept staring at the point where the blanket parted for a doorway.

Doreen stood too. "Well, I guess you could say that I

followed Isaac. Is he yours?"

She nodded slowly.

Doreen asked again. "Are you free to leave?" The woman looked at her, and, through the tears and the fear in her eyes, she slowly shook her head.

"Are you the one who put the note on my Thaddeus here?"

The woman looked at Thaddeus, then gasped, her hand going up to clasp per mouth, but she nodded.

Finally they had an answer.

"Then would you like to leave here, right now?" Doreen asked. "I promise there's help waiting for you and Isaac."

She whispered, "No, I can't. I'm not allowed to leave."

"Well, it's a different story right now," she said. "I have the police close by."

The other woman shook her head and whispered, "It's not that easy."

Realizing this was far more traumatic than Doreen had expected, and keeping Thaddeus well in view, she crouched in front of the woman. "How long have you been here?" she asked softly.

The woman looked at her with haunted eyes. "A very long time."

With her heart slamming against her chest, Doreen asked, "Did you come here as a child?"

She nodded. "I was twelve," she whispered. "I was brought here when I was twelve."

"And how old are you now?"

The woman gave her a ghost of a smile. "I think I'm twenty-two. But I'm not sure."

"Good enough," Doreen said, reaching out a hand and giving her arm a reassuring squeeze. "Putting the message on

Thaddeus was a cry for help, and it worked."

The woman looked at Thaddeus, and, for the first time, a smile broke free. "He is beautiful," she said. "It was a split-second impulse."

"It was a good one," Doreen said. She rose and gently grasped the woman's hand and helped her to take a few steps forward. "Have you always lived on this part of the property?"

The woman shook her head. "No. For a while I was inside the house, and now I'm out here."

"Is that better?"

The woman slid her a glance and shrugged. "I don't know," she said.

"Is that your family in there?" The woman gave a violent shrug. "Except for Isaac?"

Again, the smile broke free. "Isaac is mine," she whispered.

And that's when Doreen realized what was going on. "You were kidnapped as a child, weren't you? Kept here as a captive, and the man in that house forced himself on you, and you became pregnant, right?"

She nodded slowly. "For a long time, I was part of the family. But, when Isaac was born, he moved me back here. Isaac was in the house with me, and now he is out here with me."

"Ah," Doreen whispered, as she slowly led the young woman out into the backyard between sheds.

"If he sees you talking to me," the woman said quietly, "he'll be very angry."

Doreen looked at her, smiled, and said, "Let him. He is not facing a young child anymore. He'll be facing me. And more than that, Mack is here too."

The woman's eyebrows rose. "Mack?"

"Mack." As they stood here, Thaddeus walked across her arm and walked over to the young woman, then gently rubbed up against her. "Thaddeus is here. Thaddeus is here."

The woman laughed. "It feels so strange," she said, "to even talk to another person."

"He kept you isolated because it kept you as a victim," Doreen said, remembering various tactics of her own husband, even though this situation was very different. Holding this woman's hand, she gently walked her back to where Isaac had escaped through the fence. As they walked closer to the fence, the young woman said, "Why are we going here?"

"Because Mack is here."

"Right. You were going to tell me who Mack is."

"He is the defender of the innocent, a protector of the young and the old alike," she said, and, with a smile, she pointed out Mack, standing there, a confused look on his face, as the two women approached him carefully. "He is with the police, and he will help you."

"Are you sure?" asked the young woman.

Doreen nodded and squeezed her fingers, lacing their hands together. "What's your name?"

"Izzy," she said. "Isabelle, but Izzy for short."

"And where did you live before, Izzy?"

She looked at her in surprise, and, as they got closer to Mack, she said, "Vancouver." Looking around, she said, "But aren't we in Vancouver?"

Mack looked at her in surprise, then looked at Doreen. As he opened the hole in the fence a little bit, he let Mugs through to join Doreen.

"This is Mugs," Doreen said. Mugs immediately

wrapped his sturdy body around Izzy's legs.

She laughed and bent down to give him a cuddle. "He is beautiful."

Never to be outdone, Goliath came through as well. Izzy looked up at Doreen. "Are they all yours?"

Little Isaac popped out from behind the shed. "They're all hers," he said, laughing, as he bent to give Mugs a big hug.

Izzy looked at him with love, smiled, then looked up at Doreen. "Really?"

Doreen smiled and nodded. "It's okay," she said. "Someday you might get some sort of pet too."

The woman looked confused and then shook her head. "I don't think so."

"Oh, I do," Doreen said, with a bright smile. "Your future is completely different now." As Izzy and Isaac played with the animals, she took half a step closer to Mack but kept her fingers linked with the young woman. Needing to keep her moving forward. She motioned at the fence.

Mack leaned closer with a question in his eyes, and she whispered, "You need to check for a child who disappeared ten years ago—out of Vancouver." His eyebrows shot up, as he looked at her, looked back at Izzy, and then back at her again. She nodded slowly. His gaze shot to the house on the other side. She deliberately didn't look.

"And I need to get her out of here," she whispered.

He nodded slowly and pushed the wire hole open, even as he pulled out his phone. Moving the animals ahead, she gently urged Izzy out of the fence first, along with Isaac. Slowly, and as a unit, they walked down the path toward Mack's truck. He was busy on the phone, and Doreen kept Izzy and Isaac busy with the animals, as they moved toward the truck. As soon as they got there, Izzy looked up at it and stopped.

"This is Mack's truck," Doreen said quietly, her gaze looking around at everybody else.

"And does that matter?" Izzy asked nervously.

Obviously she was scared about taking this big step. "It matters a lot," Doreen said, "because Mack is one of the good guys."

"But what am I supposed to do?" she asked. "I have no way to make a living. I can't work or do anything. How will I take care of Isaac? He said I'll never see Isaac again if I try to escape."

"You don't have to worry about any of that right now," she said. Opening up the truck door, Isaac immediately scrambled into the back seat along with Mugs, who jumped up.

Izzy laughed. "How is it that the animals are so okay with the truck?" she marveled.

"You will be too," Doreen said, and she boosted Izzy up. Just then came a shout from the house and out came the man they had met at the front door. Immediately Mack stepped forward to talk to him, and Izzy started to cry. Doreen hopped into the back seat, wrapped her arms around Izzy and Isaac, and held them close.

"Come on, Goliath." She urged the big tomcat to come up for a cuddle. Almost as if he understood the problem, Goliath took his massive girth and laid it across Izzy's and Isaac's laps. In spite of herself, Izzy smiled, even though she quaked with fear. Isaac cried out in joy, as he wrapped his arms around the big cat and hugged him tight. Doreen winced, wondering if Goliath would let him get away with that, but he seemed totally okay with it. Her own throat was tight, and she hated to say she was afraid, but, right now, it was all about getting these two people away from that man.

Just then the guy came at Mack, pointing a gun at him. Mack took a step back, his hands up. She couldn't hear the conversation, but she knew exactly what was happening. She looked at Izzy, who stared at the man in horrified fascination. "Did he ever pull a gun on you?"

Izzy nodded slowly. "All the time," she said.

"Well, look at that," she said, "we'll have to deal with this bully then." She looked down at Mugs and looked at Thaddeus. "You're not going anywhere," Doreen said, as she picked up Thaddeus and plucked him off her shoulder and onto Izzy's. "Isaac, you look after these animals and your mom, okay?" And, with that, Doreen slid out of the truck, locked and slammed the door, hoping that the woman wouldn't leave. This was Izzy's one chance at freedom, and they needed to take it.

Doreen raced down the sidewalk where Mack was in a face-off. The man glared at her. But instead of stopping with Mack, she walked right past the gun in the man's hand, making him back up, as she shoved her face into his. Then she hauled back with her right arm, and she smacked him hard across the face. He started yelling. Mack started yelling. Then suddenly she was airborne, as Mack picked her up and moved her off the sidewalk. Out came his fists, and he hit the gunman hard and dropped him where he stood.

She turned to looked at Mack, then grinned. "See? We make a great team."

He stared at her in disbelief. "He had a gun," he roared.

"I don't care," she snapped. "He spent all these years tormenting and terrorizing that young woman with that gun," she said.

All of a sudden the neighbors were out all over the place. Some of them were looking at the man on the ground, and one of them called out, "Hey, what's going on here? This is police harassment."

She spun on her heels and glared at them all. "Are you people aware he's kidnapped and raped a young woman and then kept her captive inside that property for ten whole years? That Isaac's mother has been a prisoner in one of those huts in the back?" Arms outstretched, Doreen asked, "Is that the kind of people you are? That you let that happen right here under your noses? That you never once gave her any assistance or called for help for her?"

All the people just stared at her in shock.

She glared at them. Just then, the door of the truck opened, and the animals came running to her side, standing all around her. And slowly moving toward her were Izzy and Isaac. Doreen immediately opened her arms, and Isaac ran toward her. Izzy stepped up, shaking and trembling. She looked at the others, standing around.

"Neighbors, this is Izzy. She was kidnapped as a twelve-year-old and kept here as a prisoner for all these years. For ten years," Doreen said, roaring into the crowd. "Do you have any idea how this little girl feels knowing that all of you people knew she was here and didn't help her?"

One of the men blustered and said, "We didn't know anything. We had no idea."

"What did you think? That Isaac just appeared out of nowhere?" she snapped back at him. "Did you think that he just appeared out of fairy dust?"

The people looked at each other and then looked at Izzy, as if they'd never seen her before.

Then Doreen realized that it was probably the truth.

"Oh, Lord. You guys really haven't ever seen Izzy, have you?"

They slowly shook their heads. Doreen looked down at the man still on the ground and pointed. "Well, this is the man you guys have been keeping deep in your bosom, protecting Isaac, yes, but you forgot about Isaac's mother," she snarled.

At that, another neighbor started to protest. "We didn't know. We didn't know anything," she said. "We wondered, of course, but we didn't know what happened."

Doreen looked at the gunman, and Mack gave him a shake. "Are you the man who kidnapped her?" he roared. The guy looked at Izzy, then back at Mack and said, "Izzy, what lies did you tell them?"

"The truth," she said, her voice quiet but getting stronger as she spoke. "That for ten years you've kept me a prisoner, using the gun and your fists to keep me petrified." She looked at the crowd. "He is Isaac's father. He's raped me for all these years," she muttered to the horrified crowd.

At that, Mugs started barking and raced up to the man Mack was holding, chewing on his ankle. He started to scream and cry out. In exasperation, Mack tried to hold Mugs back.

Doreen looked at Mack and said, "Mugs knows exactly what he is. Nothing more than a piece of meat," she said. "I hope the inmates in the jail take good care of him," she said. "Mack, you leave us here so you can take that trash down to the station."

He looked at her in surprise, as she shook her head. "This young woman shouldn't have to be in the same vehicle as him."

"Not a problem," he said, "we've already got a cruiser coming." And, sure enough, within minutes, Arnold and

Chester pulled up. As soon as they hopped out, they took one look and spotted her in the crowd and groaned.

"Why are you always in the middle of trouble?"

"She's not," Izzy said, crying out, defending her.

They looked at her in surprise.

"She saved me," she said quietly. "I've been a prisoner on that property, mostly in those horrid sheds for ten years. She saved me." She turned and looked at Doreen and shot her a beautiful smile.

Doreen's heart melted as she raced over and gave Izzy a gentle hug. "And now you're free," she said, wrapping Isaac up in her arms too. "You both are." She looked at the neighbors and said, "Next time, do a little more than look after a little boy."

Then Randy stepped forward. "We didn't know," he said in his booming voice. "Honestly, we didn't know."

Jerry, the man with all the animals, stepped forward and said, "We're private people, but we would have helped her, if we'd known."

"Maybe so," she said. "Maybe that's true, but this was allowed to continue under your noses for a decade." They shook their heads and looked at the guy in custody.

Randy spoke again. "Martin. Is this true?"

He just stiffened his back and glared at everybody.

"Jesus," Randy said. They all looked at each other, then back at Martin, disbelief and shock clear on their faces.

"Izzy," someone called out. "If you want to live in the house—"

At that, Mack stepped forward and said, "It's not that easy. Izzy was kidnapped from Vancouver ten years ago. She has family, we hope, people who need to know she's alive. And Isaac? He needs a better life."

At that, the neighbors all nodded and offered all kinds of help. Help with rides, help with money, help with anything she needed.

Izzy stared at them in surprise. "I don't even know who you are," she murmured.

"But they know your son," Doreen said quietly. "And that's a good thing. Isaac has made himself quite a popular young man here."

Izzy laughed and, smiling, reached out and ruffled his hair. Isaac wrapped his arms around her and hugged her close.

Doreen smiled at the two of them. "You know something? Today's a pretty good day after all."

Izzy looked at her, shot her a bright smile, and said, "It is a good day."

Isaac looked up and asked, "Can I have Thaddeus?"

Doreen laughed and said, "No, you sure can't, but that doesn't mean that maybe you can't have a pet once you get settled somewhere."

He looked at his mom with pleading eyes.

She shrugged and said, "I don't know where we'll end up, but maybe we can get you something." She looked over at Doreen and whispered, "Thank you."

Doreen immediately wrapped an arm around her shoulders and whispered, "You're welcome." She turned to look back at Mack, who was with Chester and Arnold, all in a heavy discussion. Before Mack walked back to them, he looked at the crowd and addressed them all. "I'll take Izzy and Isaac to the hospital to get checked over," he said. "We'll be back to talk to all of you later on."

The neighbors all nodded. "But, like Randy said, we just didn't know."

Mack nodded. "And I understand that. Unfortunately it's much easier to not see something, than to see it for what it really is." He looked at Doreen, smiled, and said, "Well, are you happy now?"

"Absolutely," she said, beaming at him. "This is the best day ever."

"Really?" he said. "I'm pretty darn sure your gunman escaped yesterday."

She glared at him. "You didn't have to bring that up."

"Oh, I don't know," he said. "I think I did."

Just then came a shout from the sidewalk.

She looked over to see her attacker, Snoz, standing there, but he wore a black hoodie. "Mack!" she cried out. "Look out!" The gunman raised his weapon, as if to fire, but Chester, who had been standing at the side, watching the goings-on, saw what was happening and pulled out his weapon.

Mack lunged to protect the women and the child.

"Police! Stop or I'll shoot!" The gunman laughed and shot anyway, and so did Chester. The gunman collapsed to the sidewalk, even as Mack, his arms now wrapped around all three of them, blocking Isaac's and Izzy's view of the violence, stood quiet.

Doreen looked up at him. "Are you hit?"

He shook his head. "No," he said in surprise. "I'm not." He turned to find the gunman on the ground, and Chester stood there in shock, then faced Mack. "Honestly, I didn't think I would hit him."

Mack raced to Snoz, checked him over, looked up at her, and shook his head.

She hated to say that it was a good thing, but it *was* a darn good thing. She stood in front of Izzy and Isaac to block them from what was going on. "Come on, you two. Let's get you back into the truck."

"Who was that man?" Izzy asked.

"Another one of the bad guys," she said, "but, like I said, Mack is one of the good ones."

Izzy smiled and said, "I think I believe you." And, with that, everybody got up into the truck. Mack was now unable to leave because of all the chaos going on.

She looked out from the truck and asked Mack, "Do you trust me to drive this to the hospital?"

He looked at her and snorted. "Hell no."

She glared at him, then hopped into the driver's seat and turned it on. "Too bad," she said. "You're busy, and I want to get them checked out." He glared at her, and she said, "Give the hospital a call, would you?"

"I will," he said, shaking his head. "But if you damage it—"

"Oh, please," she said. "If I damage it, well too bad." She shook her head. "I don't have any money to pay for it." She gave him a cheeky smirk and slowly backed it up. As she drove, Mugs started to bark and bark and bark. Izzy was laughing, and Isaac was cheerful and screaming goodbye and waving from the window to the crowd standing there. Doreen grinned as she managed to get the huge truck out onto the road and headed to the hospital.

She looked over at Izzy and Isaac. "Like I said, it's a brand-new day." And she herself hadn't felt quite so good in such a very long time.

Epilogue

Saturday Morning...

THREE DAYS LATER Izzy and Isaac, after promises were made to stay in touch, had been dispatched to Vancouver and a family who awaited their joyous reunion. Martin would be in jail for a very long time. He had finally confessed that he couldn't take his eyes off Izzy, when he was down on the coast for a trip stocking up, and had managed to snatch the girl from her parents and had kept her with him ever since. Nobody had been any the wiser, and, when Isaac had been born, Martin just made up lies about how he'd arrived, and everybody had basically accepted it.

If Izzy hadn't caught Thaddeus and hadn't put that message on his leg, she might still have been a captive there. It just didn't bear thinking about.

As soon as she got dressed and made her way downstairs, Doreen made coffee. Three days had passed since all that. Three days and her shoulder was finally nowhere near as sore. It still hurt to lift her arm above her head, but at least the oozing of blood had stopped, and it wasn't the gut-wrenching agony that she'd been dealing with. The pain was much lighter now, much softer, more distant. As she sat outside on the deck, she heard a vehicle drive up. Mugs immediately woofed a welcome. She looked down at him and laughed. "It's Mack, isn't it?"

Mack, instead of coming through the house, walked around the back, then smiled at seeing her. He had something large in his hand. She looked at it and asked, "What the devil is that?"

He lifted it up, and she saw that it was a table—he'd been carrying it sideways. He plunked it down on the deck beside her, and she cried out, "Where did you get that from?"

"One of the guys at work was getting rid of it," he said. "I said that you needed it, and he immediately offered it up. I've got the chairs in the back of the truck too." He disappeared and made two trips, carrying two chairs at a time. She just froze. Finally she had a table with four chairs sitting on her deck. She stared in amazed delight.

"It's just beautiful," she said. It was glass and acrylic, and it looked lovely. It was also the nicest outdoor set she'd ever had, since living here. She immediately moved to sit down at the table with her coffee and grinned up at him. "Now, if only there was something to eat."

He sagged into the chair beside her and stared at her. "If only," he said. But something was strange about his voice.

"I'm really happy you came," she said, "and thank you so much for the table and chairs."

He nodded, but he was slightly distracted. He motioned at her shoulder. "How are you doing with that shoulder now?"

"I'm better," she said, cheerfully lifting her cup and taking a big drink. Mack just glared at her. "Okay. It still bothers me. But not like it did." When he remained silent, she worried. "What's the matter?" she asked, her gaze sharpening. He shrugged and wouldn't meet her eyes.

"There's more coffee in the kitchen, if you want a cup."

"I'm fine," he said.

"Uh-oh." *Something was really wrong.* "And that means something pretty ugly is going on."

He nodded. "There is, and you'll hear about it soon enough," he said, his fingers tapping the table.

"What's the matter?" she asked.

"Have you—" And then he stopped.

"Have I what?"

He sighed. "You know the marigolds in the flower garden down at the big Welcome to Kelowna sign? The old one? There's talk of a new one north of the airport."

"Yeah, the one that I spent a lot of time on, trying to design a layout for the city? It was a lovely bunch of flowers, as I remember. I can't remember all of them, but some lovely marigolds were there, I think." They are tearing that one down? Or maybe I misunderstood, and they were designing the new one." She frowned at that thought. It did explain why that scenario never moved ahead.

He nodded. "Yeah, that one. We found a body there this morning." He shrugged. "It's the first I've been there and was quite surprised the sign was gone.

Her eyebrows shot up, and she had to admit—even though it was ghoulish and wrong of her—that she was definitely curious as to what was going on. "I am too. And of course, I'm sorry for whoever it is," she said, "but don't keep me in suspense. Who was it, and what's going on?"

"Well, that's what I came to ask you about."

She stared at him in surprise. "Okay, now I'm confused."

"It might be somebody you know."

"Someone I know?" she asked incredulously. "Oh, dear, I hope not."

He pulled out his phone and slowly flicked through the

photos there.

"So, this is a delay tactic," she said, "and I admit you're scaring me."

"No, it's not that," he said, "but circumstances require that I ask you a couple questions." He proceeded to ask where she'd been an hour ago, where she'd been four hours ago, and if she had an alibi.

She sat back and stared at him in shock. "Seriously, Mack?" she said. "I woke up about an hour ago. I was home alone all night. Why? Who is dead?" Suddenly she leaned forward. "Is it one of the bad guys?"

"Well, maybe," he said. "I'm sure a lot of people would say it definitely was a bad guy, but a lot of people wouldn't."

"Stop now," she said, raising both hands in frustration. "Just tell me who it is."

Then he held out his phone.

She looked at it and stared in shock.

"That's the thing," he said. "This is our dead body. So where were you last night? And where were you early this morning?"

She stared at the picture of Robin, her former divorce lawyer. Her very dead former lawyer. "What on earth?" Doreen raised her gaze slowly to stare at him.

"And I'm sorry, but I have to ask," he said. "Did you murder her in the marigolds?"

This concludes Book 12 of Lovely Lethal Gardens: Lifeless in the Lilies.

Read about Murder in the Marigolds: Lovely Lethal Gardens, Book 13

Lovely Lethal Gardens: Murder in the Marigolds (Book #13)

A new cozy mystery series from *USA Today* best-selling author Dale Mayer. Follow gardener and amateur sleuth Doreen Montgomery—and her amusing and mostly lovable cat, dog, and parrot—as they catch murderers and solve crimes in lovely Kelowna, British Columbia.

Riches to rags … Chaos has never been so supreme … Now a suspect herself … No calm in sight …

Being a suspect in the murder of her ex-lawyer is not the fun Doreen thought it would be. And, of course, she's been ordered to stay away from the case, … but she can't help being interested. So she enlists Mack's brother, Nick—her *new* lawyer—to help.

Mack's first priority is to clear Doreen as a suspect. No one in their right mind would seriously believe she'd done the deed, of course. ... But, the fact is, she had both motive and opportunity, so clearing her of suspicion isn't the walk in the park that Mack would like it to be. Especially not when she insists on sticking her nose into his case, where it doesn't belong.

And just when Doreen is certain things can't get any worse, answering her doorbell shows her that this nightmare has just started. Who just walked into her life? None other than her soon-to-be-ex-husband, ... Mathew ...

Find Book 13 here!

To find out more visit Dale Mayer's website.

https://geni.us/DMMurderUniversal

Author's Note

Thank you for reading Lifeless in the Lilies: Lovely Lethal Gardens, Book 12! If you enjoyed the book, please take a moment and leave a short review.

Dear reader,

I love to hear from readers, and you can contact me at my website: www.dalemayer.com or at my Facebook author page. To be informed of new releases and special offers, sign up for my newsletter or follow me on BookBub. And if you are interested in joining Dale Mayer's Reader Group, here is the Facebook sign up page. http://geni.us/DaleMayerFBGroup

Cheers,
Dale Mayer

About the Author

Dale Mayer is a *USA Today* best-selling author, best known for her SEALs military romances, her Psychic Visions series, and her Lovely Lethal Garden cozy series. Her contemporary romances are raw and full of passion and emotion (Broken But … Mending, Hathaway House series). Her thrillers will keep you guessing (Kate Morgan, By Death series), and her romantic comedies will keep you giggling (*It's a Dog's Life*, a stand-alone novella; and the Broken Protocols series, starring Charming Marvin, the cat).

Dale honors the stories that come to her—and some of them are crazy, break all the rules and cross multiple genres!

To go with her fiction, she also writes nonfiction in many different fields, with books available on résumé writing, companion gardening, and the US mortgage system. All her books are available in print and ebook format.

Connect with Dale Mayer Online

Dale's Website – www.dalemayer.com
Twitter – @DaleMayer
Facebook Page – geni.us/DaleMayerFBFanPage
Facebook Group – geni.us/DaleMayerFBGroup
BookBub – geni.us/DaleMayerBookbub
Instagram – geni.us/DaleMayerInstagram
Goodreads – geni.us/DaleMayerGoodreads
Newsletter – geni.us/DaleNews

Also by Dale Mayer

Published Adult Books:

Hathaway House
Aaron, Book 1
Brock, Book 2
Cole, Book 3
Denton, Book 4
Elliot, Book 5
Finn, Book 6
Gregory, Book 7
Heath, Book 8
Iain, Book 9
Jaden, Book 10
Keith, Book 11
Lance, Book 12
Melissa, Book 13
Nash, Book 14
Owen, Book 15
Hathaway House, Books 1–3
Hathaway House, Books 4–6
Hathaway House, Books 7–9

The K9 Files
Ethan, Book 1
Pierce, Book 2
Zane, Book 3

Lovely Lethal Gardens

Lovely Lethal Gardens, Books 1–2
Lovely Lethal Gardens, Books 3–4
Lovely Lethal Gardens, Books 5–6
Lovely Lethal Gardens, Books 7–8
Lovely Lethal Gardens, Books 9–10

Psychic Vision Series

Tuesday's Child
Hide 'n Go Seek
Maddy's Floor
Garden of Sorrow
Knock Knock…
Rare Find
Eyes to the Soul
Now You See Her
Shattered
Into the Abyss
Seeds of Malice
Eye of the Falcon
Itsy-Bitsy Spider
Unmasked
Deep Beneath
From the Ashes
Stroke of Death
Ice Maiden
Psychic Visions Books 1–3
Psychic Visions Books 4–6
Psychic Visions Books 7–9

By Death Series

Touched by Death
Haunted by Death

Chilled by Death

By Death Books 1–3

Broken Protocols – Romantic Comedy Series
Cat's Meow
Cat's Pajamas
Cat's Cradle
Cat's Claus
Broken Protocols 1-4

Broken and... Mending
Skin
Scars
Scales (of Justice)
Broken but... Mending 1-3

Glory
Genesis
Tori
Celeste
Glory Trilogy

Biker Blues
Morgan: Biker Blues, Volume 1
Cash: Biker Blues, Volume 2

SEALs of Honor
Mason: SEALs of Honor, Book 1
Hawk: SEALs of Honor, Book 2
Dane: SEALs of Honor, Book 3
Swede: SEALs of Honor, Book 4
Shadow: SEALs of Honor, Book 5
Cooper: SEALs of Honor, Book 6

Heroes for Hire

Merk's Mistake: Heroes for Hire, Book 3

Rhodes's Reward: Heroes for Hire, Book 4

Flynn's Firecracker: Heroes for Hire, Book 5

Logan's Light: Heroes for Hire, Book 6

Harrison's Heart: Heroes for Hire, Book 7

Saul's Sweetheart: Heroes for Hire, Book 8

Dakota's Delight: Heroes for Hire, Book 9

Michael's Mercy (Part of Sleeper SEAL Series)

Tyson's Treasure: Heroes for Hire, Book 10

Jace's Jewel: Heroes for Hire, Book 11

Rory's Rose: Heroes for Hire, Book 12

Brandon's Bliss: Heroes for Hire, Book 13

Liam's Lily: Heroes for Hire, Book 14

North's Nikki: Heroes for Hire, Book 15

Anders's Angel: Heroes for Hire, Book 16

Reyes's Raina: Heroes for Hire, Book 17

Dezi's Diamond: Heroes for Hire, Book 18

Vince's Vixen: Heroes for Hire, Book 19

Ice's Icing: Heroes for Hire, Book 20

Johan's Joy: Heroes for Hire, Book 21

Galen's Gemma: Heroes for Hire, Book 22

Zack's Zest: Heroes for Hire, Book 23

Bonaparte's Belle: Heroes for Hire, Book 24

Heroes for Hire, Books 1–3

Heroes for Hire, Books 4–6

Heroes for Hire, Books 7–9

Heroes for Hire, Books 10–12

Heroes for Hire, Books 13–15

SEALs of Steel

Badger: SEALs of Steel, Book 1

Erick: SEALs of Steel, Book 2

The Mavericks

Bullard's Battle Series
Ryland's Reach, Book 1
Cain's Cross, Book 2
Eton's Escape, Book 3
Garret's Gambit, Book 4
Kano's Keep, Book 5
Fallon's Flaw, Book 6
Quinn's Quest, Book 7
Bullard's Beauty, Book 8

Collections
Dare to Be You…
Dare to Love…
Dare to be Strong…
RomanceX3

Standalone Novellas
It's a Dog's Life
Riana's Revenge
Second Chances

Published Young Adult Books:

Family Blood Ties Series
Vampire in Denial
Vampire in Distress
Vampire in Design
Vampire in Deceit
Vampire in Defiance
Vampire in Conflict
Vampire in Chaos
Vampire in Crisis

Vampire in Control
Vampire in Charge
Family Blood Ties Set 1–3
Family Blood Ties Set 1–5
Family Blood Ties Set 4–6
Family Blood Ties Set 7–9
Sian's Solution, A Family Blood Ties Series Prequel
    Novelette

Design series
Dangerous Designs
Deadly Designs
Darkest Designs
Design Series Trilogy

Standalone
In Cassie's Corner
Gem Stone (a Gemma Stone Mystery)
Time Thieves

Published Non-Fiction Books:

Career Essentials
Career Essentials: The Résumé
Career Essentials: The Cover Letter
Career Essentials: The Interview
Career Essentials: 3 in 1